The Last
Ms. Understanding

A novel

The Last Ms. Understanding
Published by Another Clue Publishing

PUBLISHER'S NOTE

This is a work of fiction. Names, characters, places and incidents are either the
product of the author's imagination or are used fictitiously, and any resemblance
to actual persons, living or dead, business establishments, events, or locales, is
entirely coincidental.

To order additional copies of this book or for information regarding special
discounts for bulk purchases, please contact **www.rltayloronline.com**

ISBN 978-0-578-02434-9

A message to readers:

The Last Ms. Understanding promotes real emotions that reveal the power of what a true misunderstanding can unleash. Misunderstandings can trigger feelings of rejection, loss, pain, confusion, and sympathy.

For men, this book is a true example of how a man can feel once he makes the decision to change for the better and take ownership of any misunderstandings caused on his behalf. For women, this book tells both sides of the story...

As women we hold the power of love and carry the torch of determination and strength. We are strong women with strong minds; we encourage, empower, strengthen, and support women through their journey of life... ~We are Serenity Women's Circle~

-Shana M. Jackson-
Founder and President
Serenity Women's Circle

Serenity Women's Circle is a nonprofit organization founded by women for women. They provide special programs in order to empower, educate, and serve the entire population of Mississippi.

Serenity Women's Circle especially dedicates their organization to reach out to women and children due to the high percentage of women and children issues in the state of Mississippi.

Serenity members are involved to help become positive role models for women and children.

Serenity Women's Circle Mission Statement:
As a member of Serenity Women's Circle, we will dedicate ourselves to being strong women with strong minds. Our goal is to educate, empower, support, and build circles of friendship while providing endless service to our community.

For more information or to get involved visit their website today:
www.serenitywomenscircle.org

For the real Ms. Understanding

Prologue

One Month Earlier

I can't believe I'm leaving L.A., Rita thought as the airplane began picking up speed, in preparation for take off. Flying still made her nervous despite all her travels, both foreign and domestic. Her new job would require travel, sometimes on a weekly basis. The plane began its steady ascent skyward. Her fingertips gripped the leather seats tightly. Her breath grew short until the plane leveled off and stabilized, giving way to her sigh of relief.

She opened her eyes and slothfully looked around at the other passengers. Who was that handsome face to her left? How did she not notice him? Across the aisle sat a remarkably attractive man, with broad shoulders, and a muscular chest, noticeable even through his pin striped suit. He was dressed casket clean, perfectly coordinated from his scarlet colored tie down and his ruby cuff links. His spit polished black Allen-Edmonds dress shoes completed the ensemble. She was too busy distressing about the planes takeoff to notice him.

He detected her the moment he boarded the plane, taking his seat in first class. He saw the perfectly made up face, although it needed no assistance to display beauty. He saw the silk like texture of her skin, freshly cut style of her hair, on down to her lengthy limbs and open toe Prada shoes. Rita was already seated with her eyes pressed shut when he boarded.

He like most other men noticed her and became infatuated from the onset. Men based their attraction on her anatomy and facial features despite her gifted intelligence. Rita possessed the ability to turn heads even amongst a crowded room of Hollywood's finest. At the same time she could easily hold her own in a Wall Street boardroom.

Seizing the opportunity, the stranger occupied the open seat to her left. He leaned over and moistened his lips. "I couldn't help but notice you sitting there looking so divine. May I have your name?" he asked.

She smiled back. "Rita," she said. His obvious sophistication grabbed her attention.

"Nice to make your acquaintance, I'm Jeffrey DuPois, and I think I might be the most fortunate man to ever board a plane. How did I get to sit across from an angel?" he asked.

She smiled again. His approach was far different from most men with their inappropriate sexual advances and innuendos. This gentleman was just that, a gentleman.

He explained his career as a business attorney, flying across country weekly to settle union disputes. Rita traveled on business as well, hers of a permanent nature.

"I've accepted the COO position at Jackson & Fitz. They're just breaking in the international market, and I hope to grow with the company," she said.

"I love a woman with ambition. Perhaps when we land, we can get together for dinner. I'll be in the city for a few days. I'd hate to be there lonely...," he said. Rita viewed the cross country move as a chance for business growth, and maybe even opportunity for a love life, which at the time was nonexistent. She'd been burned many times in the past.

The charming stranger glanced around, nervously excusing himself. As he disappeared from view, the planes curvaceous flight attendant rushed towards Rita as if her life was being threatened. "I don't want to be all up in your business but *that man* is married. He's on this flight every week trying to pick up some new woman," she cautioned.

Rita couldn't believe it. He seemed so sincere.

Rita frowned with a face full of doubt. "Excuse me, but how would you know?"

The flight attendant replied by rolling her eyes. "He fooled me once..." She shot Rita a frown and walked away swinging her hips back and forth in dramatic fashion.

Moments passed until the handsome face returned. Rita's body became tense. "Are you married?" she asked as he settled into his seat.

"What?" he asked. His cover was blown, it was true. Right on cue the sassy looking flight attendant sashayed back through the aisle smiling deviously at the man who appeared more repulsive than appealing.

"Are you putting your nose in my business Pam?" he asked as she walked by.

"Go home to your wife...," she replied as she entered coach seating.

He sat down humiliated and whispered discreetly. "Let me explain...look, it doesn't bother me if it doesn't bother you."

"Please, don't talk to me," Rita said, sucking her teeth with her eyebrows slanted south.

"Hey...wait," he whispered again.

"Shut your mouth," Rita yelled. The remainder of the flight she reflected back on all the men she dated. Most were like this man. They were flawless on the outside, but their interior grotesque and vile.

All the men in her past were successful. Doctors. Lawyers. Executives. None of them treated her well, none of them lasted. She vowed for change. This would be a new city she was moving to. She'd be open to new experiences, new outlooks on life. She'd definitely be open to new types of men. Maybe she would find love with someone considered ordinary, or regular, someone real?

Chapter 1

Another week quickly dissolved and the inevitable routine was happening all over again. Another Friday spent just hanging out at the bar idly passing time. In no way was it distinct from any other Friday night. The weekend unfolded slowly leaving Lee and his longtime friend Keith partaking of their usual routine.

The two had been appearing at that location every Friday for the past ten years as if it were some sort of ritualistic ceremony. The fact of the matter was Lee's uncle owned the lounge so the drinks were at least half off, and most of the time free. The pair came and went as they pleased, recipients of royal treatment. The town they called home bordered against the fringes of the big city. Sky rise lights could be seen flickering hastily in the distance just past the interstate located a few blocks from the bar.

Every so often a few city folks shuffled in to hear the jazz or try the catfish. For the most part the lounge was supported by locals. The crowd remained eager to drink, and hesitant to leave. Friday nights gave way to live music which accompanied the low lit dusty lounge type ambiance.

"Would you look at the ladies in here tonight," Keith said.

Lee nodded unenthusiastically while staring face down into his usual mix of Crown Royal and Coke. "Yea sure," he said.

"What's wrong?" Keith asked while smiling.

Lee quickly changed the subject. "Nothing. The band sounds good tonight," he said. He sampled the well mixed concoction from his ice filled cocktail glass.

Something submerged inside Lee had been eating away at him lately, and he couldn't quite distinguish what it was. Perhaps it was the monotony of his job processing bulk mail where he worked for the past decade?

At age thirty-one he was ready to settle down. Keith his friend since elementary school seemed perfectly content with continuing to chase women. Lee desired more. He'd grown tired of the games and drama associated with meaningless relationships. His life had been riddled with enough disappointments and missed opportunities he could write a book.

Fortunately, he'd dodged having any children out of wedlock which by some standards made him an eligible bachelor. On the other hand, what did a guy with a $15.00 per hour job and bad credit have to offer?

"They're out tonight, they're out, look at this place…nothing but ladies," Keith said. He chuckled and rubbed his hands together.

Lee stared blank. "Can we talk about something else? I'm tired of the same old thing." Lee crumpled up his napkin and pitched it towards the trash can behind the bar.

"You trashing my place now?" a familiar gruff voice said in a playful tone. The voice belonged to Uncle Charlie, beaming as usual. Some people thought his face was permanently contortioned that way. Charlie was a big man, but the one thing he could do was dress. He had a standing reputation for being cleaner than hospital carpet. The clothing he wore stayed immaculately coordinated and as a rule never left the house without at least two buttons on his shirt undone to expose his chest hair. The big bushy coal shaded moustache that covered his lip, made him appear to be the last member of the Whispers.

"What's wrong Lee?" Charlie asked in a tone loud enough for the whole club to hear.

"Nothing's wrong, I'm cool," Lee said, straightening up like a man gone sober.

"Hold that thought Playa," Charlie whispered low. He motioned his arms the same way football players do when trying to calm a raucous crowd.

"Okay who is that and what her name is?" Keith asked in a similar breathless tone. Half of the time the two spoke identical foolish thoughts. Lee lifted his head to see what the commotion was all about. These two were carrying on as if they witnessed someone find the cure for cancer. He needed to know why. What was it that intrigued this pair of men? Probably nothing worth responding to.

Wrong.

The instant Lee lifted his head from staring into his drink, he saw her. His mind shifted expeditiously as he sat up trying to keep a cool look glued to his face. Keith and Uncle Charlie both already needed to wipe the drool from the corners of their dry chapped lips. Those two talked a good game but usually settled for local regulars who were odd shaped and low on intelligence.

He desired to meet someone with substance, a lady with classy style. Someone like this mystery woman who just walked in was exactly what he envisioned for himself. You could tell by the way she glided across the floor that she wasn't from around there. He kept thinking to himself that she had to be lost. Somehow she just didn't fit in with the crowd filled with locals who grew up together but never found the courage to leave. He knew if he didn't act fast, that some ridiculous looking clown, clad with polyester pants and knock off cologne would approach her, equipped with an act of buffoonery within minutes.

Without speaking, he instinctively removed himself from the bar progressing towards the stranger whose enchanted face danced beneath dim light. Her body language exuberated confidence. Her face was to be desired. Everything about her from the way her wavy hair complimented her face, down to her model like shape was in perfect place. Even her feet were gorgeous as he watched her take a seat. She sat alone at a table near a window, looking slightly bored.

"Where's he going? Where's he going?" Keith asked as he and Uncle Charlie slap boxed playfully, bouncing up and down like children wanting to be picked up.

Lee knew exactly where he was going and he wasn't about to blow it by hanging around with his usual crowd. He dispersed from their vicinity, eager to approach her. Out of the corner of her eye, the lady noticed the well built former athlete moving in her direction. As a waitress passed by shouldering flutes of Moet & Chandon White Star champagne Lee grabbed two glasses and kept moving like you see in the movies.

Perhaps being Charlie's nephew had its perks to go along with years of poor advice? Lee's father died young and Charlie was his mother's brother who to his credit stepped in to fill the void.

He stepped within a few feet when she glanced his way her eyes looking up at him, leaving him momentarily paralyzed. Her long eye lashes hovered over her light brown Asian inspired eyes.

Lee extended his hand. "Oh I'm sorry, can I sit down, I mean are you..." He stumbled over his words like an old drunk at midnight. Feeling sorry for his audible error, an invitation was extended to sit down by way of a hand gesture. She moved so gracefully, almost like she was below the oceans surface. Her jewelry shined radiantly, a tasteful mixture of gems and semi-precious stones adorned her neck, wrist, and fingers.

She shook his hand. "Rita Clark, nice to meet you," she said. Her voice sounded better than she looked. The smoky sound was laced with proper tone and pronunciation.

"Lee Johnson. The pleasure is all mine," he said. One thing was for sure, Lee had to step his game up, and it was unequivocally clear by the Burberry perfume that intoxicated his nose she wasn't like the ladies from around town. He breathed deep to take in the fragrance again. She sipped her champagne slowly.

"I've been in town for a few weeks now," she explained, "I bought one of the new lofts not far from here and commute to the city for work."

Lee was familiar with the lofts she was referencing. He used to play baseball behind those once abandoned buildings as a youngster. He toured one of them at an open house when they first remodeled the once vacant furniture factory. Reality was he couldn't afford half of a payment they were asking for the loft.

The brief conversation was moving along exceptionally. She was smiling and laughing at his usual charm while he continued to speak with confidence. Keep your cool he kept telling himself.

"What do you do for work?" Lee asked, doing his best to sound professional.

"I'm a CPA, I just started a job with a firm in the city but I wanted to live out a little. I'm tired of the hustle and bustle of the city. I needed a change," she continued, "and when the opportunity came to head up

Jackson & Fitz Accounting Division, I jumped at it."

"You run the company?" Lee asked.

She laughed playfully with a sparkle in her eyes. "Oh, you don't think a woman can handle her business?"

Even her teeth were perfect, along with her laugh. Perfect.

"I'm the first female COO in the company's eighty-five year history and I'm proud of that," she said. She took another small sip of champagne. Her glossed lips shined as Lee watched them closely. "Enough about me, what do you do?" she asked.

Lee froze. Panic stricken, he felt his body temperature rise and a little trickle of sweat slowly rolled down the center of his back. "I work at Home Towne Mailers as the first shift supervisor." Lee looked down; his eyes fluctuated left to right.

"That's great, have you been there long?" she asked with interest.

"Yea, ten years now," he said while shrugging his shoulders. The player façade he once had was now removed, and Lee didn't feel much like conversing. Somehow ex-baseball player and bulk mail supervisor didn't seem so fascinating matched up with accounting firm COO.

"Stability...I like that in a man," she said. Rita smiled as she talked. "I'll tell you what Lee, I have an engagement in the morning and I just wanted to check this place out. A girl at work recommended it to me. Why don't we exchange numbers and talk sometime." She reached into her pecan brown leather Coach bag and handed him a business card.

"I'd love to talk again. You know what... I'm all out of business cards here's my number." Lee tried to sound cultured as he scribbled seven digits on a soiled wrinkly napkin. Within moments she was gone after politely thanking him for the champagne.

As he walked back towards the bar, he watched her pull out of the parking lot in a brand new silver two door Audi TT 3.2 coupe. Lee lethargically dropped his head, still rubbing the business card she gave him as if he was consoling it. Inside his head he was thinking, maybe this time he was in over his head, and perhaps out of his league. His good looks could always get his foot in the door, but this door wasn't like any other he'd knocked on.

Chapter 2

As Lee watched the car disappear from view Keith came scurrying over towards him. "So what happened?" Keith asked while staring at the business card. Without warning he reached out and snatched the card examining it and holding it up to the light as if it was counterfeit currency. "He got the digits Charlie, he's still got it!" Keith hackled out with all of his teeth showing.

"That's my nephew," Charlie said as he spun away heading back into the kitchen.

"Give me that," Lee barked, grabbing the card back and placing his champagne flute down on the bar. Most times his friend and uncle could use a lesson or two in tact. "I'm calling it a night. I'll call you tomorrow man," Lee said. He patted Keith on the shoulder as he walked off.

Keith yelled out in laughter. "Hey, she's got money man, she's big time. What's she going to want with a low budget player like you? It's probably not even the right number." In some strange way he was trying to be persuasive.

Lee didn't feel like responding as he calmly pulled out his keys to his six year old Chevy Trailblazer. He stepped out into the night. The autumn air was brisk. It woke him up as he hopped into the SUV. He instinctively kept checking his pocket making certain the business card was still there.

He couldn't get that woman out of his mind no matter how hard he tried. It wasn't just her physical attributes; there was a way about her that he liked. Lee had become a regular ladies man over the past few years, and as a rule never even let a thought of a real relationship enter his head. He'd been hurt before, and vowed it would never happen again.

Ms. Rita Clark possessed something distinctive and exclusive about her that intrigued him. He tried to rationalize his fascination on the short ten minute commute home. As he pulled up to his duplex and cut the engine the SUV idled a little rough. There was a beep heard from inside of his sports coat where his cell phone was a mainstay. The time on his dash read 10:45. He couldn't remember the last time he'd been home so early on a Friday night. He checked the text message on his phone.

He didn't recognize the number or even the area code for that matter. His brain kicked in. He frantically reached into his pockets sifting through ATM receipts and gum wrappers, searching for the business card he received earlier that night. Did she send a text message to him? Not many women would even bother to show interest in making the first move regardless of how miniscule. He patted each pocket like a poor man searching for a winning lottery ticket.

The card was still there. He flipped it over.

Unbelievably, the number on the card matched the phone. He pushed repeat on his phone, just standing there staring. The text simply read; *Goodnight.* He contemplated his options and found himself mystified as to what to do. He could call back, or text her, just ignore it, he wasn't sure. He smiled and began to walk in a masculine manner as he began up the steps. He turned the key to his place and toppled down on the tan leather loveseat that sat next to the door.

He hit the fridge within minutes grabbing a perfectly chilled Michelob. Lee decided to text her back; *Goodnight Miss Clark.* On the other side of town the simple little message appeared across the screen on Rita's phone. She couldn't help but blush. In some ways she felt embarrassed for being so forward.

She was under the impression men should make the first move in showing interest. All these years since grad school and she never had been able to have a relationship with stability. Most men were intimidated by her, or her salary to be specific.

Rita Clark was an alluring woman, well educated, cultured, and a lot of fun to be around. Still, the fact remained that most men hesitated to talk to her for one reason or another. At age thirty-two she had an urge to settle down. Though far from desperate, the desire was undoubtedly there.

She laid back in her king size pillow top bed and thought about how nice and genuine Lee seemed. He wasn't pompous or arrogant like most men she had dated in the past. Other men's behavior suggested interest solely in their image and growing their retirement portfolios.

She'd heard all the discussions and read all the articles about how hard it was for a successful woman to find a man. But all she needed was someone to hold her tight and to care about her. She thought about how nice it would be to talk to someone understanding after a long days work. All she could do now was look forward to an outstretched conversation with her mother, and she wasn't always full of compliments.

Lee intrigued her as she laid in bed thinking about him. He had such an appealing smile and seemed to actually be listening to her as she talked, not ogling her. A regular guy with a regular job was just fine with Rita. She made enough money to not care about Lee's income. She only sought companionship.

The initial vibe between Lee and herself was like high voltage electricity flowing between them at each glance. Sometimes when you know you just get the feeling inside that things could work out. Rita's phone began to ring and broke her concentration. She lunged across the bed snatching the phone off the nightstand.

To her disappointment it was only her mother calling late at night, true to her usual routine. She let her mother leave a voicemail. Maybe her mother would think that she was out on a date.

Rita shook her head and laughed in silence to herself. Her curly locks tickled the back of her neck. Maybe this time she would find a man? If Lee couldn't give her the world on a silver platter she wouldn't mind, rather she would understand he still could possess other qualities.

Rita had become comfortable enough with herself and her career to not need a certain type of man for validation. Lee stayed in her mind over the next few minutes as she flipped aimlessly through television channels.

He was so different from the crowd she was used to associating with and she found that refreshing. She closed her almond shaped eyes to lie down to sleep. Just as she drifted off her phone rang again.

Chapter 3

Saturday morning rolled around sooner than expected. Lee spent the whole night sleeping out on the couch in front of his large screen television set. Sports Center highlights were the first sounds that he awoke to as he crawled out from beneath a blanket of half a dozen empty beer bottles. He thought about the time as he stood and wobbly walked through the cluttered room in a worn cut off tee shirt and old faded sweat pants. He glimpsed at his cell phone. The bright sun shined through the window blinds like reflective mirrors aimed at his eyes. The burning reflection bounced off the television screen causing him to squint. 12:30 already?

Lee thought about calling his Uncle Charlie but it was already in the afternoon. Uncle Charlie was most likely already in the city picking up food for the jazz lounge. He had what he called, a hook up with some Asian people who could get him goods for cheap, whatever that meant.

Lee shifted subjects in his mind. He thought about Rita and what she might be doing. His mind wandered and churned as he recalled their conversation and reminiscing on that beautiful face of hers. It was hard to believe that she was real and not just a figment of his imagination. He hoped to see her again even though a full day hadn't passed since they'd met.

Acting on a whim, he pulled the business card she gave him out of his wallet and dialed the number. He punched each button with concentrated precision. He couldn't get control of his hands, which were shaking, or stop the butterflies from fluttering in his stomach. The phone rang while he nervously waited for an answer.

A smooth professional voice answered. "Hello, this is Ms. Clark."

Lee hesitated for a moment. "Yea, Rita how are you, it's me, me Lee. We met last night."

"Can I call you back Lee?" she asked, her voice short and hurried.

"Sure, sure," Lee said.

Just like that, it was over. She was gone.

His sulking ended abruptly as his cell phone rang, startling him. He flinched, and then answered the phone.

"Hello, hello," Lee spoke calmly. He needed to impress his new female acquaintance.

"Hi Lee. I'm sorry about that. I was just finishing up goodbyes with some important clients that were in town from the Netherlands. Their flight was just leaving. I'm so sorry. I hope you understand."

Lee understood just fine, but he couldn't help but wonder. Who does business with people from the Netherlands? He wasn't even sure he knew where the Netherlands were.

He exhaled into the phone. "No big deal, thanks for calling back." His nerves finally settled as he took a seat at his kitchen table. While they talked he fiddled around nervously with the apples sitting in a bowl. The conversation got underway so natural, like two old friends catching up with each other.

Rita took charge. "So tell me about yourself. Any siblings?"

"Actually I'm an only child."

"I am too," she gushed, "What a coincidence."

"Yea, that's cool. My mom actually moved away a few months ago."

"Job relocation?"

Lee's voice changed a little. "No, she retired from the school district and wanted a change. So, she and her sister moved down to Cancun. They're teaching English to kids down there."

"Something tells me you all were really close."

"Yea, we are. I miss her, but I told her I'd be fine up here with my uncle."

"He's the one who owns the nightclub right?"

"Right. Uncle Charlie. He's like my father. My dad died when I was...three, yea three."

"I'm sorry to hear that."

"Thanks." Lee switched gears, and avoided more explanation. "Enough about me and my boring life. You told me about the move from

L.A. to this cold place last night. Where did you grow up?"

"You mean, where was I raised?"

"Yea."

"In D.C. I mean right in the thick of it too. Not too far from the White House."

"Seriously?"

"Yes. My parents met at Georgetown and settled in the area after graduation. My dad got into politics."

"Who's your dad...Colin Powell?" Lee chuckled out loud.

Rita giggled. "Come on, don't be silly. My father handled some administration for the House of Representatives. He recently retired and relocated to Connecticut. He's teaching at Yale. It's kind of funny, both our parents are educators."

Local school district fourth grade teachers were more than slightly different from Yale professors, but Lee played along.

"Yea, that's something. How about your mom?"

"Oh my mother, she's something else. She's a cellist."

"That's cool. My mom is real religious too."

Paula started laughing. Lee looked perplexed.

"You are *so* silly."

"What?" he asked.

Rita sensed his confusion and straightened up. "I'm sorry, let me explain. She's a cellist, the instrument...in an orchestra. They tour all over the world and perform."

"That's my fault. I thought you said...never mind."

"Nessuno problema."

Lee wrinkled his forehead. "Okay, now I'm hearing things."

Rita laughed. "I'm sorry. I always do that."

"Do what?"

"I'm speaking Italian again. My mother and I talk everyday and she prefers to speak Italian."

"Why? No offense but I didn't take you for an Italian at all."

Rita smiled. "I'm not. My mother is from Eritrea."

"What's that?"

"It's a small country in Africa, just north of Ethiopia. They speak many languages there. Italian is one of them. My grandfather was an Eritrean diplomat. The Italian government colonized the country in the forty's. It was an Italian African Province until the sixty's. He stayed there and worked for the UN."

"Wow. Talking to you is like turning on the History channel. Are your grandparents still there?"

"Yes, they're still in Eritrea, but their health is fading. When I was born my mother decided to teach me Italian so I could communicate with them. They speak Tigrinya and Arabic too, but mother thought it'd be most useful in the western world to speak Italian. It's especially handy for when we visit Europe."

Lee sighed. "You just said a mouthful. All I can tell you is that I've been here my whole life, except when I played minor league baseball. The team traveled all over. My dad went to high school here and my mom is from Cleveland. Impressive huh?"

"Actually, it is. Explaining my life can be difficult sometimes. I like the simple side of things."

"And I like listening to you talk. You're amazing."

Rita blushed. Each word he spoke with his smooth voice was so sweet, but didn't seem rehearsed. By the time either of them noticed it was 5:00 pm and Lee was famished. He could hardly believe that he had been on the phone for four hours talking to this phenomenal woman.

Lee made a suggestion. "Let's go out to dinner tonight," he said.

There was a pause on the other end of the phone as Rita dimmed her eyes. "If I didn't know any better I'd think you were asking me out."

"Yes I am Ms. Clark, will you accept?"

"Of course, that sounds great," she said. Her dose of enthusiasm surprised him.

"I can't wait to see you. I haven't stopped thinking about you since the moment we met last night."

"If I didn't know any better I'd think that you were falling in love with me," she teased.

Love? Please, that word wasn't in Lee's vocabulary.

He laughed shyly. "I'll see you soon."

Rita began a deep self inquisition herself over her last comment.

Why did she say that word she kept asking herself? How could an individual fall in love in one day? Most people would think that's just asinine, but most had never met Lee Johnson.

As Lee started to get dressed he pulled out of his closet a navy blue suit laying it across the bed. Then he grabbed his burgundy button up Kenneth Cole shirt matching up the outfit, thinking deeply.

He couldn't help but have that word love stir around in his mind. As he ripped the tags from the cleaners off his suit jacket he entertained the idea that for the first time in a while. Maybe this could be something real?

Chapter 4

After the first night at dinner the next six months would pass with both of them experiencing unusual feelings of exuberance. Things progressed marvelously as Lee began spending less time with Keith and Uncle Charlie. The two comrades were less than enthusiastic about Lee's new found romance. The trio of men had been reduced to a duo and perhaps they were victims of jealousy, it was hard to tell.

Every once in a while one of the two would call Lee giving him a hard time about dating Rita. Their claim was that sooner or later she would wake up and leave him for some wealthy tycoon with more to offer financially.

Despite her busy work schedule they managed to spend every weekend together and stayed on the phone incessantly. Lee watched in amazement as she fit him into her hectic life. At least once a month she traveled on business trips to Chicago, New York, or Montreal to handle the exorbitant accounts for the firm. This left Lee back in town, alone on some weekends.

Uncle Charlie made it a point to remind Lee that there was no proof Rita was where she claimed to be. Keith rattled on persistently, asking what it was like to date a woman who didn't need him. Their negativity slowly ate away at him like an old home infested with termites, crumbling his confidence, and shaking his pride. Inside Lee questioned his own machismo, but his exterior was still hardened as steel and he appeared more than self assured. Despite the negative borage he was ambushed with Lee fought to dispel any doubts from his mind and focus on the positives.

He brought a lot to the table. For starters he was a sincere, caring man that had fell head over heels. If she was a diabetic, he quite possibly could've killed her by being so sweet.

Rita never discussed money or anything remotely financial. They were both too busy enjoying one another's company to dwell on paychecks and bank statements. They had become so close over the past six months that Lee began to say the famous three words. I love you.

Rita told everyone in her life about this new man of hers and how incredibly happy she was for once. Perplexingly, no one else seemed to share her enthusiasm for Lee. Her mother in particular was livid and refused to meet him. Her mother referred to him as a bum. As usual her father sighed heavily and issued no strong opinion on her life. Her secular success mattered, nothing more.

Lee conveyed to his mother news about this special lady, Ms. Clark. His mother was not exactly thrilled by the news, rather cautious. What did a powerful career woman want with a washed-up baseball star that held down an average job? That question haunted Lee when he sat alone with his thoughts.

He had indeed fallen in love with Rita and her likewise but he still has his reservations. His mind drifted in a sea of self-doubt. Rita routinely picked up the bill when they went out on a more extravagant date. Though it felt weird, he never spoke up in objection. He did however continue to reassure her that he was more than comfortable with that arrangement.

Deep down inside it became a cause of vexation.

Why not speak up? Why not tell her the feelings inside? Honesty has always proved to be the best policy with Rita. She made it clear several times that she paid no attention to their difference in income. Lee brought the subject to the forefront just weeks into the romance. The issue was quickly dismantled. Rita declared on several occasions she couldn't deal with an insecure man.

He had to come clean. He had to confess.

Unable to withhold the secret that burned within his heart each night, he reached a conclusion. It would be best to let his true feelings out slowly and under control, rather than erupt later in a volcanic meltdown.

He hadn't contemplated about a long term romance in years, but no one had become worthy in his eyes except Ms. Rita Clark.

Lee gazed over at Rita's framed picture sitting on his nightstand. He lay in bed, distraught and confused. The warmth from the covers weren't enough to erase the cold chilling seed of self-doubt planted within his soul. He laid there for at least fifteen minutes easy, realizing how fortunate he was to have this refined attractive woman walk in his life six months ago.

The morning sun slowly became more visible. As he sat up in bed at early dawn, he knew that night at dinner he would open up and convey his deepest sentiments of low self worth and doubt. He wanted desperately for the love to last with Rita, and he would give his last breath to have those feelings endure. She, simply put, was all he desired in a woman and didn't wish to blow his chance due to his own insecurity. Within his reach was a prospect presenting itself to truly be happy and he sought to put forth effort that very night to solidify that notion.

It was a night Rita regarded as their six month anniversary. If he expressed what he was wrestling with inside somehow he knew Rita would understand, just like she always did.

Chapter 5

As planned, they dined at a luxurious restaurant Rita had heard so much about. As the two were being seated at their reserved corner table Lee looked around nervously at his environment feeling out of place. For some odd reason it occurred to him that everyone was staring at him as if he didn't belong amongst their crowd of upper crust professionals. Rita on the opposite end of the spectrum was excited to be out celebrating their six months of exclusivity. She had heard so much about this restaurant, Chateau Le Blanc.

It was an upscale French Bistro tucked away in the city that provided an intimate setting. Everywhere his eyes looked they were greeted with dancing candles aflame and crisp white linen. There was even a woman in performing on a harp in the establishment's northwest corner. Rita expressed to Lee her love of French cuisine, and the semi-sweet champagne that was famous in the region.

Lee recalled the familiar tale of how she had spent the summer in France after graduation. Her father shelled out the money for the trip sending Rita along with her best friend on an all expense paid excursion into a foreign land so full of culture and delicacies. Her father may have never spoken much to his daughter, but had no qualms about spoiling her with elaborate gifts, to make up for his absence in the home.

Lee cautiously sipped water from a crystal glass thinking to himself nervously of the cost of dinner at this regal restaurant. He'd never even heard of the Chateau Le Blanc.

The pricy evening included a $221 bottle of Louis Roederer-Brut champagne. Her taste for fine food had direct impact on his wallet. He finally mustered up the courage to divulge his feelings and insecurities.

He started to speak. A waiter interrupted. "My name is Pierre, I'll be serving you tonight." A petite man with dark hair and enormous nose spoke; the remainders of his words were indecipherable. The man spoke French, the whole time he looked unswervingly at Lee.

Perhaps it was the blank stare that gave way to the fact Lee was not slightly skilled in that tongue. The waiter became discontented and bothered with Lee turned his attention towards Rita awaiting a response. Rita spoke a fair amount of French and took the liberty of ordering for them both. After a curt bow and a cut of the eyes towards Lee the small tuxedo clad waiter with the large nose was gone.

"Oh, so you speak French too?" Lee asked. He nodded his head.

She gestured a pinch with her fingers. "Well maybe a little." She smiled shyly.

Lee smiled back. "Well, any other languages to tell me about, or do you want to just surprise me next time we order Chinese?"

Her answer quickly erased the smile, startling him and going on to explain. "I speak Italian, of course. But also some French as you've seen, Spanish, and yes a measure of Chinese."

Six months together and he was still finding out so many vast differences between them. They started to outweigh the similarities. She was always revealing things about her past and her travels that were so engrossing while his history was lackluster, and dull as old brass.

Rita reached out touching his hand in a gentle way as if to say she had something weighty to ask him. "Lee, there's a job opening where I work. Now, don't take this the wrong way, but I think you should consider it. You always say how you're tired of those people you work with at Home Towne Mailers." Rita was cautious in her choice of words.

Lee sat back, perplexed, since he had no accounting experience.

"Okay...," he said slowly while waiting for more information.

"We have a mailroom at our firm and they are looking for a new manager to oversee the department. The last one was hopeless to deal with, but nonetheless. Frank was telling me about it and asked if I knew anyone, so I told him about you, and..." Rita paused and smiled intentionally. She knew he loved her naïve look.

He found her irresistible as he smiled back, "And, what? What's the catch? Let me have it..."

"No catch, Frank just wants you to forward your resume over. So email it to him next week...well, if you choose to." Rita was smiling again.

Lee paused. Who was this Frank character? "Working together would be a bit much though baby, I don't know," he said.

"Well we wouldn't be together per se, it is a sizeable building. You would be on the third floor and I'd be upstairs, besides it's a great opportunity with great benefits," she rebutted.

Benefits would be nice Lee thought. Home Towne Mailers wasn't in the habit of providing insurance for employees.

"Your appetizers sir," a voice said, this time in English. The waiter handed Lee a small plate with a slimy substance on it covered in a light brown sauce accompanied with garnish of fresh thyme and rosemary. His mind churned wondering what it was and how he was supposed to eat it.

Rita's voice sounded roused as she sampled what she explained was a delicacy. "Escargot baby, hope you like it."

Lee awkwardly handled his silverware attempting to enjoy the appetizer in small portions. All the while his silverware clanged and dinged against his plate drawing stares from the wealthy patrons who dined alongside. Rita overlooked the clumsily manner in which he dined. Many people were unskilled in the etiquette associated with fine dining. He was at least trying. As the slippery fragment of food slid down his throat, he picked up on the conversation.

"So, about this job... Is the salary listed? I'm just wondering the pay scale for manager at Jackson and Fitz." Lee put on a fake British accent, attempting to be humorous. At the same time he was trying to gage what kind of money Rita made. She never discussed her income with him, but he concluded she was very wealthy. He saw her new Audi, the fancy degrees that graced her walls, the title COO and the expensive condo that she lived in.

If she was well off, she was modest and never seemed judgmental. Honestly she was the most understanding woman he had ever met in his life. Shame quickly came over him like a fast moving desert wind storm as he felt regret for feeling intimidated by her salary.

Rita never talked down to him and always treated him as the man in their relationship despite their obvious financial differences. Undoubtedly, she came from a family with a background of wealth and distinction but she reassured him that his sincerity was a breath of fresh air in her life once clouded with pollution.

She continued the company description, going on to explain the monetary benefits of working at Jackson and Fitz. There was the 401k, the life insurance package, three weeks vacation, paid holidays, sick leave and the $50,000 a year salary for the mail room manager. *Really?*

Lee knew he could handle the job. Could he handle the situation? He couldn't help but wonder what type of compensation Rita earned if mail room manager started at $50,000. She had to make at least $90,000 a year minimum or maybe even six figures. His imagination ran wild in regards to her earning potential.

Rita picked back up the conversation. "Just think about it Lee, change can be good occasionally. It has been for me. These last six months I've never been happier, thank you so much darling, I love you."

Lee felt a big wave of shame crash into shore. The feeling cut into his heart making it strenuous to breathe. "I love you too babe, I'll think it over, it does sound like something to look into." Lee spoke softly with his eyes looking down and starting to glaze over as he blinked rapidly.

He decided to dismiss the negative thoughts he originally sought to discuss, suppressed those feelings. How could he bring them up after this kind of opportunity was presented?

Lee seemed somewhat distraught and the conversation slowed.

"Everything okay Lee?" Rita asked while rubbing his hands with her sleek honeyed skin.

"Everything is fine Ms. Clark, everything is fine....including you. You look breath-taking tonight." She viewed it as so cute how he affectionately called her Ms. Clark from time to time. It made her reminisce over the night they met.

Throughout the remainder of the dinner Lee's soul was conflicted and torn in every direction imaginable. The last thing he wanted to do was hurt her. He couldn't promise himself that wouldn't happen.

Chapter 6

The next week arrived and Lee decided to submit an application for the mail room manager position at Jackson & Fitz. It was a great opportunity and a chance for a needed change. After going through the application process and two interviews he finally heard those sought after words.

"Congratulations Mr. Johnson, welcome to the Jackson & Fitz team." Those were the words ushered out by Mr. Ed Flannigan the assistant director of employment. Ed was a skinny older man with bad posture, thin hair and an antique gray suit.

The twig like man went on giving him a laundry list of people to remember that were important players as he put it on the Jackson & Fitz team.

"I'll have you know Lee, you beat out seventeen other applicants for this job, you ought to be proud," Mr. Flannigan said. Lee felt a sigh of relief more than anything.

"Thank you sir," Lee said.

"It's not often we find people who can run all our mailing equipment, let alone have the savvy and experience you possess." Mr. Flannigan spoke as if he was impressed by Lee's repertoire.

No mention was made of Ms. Clark and his relationship with her. Lee was almost sure he got this job due to her, feeling she must have had some impact on him being hired. She continually assured him she would have nothing to do with the hiring process at all. She preferred to keep her business and personal life absolutely separate.

Rita did express concern about them working in such close proximity but Lee assured her he could handle it. She suggested they kept the relationship discreet as to not cause a stir amongst fellow employees. He kept thinking about all the times he doubted Rita and each time she would prove those very doubts that plagued him to be unfounded. She provided support, applauding his efforts on trying to land the job.

He told himself for the last time to believe he got this on his own. Rita told him it would be unethical to tip the scales in his favor, especially when coming from someone of her business stature.

Lee stood to leave. "Thank you again."

"Hey Lee, before you go, I've got to warn you my man. I shouldn't be telling you this but listen, man-to-man. We've got a new COO her name's Ms. Clark and boy is she a head turner. I just want warn you, because a couple guys upstairs asked her out. She shot them down dead in their tracks. She can be cold. I'm talking brutally mean."

Lee cracked a nervous smile. "Thanks for the advice."

Ed Flannigan patted him on the shoulder, moving him towards the door. Lee and Rita had been dating for almost seven months and he never saw that tough personality Ed Flannigan mentioned.

"Oh yea, one more thing... Frank Harrison, my boss. He's head of Human Resources by the way. He's been going around telling everybody Ms. Clark will be his in just a matter of time. He said pretty soon they'll be going out with her on the back of his Harley. See you soon Lee. Congrats again."

Frank Harrison was a bigger built middle aged man who had been divorced twice. He was your standard blue suit, red power tie kind of boss. He always rubbed his chin like an evil dictator, trying to appear intimidating. There were several rumblings around the office of how he was showering some new young secretary with gifts or spending weekends with one of them at his infamous lake house.

After hearing the last bit of news Lee wasn't smiling. He neglected to say goodbye as he walked out the door heading towards the elevator. His mind began to wandering again. How much time did Frank and Rita spent together? He thought about Mr. Flannigan's comments about all those men at the office who pursued Rita, especially with their relationship being a secret. He wasn't sure he wanted to deal with the situation.

Questions ran through his mind turning and twisting like cyclones. Was Rita ashamed of him? How close was she to this Frank character? Could her intentions with him possibly be that conniving and sinister?

Should he have taken the position at Jackson & Fitz?

He'd already become slightly disturbed about the attention Rita drew from men when they went out. Now he'd now have to deal with it at work.

Lee realized the stares and looks given to them came with the territory of dating a woman with superstar looks. She was far different than some of the girls Keith tried to hook him up with. Those women seemed to always have relaxed brains, and faces perfect for radio. Ms. Rita Clark was nearly flawless. She was also honest with him, giving him no reason to be skeptical, but part of him was.

As he observantly walked through the parking lot filled with endless rows of expensive foreign vehicles he contemplated if it was her he doubted? Was it himself? That evening Rita was busy entertaining clients again. This time she dined with investors from China.

By the time she set foot in her condo and returned Lee's phone call he fast asleep. Lee groggily answered the phone. "Can we talk later babe? I'm just now getting to sleep."

Rita's smile came all the way through the phone. "Sure, I understand." Her gentle voice gave way to pleasant dreamscapes.

The next day was Thursday. Lee agreed to start mid-week. He wanted to become acclimated to his new surroundings as soon as possible. Part of him felt bad about leaving Home Towne Mailers with short notice, but that place had more turnover than a restless night of sleep. All those years on the job feeling so dissatisfied left him emotionally drained. The minute he could remove that monstrous burden from his life, he did so. That change would allow him to breathe again. It felt good.

He rolled over in bed, half sleep. Sometimes he envied Rita and the times she entertained international clients. Other times he realized the significant position she played for the company.

Jackson & Fitz was an international company with locations abroad. The company had interests in account management, international banking, and real estate investment. They sought out bright young minds like Rita Clark. Lee wondered what he sought. He wasn't sure.

Chapter 7

Thursday morning at 7:30 Lee met Ed Flannigan in the pristine lobby of Jackson & Fitz. The huge glass building sat amidst downtown. Taxi cabs and hurried traffic could be seen whizzing by outside of the buildings glass entrance.

"Well Lee, you look good. Are you ready to meet the employees you'll be supervising?" Mr. Flannigan asked as they moved towards the endless row of elevators.

"Yes, definitely sir," Lee said. His voice carried a rigid tone.

"Well good, they're a nice bunch, I'm sure you'll like them," Mr. Flannigan said as they took the brief elevator ride. "Third floor, ah yes, here we are," Mr. Flannigan now gestured towards the large grey double doors just off the elevator that read Mail Room. Directly adjacent to the door was a new name plate reading Lee Johnson, Manager.

Lee liked the sound of that. He smiled to himself. The title rolled nicely off his tongue. They stepped into the mailroom. Look at this place Lee kept thinking in disbelief as he walked around inside the wide open floor plan.

"See, all the latest equipment, just like I told you. Everything at Jackson & Fitz is first class, including the mail," Mr. Flannigan said. He slapped his bony hand against Lee's back leaving it stinging.

"Over here's your office," Ed said pointing, "and feel free to call me if you need anything. My door is always open. Welcome to the team partner." Mr. Flannigan spoke with his breath reeking of coffee while extending his hand. After a firm handshake, he was gone and Lee was left to wander around for about ten minutes before the staff arrived at 8:00.

One by one, each employee came dragging in, with their own distinct traits. There was Javier, a clean cut gentleman who was Lee's age and seemed eager to do his work and go home. Next entered Sharon, an older woman carrying a thermos and a lunch bag almost waddling as she walked. She reminded Lee of penguins at the zoo.

Scott arrived dressed in his usual tight blue jeans and flannel shirt tucked in. Lee noticed his badly worn off brand tennis shoes. "Excuse me; I didn't get your name please."

Lee pivoted towards the three and introduced himself. He'd been a manager for years at Home Towne Mailers and knew the proper way to keep a staff in line. This would be a breeze compared to the group of slackers, ex-cons, and high school dropouts he worked with previously.

That's when he heard the voice.

"Sorry I'm late."

Lee turned around and saw Liz Hart, an old family friend. All through high school and well into his twenties he dated her younger sister Simone, until their ugly breakup.

That separation shattered Lee's heart into a million minuscule pieces. At one time he planned to start a life with Simone just as soon as she was finished with college. She attended school in Atlanta and the distance proved taxing.

He leaned in and hugged her. "How are your parents doing?"

"Good. Mom retired, no more counseling teenagers for her and dad is still fighting fires."

Mr. Hart, their father, was a tall strong man who was well respected around town. Mr. Hart grew up together in town with Lee's father. They also worked together as fireman since graduating from High School.

"That's cool," Lee said.

"I saw your mom's house is for sale."

"Yea, I'd like to buy it, but right now's not a good time."

His mother and the Hart family in spite of everything were family, talking on a weekly basis. The families lived only one street over and their backyards backed up to one another.

"I just can't believe we're going to be working together, and you're going to be my boss."

"Funny huh?"

"Yea it is. We go way back."

Mr. Hart took Lee and his mother under his large wings with open arms. They would spend a massive amount of time together growing up, going on family trips and throwing hundreds of backyard barbeques. They pretty much did everything as one family unit until Lee and Simone split apart.

The Hart's younger daughter Simone was the love of Lee's life since childhood when he first discovered her beauty. Simone was always considered gorgeous in everyone's eyes. Maybe it was her electrifying smile, and those deep dark eyes? Whatever it was she seemed to be the complete package from head to toe.

"Mom and Daddy are always asking about you Lee. I can't wait to tell them the good news. Simone is going to flip out too. I'm going to call her tonight."

Lee winced.

Noticing Lee's expression Liz smiled. "I'm sorry Lee. I don't want to go there, but Simone still asks about you almost every time we talk. She still loves you. I know that for a fact. You guys are still perfect for each other, you always were." Her words trailed off considerably at the end of the sentence.

Lee made an attempt to change the subject. "How long you been here?"

"For about a year now, I started after I moved closer to the city with Ray." She held out her hand exposing a wedding ring.

"Okay," Lee said playfully, squinting as if the diamond was blinding him. Lee had a certain way that made everyone feel comfortable.

"We missed you at the wedding too, don't think I forgot," Liz frowned pulling her hand back and placing it on her rounded hip.

"I'm sorry Liz I wanted to be at the wedding, but..." He stopped short. He couldn't think of a good excuse.

"I know you didn't want to see Simone, but come on. Even your mom was sitting with us at the family table. That's alright though cause you going to have to see her soon. She's moving home in a few months and she's going to stay with Mom and Dad until she finds a house to buy. You should see Shawn too, he's getting so big. You know he's ten now and he plays baseball too. Just like you."

Lee was a star baseball player in high school and played triple A minor league baseball while Simone was at college on scholarship. He played the game with so much passion and intensity back then it was intimidating. His high school dreams of becoming a professional were crushed after he lost his head and physically attacked a coach. He viciously attacked the older man breaking his nose and fracturing his cheek bone. Lee was branded as a player unable to be coached in baseball circles and eventually was pushed out the sport, moving back home and pursuing a nine to five job.

Once back home, his dreams faded fast and fizzled out. Lee always maintained the story that the situation was all a big misunderstanding. He was okay with how things ended up he convinced himself, admitting he had trouble hitting a curveball consistently anyway.

Lee processed the news about Simone's return. He paused and shook his head. So many different emotions ran in his head. So many varying memories lingered. The last thing he wanted or needed was to catch sight of Simone again, but he was sure he'd hear about her everyday because Liz and the Hart parents wanted the two together. Lee knew that was never going to happen, not even in a million years. Even after the initial break up the couple was off and on for around eight long years, until he just couldn't take it any further.

Simone pleaded to make it work out, but the long distance, plus the past frustrations ran interference with his heart. They flirted with the idea of marriage several times but Lee just couldn't go through with it. Around two years passed without any extensive contact at all besides an occasional email, text message, or brief chat. Rita replaced her memory and healed his wounds.

Liz grabbed his hand and then letting go turned and started to join the rest of the group. "I don't see a ring on your finger Lee. You better keep your options open. Things change."

Chapter 8

Over the next six weeks time flew by and things were going fantastic on the job. The entire staff had warmed up to Lee, even the notoriously grumpy Scott. They realized he wasn't a control freak like the previous manager. Everyday Liz would be cracking jokes, and making him laugh, just like she did while they were growing up.

It made him think back to the good old days and the great times he had being with the Hart family. Of course, every so often Liz would tell him how her Mom or Dad was asking about him or telling him hello. The Harts missed Lee so much, especially since his mother was now living in Mexico and the lot behind them was vacant. To his surprise though there were never any messages from Simone, which baffled him. He did call to mind telling Liz he didn't want to discuss her, but on the other hand he wondered if he ever crossed her mind anymore.

After work he did his usual routine of heading back into town and calling Rita on the phone during the commute. He instinctively fulfilled that task daily. Most of the time, she would still be back at the office working late.

Unknown to him, Rita was being groomed to take over the International Banking Division position that would be opening up within the company at any moment.

Everyone in the executive offices anticipated a retirement announcement from a Mr. Donald Sander, Vice President, International Banking Division for Jackson & Fitz. Rita prized this idea of climbing yet another rung on the corporate ladder, but it came with a cost. Of course the salary would increase measurably, but would require relocation to London. Rita realized Lee probably would not be interested in moving across the Atlantic Ocean. She still at the same time been thinking that they've been together for nearly eight months and Lee seemed content with casual dating.

She wondered why. Was it her?

They had a few conversations surrounding the subject of marriage but Lee had the appearance of someone truly unsure. Keith continued to refer to Lee as a player, even in Rita's presence. She didn't know if it was a term of endearment or Lee's true character. She wondered. Over the past few weeks there had been several arguments over Lee's noticeable insecurity. That was an accusation he constantly denied sometimes raising his voice to the point of yelling.

Rita began to wonder if his raised voice was due to his habitual nightly drinks. He claimed they helped him to relax. Rita was all too familiar with a man and his temper. Her father had a alcohol issue, gin to be precise. She still couldn't stand the scent of that evil liquor. Her father would come home frazzled from conflicted interaction with bickering politicians all day. His physical violence caused her parents to divorce.

Rita's fathers dinking reached a culmination point resulting in her mother on the receiving end of several well placed backhands to the face. Her mother left and never looked back. She raised Rita to respect herself and to never let a man demean her in anyway. Her father eventually got help for his hindrance, remaining sober for years. Even with that being the case her parents weren't on speaking terms.

These were family secrets that no one knew, not even Lee. Rita had been programmed to shield those harsh realities out of fear of doing damage to both parents flourishing careers.

With those thoughts in Rita's mind she kept suggesting Lee needed to slow down on his alcohol consumption. Lee made sure to let her know that it was the stress of the new job that was getting to him a little bit, resulting in after work cocktails. Rita suspected that much more disturbed Lee than work.

Lee was at home after work when his phone rang. His mother voiced her concern, "Baby, I don't want to see you get hurt. You hear me talking?" His mom spoke as if he faced real danger.

You would've thought that dating Rita was equal to being placed in a Vietnamese prison camp.

"Mom please, I'm a grown man. I can handle this," Lee explained.

"Charlie says the girl's real snobby. I just wonder what she wants with you that's all."

"What's that supposed to mean? You think I'm not good enough?"

"No, it's not that, you all are just from two different worlds. Besides Charlie said half the time she'd speaking in Chinese or something so nobody can understand her."

"Okay mom, Charlie says a lot of things. Besides it's Italian. Charlie's no expert on women, believe me."

"My brother could have been married Lee. Charlie says it's his high blood pressure, you know he's got stress from running that Lounge. Stress from a marriage is too much for him." His mom was now defending her older brother, making the conversation hopeless.

"I gotta go mom, Rita's calling me right now." Lee hurried his mom off the phone and clicked over taking Rita's call.

"Hey, how'd it go at the board meeting today?" he asked her, pretending to be interested.

"Fine Lee, just fine. Listen, I was hoping we could talk today about where we're going as a couple. Where do you see us in the next year?" Rita said those few words as if she'd been rehearsing those lines all day. She tossed her keys aside, shedding her coat and flopped on to oversized chocolate leather chaise in exasperation.

Lee thought, what about a hello? Despite her attitude he journeyed forth trying to pour on his customary charm and change the subject.

"I don't know about a year or so, but I know where I'll be Friday night. We'll be at Uncle Charlie's Lounge baby. He finally got Marion Meadows to come perform his new jazz set." He hoped that good news would be enough to dodge this conversation again.

Unfortunately, she wasn't giving up so easily. "I'm serious. We always dance around this topic of marriage and commitment. What do I have to do, propose to you?" She pouted in a sad voice that made him feel guilty.

He cut her off with another joke. "Yea, that might work." Lee chuckled in another desperate attempt to change the subject.

"Okay Lee, if you want to be a comedian you go right ahead. I've got more important things to do than beg you for an engagement ring," Rita said, her voice disgusted. She sat cross legged leaning back in the lounge seated as soft piano music played lightly. Her left shoe was dangling off her foot as she concentrated.

Lee quit playing and heavily cleared his throat, "Rita, I just want to go slow babe. I've been hurt before that's all."

That was the wrong thing to say because Rita never missed a detail.

"Really? Well, this is the first I've heard of this mister-never-been in a serious relationship. I can't believe you lied to me Lee. You lied!" Rita's tone was now more business than casual now as she rose quickly from her lounged position. She went from poodle to pit bull in the blink of an eye.

Lee slipped up and let a secret out, he realized that at this instant. How could he have been so sloppy after all those months of well placed deception? He had always told Rita that she was the first bona fide relationship he'd been in because he wouldn't even reflect on how Simone flattened him years ago.

Sensing her disappointment he responded. "Well, I mean. It wasn't that serious don't get me wrong." Lee back peddled faster than a NFL cornerback, trying to stop a deep pass.

"You lied to me Lee; it was a classic Freudian slip. I can't believe you. All of a sudden you're so sensitive and scared to get hurt. You? Give me a break. I've been nothing but honest with you from day one. I don't need this after the day I've had." Rita's last words were breaking up as she began to sob.

He straightened up, his eyes staring a whole through her picture on the nightstand. "What's wrong baby?" His heart beat rapidly. He knew something was wrong. He held his breath while waiting for her to reveal the details.

"At work, they're talking about promoting me to the International Banking Division as a VP but the job is in...," Rita sniffled.

"Whoa, that's great. What's wrong with that? You should be proud." Lee was encouraging as he spoke but in the back of his mind he had his own doubts.

"England Lee, London. They want me to move to London. I have to go in a few months to administer some auditing work and if everything falls into place I could accept the VP position." Rita continued to whine. "I don't know what to do. My parents would kill me if I didn't take this opportunity. The truth is, I want to be with you. I just don't know what you want. I just don't know."

Her hair fell into her face as one hand held her forehead, her elbow braced against her knee as she stared trance like at her red toe nails. Her shoulders shook as small whimpers were heard through the phone. The problem was Lee didn't know what to do or say either, except for one thing. He wasn't about to move to a whole new country and follow her around like some little lost puppy. What did he know about life in England?

He knew Rita was a savvy businesswoman and he didn't wish to prevent her from smashing through the glass ceiling which she was doing with the force of a sledgehammer no less.

Lee swallowed hard. "We'll work something out." He did his best to be a shoulder for her. He already had an engagement ring he once purchased while planning on marrying Simone. It was an especially beautiful princess cut two karat diamond that he bought in the New York diamond district while playing baseball in the minor leagues. As he contemplated the ethics of giving a woman a ring once bought with another in mind, she said something that brought him to his feet.

The next words exploded through the receiver igniting response, as she cried. "He grabbed me today Lee, that jerk put his filthy hands on me." Rita sobbed uncontrollably, her cheeks fully flush.

"Who? What? What are you talking about?" Lee shouted, charging ahead like he was coming out of a boxing corner

Rita rose from her seated position and approached the window that overlooked the tree lined park. "Frank, at work. He grabbed on me today, and then he tried to play it off as if it was some sort of accident. I'm so sick of him bothering me everyday. I told him I had a man but he just...." Rita was obviously traumatized and upset, in necessity of Lee's listening ear.

He might as well have been deaf at that moment. All he could think to say in an outraged tone was, "I'll kill him!"

Chapter 9

"I'll kill him Rita, the next time I see that guy I'm going off. I straight up don't even care!" Rita could tell his words were not idle threats thrown about carelessly like leaves tossed in the air by children on a windy fall day. She pondered momentarily of how this man she had grown to know and love could be so easily transformed from a laid back person, into a man full of rage.

Rita sighed. "Lee that's not going to help things. Let me handle this. I already placed a call to my lawyer, I need proper legal counsel. He's supposed to get back with me soon." Rita sat once again entering back to her usual self, polished, poised, and under control. Lee paused wondering why she would choose to call her lawyer before talking to him.

Wasn't he supposed to be the shoulder she could lean on? For just a split second he entertained the idea that maybe Uncle Charlie and Keith were correct over these past months and for once the girl was the player and he the one being played.

"Lee I should've talked to you first, I'm sorry. I just didn't know what to do." Rita sniffled. It was as if she had the ability to peer inside his mind, open it up and know what he was thinking, therefore excluding herself from any blame.

Lee sat back down, "I feel you. You probably did the right thing. I don't even know how I would've reacted while at work you know." Lee shook his head up and down while he was talking. He had realized how unsettled he was and knew he could possibly spiral out of control, as he now slowly rocked in his seat.

"Thanks for the support. Oh Lee, sorry, the lawyers calling right now. I've got to take this call."

"I'll hit you back," Lee said.

"I'll be downstairs afterwards to get a spa treatment okay? I need to relax, call me later love." Rita rushed through that sentence so fast while picking up her coat from the entryway floor. She hung up.

Lee heard a dial tone as he pulled the phone away from his ear and looked at it puzzled. "Bye to you too," he said.

Rita's building housed a spa and fitness club. There was also a bookstore and coffee house on the ground floor. These were one of the many perks that went along with ownership in the renovated old warehouse. He never went over to her place much and sometimes forgot all the related amenities.

Lee sat there understanding that she had to take the phone call, but goodness. Did she have to rush him off the phone like he was some kind of irritating pest? Here he was trying to have her back and she's running break neck speed to some lawyer acting like Lee was bothering her.

"You called me!" Lee yelled out loud. He threw his phone down on the couch as he reached the bottom stairs. He became infuriated all over again. Lee had always been the type of guy to hold things in, but once that ball of anger got rolling it took a while to bring it to a halt. Lee knew he had to cool off before he did something dim-witted again.

He looked back on the situation when he attacked one of his baseball coaches, because he kept referring to Lee as a momma's boy. The third base coach overheard Lee talking to his mom a few times telling her how much he missed her and being at home. The coach would laugh, telling Lee to grow up and stop being so soft. Lee warned him enough times in his own eyes, it was the coaches fault it happened. Sure, it did blow his shot at a baseball career but it was all a big misunderstanding.

Then there was the time he and Keith battered those punks in Charlie's Lounge that wouldn't get out of their booth. Everyone knew they always sat there, those guys were asking for it too. Lee and Keith were arrested for disorderly conduct. It wasn't like it was a felony or anything.

Then he couldn't possibly forget the DUI he got busted for about a year earlier. The reason for that was because that night Uncle Charlie was practically passed out and Lee had to drive him home, all the way to the other side of town.

If he had just gone to his house near the Lounge he never would've got caught. That's what he kept telling himself anyway.

Feeling stressed out by Rita's quick dismissal Lee did what he always did after work when he needed to dampen down. He went to the kitchen and opened the fridge looking to wrap his hands around an ice cold Miller Highlife. He had forgotten that he finished the six-pack he brought home yesterday while watching the game. Yes, a whole six pack.

Lee was in the kitchen hovering over the refrigerator shelves when he decided to call Keith. The two old friends had not hung out together in quite some time. He knew his friend would be up to a few drinks and some food at Uncle Charlie's Lounge. He dialed Keith's cell phone.

"Keith what's going on man? You feel like going to Charlie's?"

Keith laughed on the other end of the phone. "Did you ask Rita if you could go? I don't want her to cut off your allowance."

"I do what I want fool. You see a ring on my finger?" Lee snapped back sounding put off.

"Ok, ok, that's the Lee I know. Meet me there in like half an hour. I gotta drop a couple CDs off at the barbershop. I'm trying to get paid real quick. Hey you want that Jill Scott? Five dollars...," Keith said quickly.

"I'm cool, see you there." Lee grinned while declining the CD offer. Keith always had some type of money earning hustle going. This month it would be bootleg CDs, last summer it was knock off designer purses and scented body oils.

As Lee got dressed into proper attire he realized he couldn't honestly remember the last time he'd been out with Keith and Uncle Charlie. In a lot of ways he kind of missed the times when life was so care free and laid back. Being with Rita was great in its own right as she did expose him to another way of living. High class living to be specific.

Lee just wasn't sure he could deal with all the added baggage that seemed to come with it. As he drove to Charlie's he decided to give her a call to see how things were going with the lawyer. "Hey, how'd it go with the lawyer?" Lee asked showing a serious level of interest.

"Fine, just fine, I'll file a complaint tomorrow morning and submit it to Personnel. Thanks sweetie I have to run okay. I just hit the spa. I don't want to be rude and talk on the cell phone in their waiting area. Bye." She shuffled anxiously giving a hand signal to the receptionist.

Lee didn't hold back his tone in expressing his frustrations. "Oh okay, you can be rude to me though and not the people at the spa? I get it now. Sorry I called then. I don't wanna bother you again."

"I don't like your tone Lee, nor what you're implying," Rita responded stiffly. She was now uncomfortable in the busy lobby, covering her mouth so passers by wouldn't hear her arguing.

"First off, you're not my mom alright. I'll use whatever tone I want. Who uses the word nor anyway?" Lee was now totally fed up with her quick remarks to him.

"This is neither the time, *nor* place," Rita was growing louder.

"It's never a good time for you is it? You stay busy. Can you fit me in your schedule sometime so we can talk?"

"I told you my job requires a great deal of time, and you said you could handle it. You said you could deal with my lifestyle. I didn't twist your arm into getting involved with me. I won't do this Lee. Not after the day I've had." Rita walked briskly out of the spa and into the parking lot.

"I tried to help you with your day. What are you talking about girl?"

"Please! You were carrying on and on, acting like some sort of thug. I don't believe in violence, not at all," Rita sighed. "Where are you going anyway, may I ask?" Rita heard the wind passing through Lee's windows as he drove along en route to Charlie's Lounge.

"I'm going out with Keith tonight," Lee said while bobbing his head to the infectious beat coming from his radio.

"It's a work night. You shouldn't be out drinking and hanging with, with...," Rita paused.

"With what? My friend? My uncle? Work night whatever, I don't care. I'm grown baby girl!" Lee laughed feeling cocky as he talked.

"My lawyers calling me back. I have to take this, we'll talk later." Rita again sounded snippy hanging up on Lee.

Again, there was no farewell only another dial tone. Lee lobbed his cell phone into the empty passenger seat, watching it roll to a stop.

Eight months together and things were beginning to crumble.

Chapter 10

As Lee roved into the bar he was taken back to the familiar smells and sounds. Not to mention the delightful sights of the ladies that lie inside the friendly oasis. Everything he used to love was all wrapped up into one inside this place. The lounge was unusually packed for a Thursday night. The band played on with their funky grooves as Lee made his way to belly up at the large mahogany bar which was crowded with patrons ordering drinks with crumpled dollar bills extended vying for the lone bartender's attention.

Awaiting his arrival Keith and Charlie were standing in a trance bobbing their heads to the beat trying their best to look distinguished.

"It's just like old times." Charlie smiled broadly giving his nephew a hug. "You finally got away huh?"

Keith erupted in laughter spilling a bit of beer on his loud canary yellow button up shirt. "Let him see your business cards Lee," Keith said. He acted as if business cards were some right of passage, stating you've arrived in the business world.

"I bet it don't say CEO on those. No, just kidding man, how you doing on that new job of yours?" Charlie laughed while he talked.

"It's going good ya'll, real good. Liz Hart works in there too, we've been having a good time," Lee said.

"You mean Simone's sister Liz?" Keith asked with his mouth open.

"Yea."

"Man, she was fine back in the day, but not as fine as Simone though. You blew that Lee! You blew it! I don't care man, I would've went down there and got my woman."

"Shut up fool," Uncle Charlie said, slapping Keith in the back of his head. Charlie instantly started to wipe his hands on a napkin as if by touching Keith he risked picking up some unwanted germs.

"Yea I know that job is more than alright, your mom told me you traded in that Trailblazer for a new Durango," Charlie said.

"Yea, I'd have a new car to if my girl was CEO at some fancy company, and got me a nice job too," Keith added, sucking his teeth.

"It's *COO*," Lee corrected him. The smell of smoke, fish grease, and mixed drinks continued to fill the air as they conversed.

"How'd you get out tonight anyway? Where's your girl at?" Uncle Charlie asked, leaning in like Lee was about to tell some hot gossip.

"She's at the spa tonight, she's all stressed out over work and stuff," Lee mumbled while flagging the bar tender down for a drink. "Gin and tonic, thanks," he ordered half ignoring their inquisition.

"If she was my girl, she wouldn't need no spa." Keith laughed again, flexing his hands in and out, "I'd put on a Maxwell CD and light some candles."

"Shut up!" Charlie and Lee spoke in choir like unison.

Keith straightened up and started explaining. "Look though, seriously, we gotta get together more often man. We haven't kicked it like we used to lately." Keith suddenly began to walk away and looking back over his shoulder winking, "I'll be back." He headed to a table filled with women, regulars at the lounge.

"Can he ever make sense?" Charlie asked, while grabbing Lee by the shoulders. "Let's talk, come on." Charlie turned towards the kitchen.

Maneuvering through the busy kitchen they dodged the splattering grease and busy cooks. The pair walked down the hall to Charlie's private office. "Sit down," Charlie commanded, "We gotta talk."

"What's wrong?" Lee asked leaning forward with both eyebrows turned in. Uncle Charlie never got serious unless things were a big deal. Charlie fooled around a lot, but he always took care of his business and personal affairs.

"Lee I'm going to level with you. Business is good lately, and I mean really good, you hear? I've got a deal with those Asian dudes in the city. I bought an old warehouse off of them...cheap. I'm planning to renovate that bad boy and open up a new club downtown next year. All I'm waiting on now is the building permits and all that jazz. I need to get the liquor license finalized and I'll be rolling baby." Charlie was speaking rather slowly so Lee could follow his every word uttered.

"Alright, congratulations," Lee said and extended his fist.

"Hold up, that's where you come in. I'm looking for a partner. Fifty-fifty split on the new club. I'm getting too old to go it alone. This is an opportunity for you to own your own business and get out that silly mail room man." Charlie was almost begging. His hands were outstretched as he hunched over in his chair. Lee was overwhelmed, but knew there was no way for him to accept the offer presenting itself. No matter how he looked at it, the fit wouldn't be quite right.

"I can't do it, I'm sorry man. There's just no way, but I'm glad you thought of me. For one, I like my new job and two Rita..."

He was rudely interrupted by Uncle Charlie jumping up and almost knocking over his chair. "Forget her boy, can't you make up your own mind for once. We're family and I need the help."

"I can't do it. Why not ask Keith?" Lee shrugged off Charlie's emotionally charged display.

"Keith? Are you crazy? Have you lost your mind?" Charlie asked making a terrifically ugly face. After a few seconds his face began to become unwrinkled. "That's cool," Charlie said. He cooled off faster than a wintry wind gust. The big man sat back down in his old leather chair behind the mammoth metal desk, which was covered with invoices, magazines, and papers of all sorts. The damp long-standing office with wood paneling gave a smell of must.

"I thought I'd put it out there that's all. I wanted to ask you first. I know you gotta live your life. Truth is, you don't wanna be like me. I'm old and single, I've got no one, just you and that fool Keith. Family Lee, that's what's important."

"Yea I know. I'm trying to make this work with Rita and all," Lee started up.

He was interrupted again by Uncle Charlie and his fat index finger thrusting out into his face. "I told you, she's nothing but trouble Lee. You already had your heart ripped out once. You wanna go through that again? Do you? Women like her don't settle down with regular guys like us."

"How do you know?"

"This is a fling Lee, a fling! She won't even tell people you're together man. That's scandalous, why can everybody else see that and not you? Wake up!" Charlie shouted a little bit at the end of his statement to drive his point further into Lee's tormented brain.

Lee questioned the fling statement. If it was a fling, eight months was close to a world record, and so he must've been doing something right.

"I don't like her, and your momma doesn't either. That oughta tell you something," Charlie said.

"But mom never even met her," Lee said. His voice grew quiet.

"It doesn't matter, she heard about her. Want a brew?" Charlie asked, ignoring Lee while grabbing two long neck beers out of the mini fridge he kept next to his desk. His statement and question ran together as if they were one in the same.

"Yea, I'll take one," Lee said as he flopped in his seat. The look of defeat was plastered to his face. It seemed to be the general consensus that no on liked his girlfriend, and none of her family was crazy about him. Maybe Uncle Charlie was right for once?

"Another thing, listen up. I'm buying your mom's old house. It's been on the market almost a year now. So, I'm gonna rent it out. That's still a great neighborhood over there. If you want you can get up in there and we can work out some deal. Something like rent to own, when you get the financing just let me know, okay." Charlie explained, while slightly smiling at Lee, knowing his nephew would be keen.

Lee scooted up in his seat. "You mean that? I'd love to be in there."

He desperately wanted to buy his Mom's old house but couldn't get the financing or swing the payments before. With this new job he started, he could afford now to make the payments and at the same time clean up his credit issues. This was like a dream coming true before his eyes.

"That's a family house Lee, four bedrooms, two baths, plus the family room addition. You get in there and before long you'll be a lonely man. It's about time you settle down. Like I said, you don't wanna be like your Uncle here, old and alone, hanging out with that fool Keith."

"Yea, I know, but my lease isn't up for a few months though."

"It's alright. I'll have the place repainted inside and do a couple repairs first. Then you can move up in there okay. How's that sound?" Charlie was laughing once again. He was more than glad to help because he loved Lee and wanted to see him happy.

Lee stood. "Sounds cool."

"Remember what I said Lee. Don't get played by this girl. She's about business that's all. I promised your mother I'd look out for you. When you get that house, find you a good woman and settle on down. You hear me?" Uncle Charlie playfully grabbed Lee by the back of the neck.

"Yea I hear you."

"Come on let's celebrate. Drinks on me!" Charlie yelled, throwing his head back as they walked back down the cramped hallway towards the bar. "Top shelf, whatever. It's all on me tonight!"

Chapter 11

The next morning, a modern day miracle occurred in the fact that Lee was able to drag himself into work. Uncle Charlie and Keith crashed at the lounge while Lee somehow made his way through the thick morning traffic into the city. Unfortunately he was still in his smoke filled clothes from the night before and didn't have time to even change or go home to shower.

He looked hideous and felt an ice pick jabbing against his brain while the whole world continued to spin too fast. Surely his unsavory aroma would cause a stir at the office. His plan was to get to work before everyone else and hand out the days assignments. From there he'd slink away into his office with his door shut for some much needed rest. Uncle Charlie kept his word about free drinks and Lee was much obliged increasing his normal intake three fold.

He planned to advise the staff there was a lot of important paperwork he needed to get caught up on. He made it, amazingly by 7:30 beating everyone to the copious downtown office building. Everyone, except Rita, that was.

She was standing smack dab in the center of the lobby near the elevators, pacing around with a disgruntled expression masking her usually angelic face.

"Where in the world were you last night? Can you explain this to me? And why are you dressed like that? Where are your work clothes? You stink, you smell like stale beer and smoke," she said all the while tugging on his crumpled and soiled button up black shirt. Rita's nose wrinkled up as she waved her hand in front of her face. Rita was beyond livid as she yelled in a whisper, scolding him as if he were a nineteenth century school boy wearing knickers. Lee was caught off guard, never expecting to see her there that early. Most of the executives made their own hours coming and going as they pleased, sometimes in at 9:30 or later.

Lee made desperate attempts to explain but instead he just talked in circles. "Well Rita, look what had happened was."

"I called your phone a dozen times easy. After I left the spa, I felt bad for jumping all over you and I wanted to talk, and to apologize. But now I see where you were, out with your boys I take it," Rita rolled her eyes while she looked at the pitiful man before her.

"I left my phone in the car by accident, my mistake," Lee mumbled. His head continued to pound. He massaged his temples.

"Uh huh, how convenient. All of a sudden you're forgetful huh? You didn't even have the decency to call me back to check on me. I told you about my day. I needed you." Rita was crying once again. "No, not here, I'm not doing this," Rita said and walked off. Her black paten leather high heel Gucci pumps clicked across the marble tile, ringing in Lee's sensitive ears.

She stormed off leaving Lee standing alone looking filthy as well as foolish. Rita quickened her pace almost to a jog and hurried off into the ladies room wiping tears that fell from her eyes like dewdrops from a rose petal.

He'd really done it this time he thought as he leaned back against the cold concrete wall in the lobby. By now employees had begun hustling into the building, some moving fast others scooting along sluggishly as if their feet were sulking. 7:30 soon turned into 7:55 while Lee waited around for his lady to emerge from the bathroom. He stood there watching trying not to look perverted, just staring at the women coming and going but she never exited.

Fearing the worst Lee hurried up the stairs, bypassing the crowded elevator, skipping over steps making his way to the third floor to start his already dismal day. Once again Lee had misjudged this understanding woman who always seemed so inclined to forgive.

He realized Rita was right. He should've showed more concern and went over to see her in her time of distress. Maybe even some flowers would've been appreciated and appropriate considering what happened?

How could he blame her if she wanted to take a step back and cool things off? He realized he was no support at all, only a cause of irritation in her already hectic life. As soon as the mailroom was up and operating at full capacity he slipped into his office and it seemed no one really even noticed how totally ridiculous and unprofessional he looked.

Quickly he raced to his computer, logged on and emailed Rita. He apologized extensively over his incredulous error and seeking her forgiveness. He told her how he knew he messed up and all about the news of how he would soon move into his Mom's house.

One minute he was ready to throw in the towel and the next he was begging on bended knee that she would stay. All the back and forth emotions about Rita and his insecurities grew old to both of them. He made up in his mind right then and there that they could make things work. It would be up to Rita if she felt up to dealing with his rollercoaster of emotions. One day Lee would be so loving and gentle, but the next he'd be cold and distant.

Time elapsed with Lee becoming nervous as the minutes went by. He ordered flowers to be sent to her with an apology note attached. He wondered if she received them, or if it even would matter? As 11:30 rolled around slowly Lee was barely hanging on, operating on a few hours of broken sleep. In a half an hour he planned to sleep through lunch and finally totally sober up. An email alert went off on his computer indicating one new message.

Lee's heart came to a complete stop as he clicked open the new email. Ms. Rita Clark finally responded, telling him she'd been meeting with Personnel all morning and discussing the Frank Harrison incident. He forgot about that situation of hers, since he was so flustered over loosing her love all together. It didn't take more than a second for his memory to be refreshed transferring him into a angry spell all over again.

Rita explained briefly how Frank was to get off lightly with a written warning and reprimand because of no witnesses. It was her word versus his. Frank plainly denied the altercation by saying it was a mistake or miscommunication of some sort. It was relayed to them both that any further complaints and Frank could be terminated, subject to board approval. She also reminded Lee about the assignment given to her by Jackson & Fitz International to go to London in a few weeks to perform an important assignment.

She would be stationed there and put up in a fine luxury five star hotel for upwards of four to five weeks. Before she left, she sincerely hoped to clear all matters in their turbulent relationship. Deep in her heart she wanted for things to work out, but her level headed mind had doubts inside. Lee was overflowing with excuses and still seemed to be insecure at various times, which was a turn off for Rita.

The opportunity to become a Vice President of Jackson & Fitz International Banking was still there and she had to opt between love and career. She figured over the next two months she would be able to sort things out. Lee had once cemented his place in her heart, but his recent behavior and attitude had begun to chisel away that once sound structure.

That night they were supposed to go to Charlie's Lounge to see Marion Meadows perform, but as much as she loved his music it didn't seem to be the finest idea. Rita suggested that maybe the two could spend some time alone and hash things out. Lee agreed to that idea, and planned on going to her condo where they'd meet in the bookstore and have coffee together.

Lee sat at his work desk clicking away on his saved files, looking at a photo gallery of him and Rita posing happily together.

Memories buzzed around in Lee's head as he drifted off to sleep face down on his desk during lunch. Liz saw just how Lee looked earlier that morning and thought that she would take the initiative to be nice.

Liz stood outside his office and lightly knocked on his door. There was no answer. "Can I come in?" she asked. Liz slowly pried open the heavy wood door.

Lee laid face down on his desk, knocked out cold. Liz knew he was struggling that day and hung-over from last night. Lee may have thought he could fool everyone else but she was family. She just looked at the dehydrated little brother of hers and kind of laughed to herself, Lee, when are you going to grow up?

Liz figured the least she could do was be nice and get him some water and aspirin to take when he awoke. She retrieved the items and entered the room again. He was still sleep in the same position with his mouth open on the desk. As Liz cautiously moved around the desk being careful not to wake Lee she saw his computer screen flashing a slide show filled with pictures of he and Ms. Clark, the much loathed COO from upstairs.

She couldn't believe it. Her mouth dropped and she covered it instantly as if to block a ferocious sneeze. She stumbled backwards nearly bumping into the window sill behind her. Lee never said to her he was dating anyone, let alone the COO from upstairs in the executive suites. This was bizarre, and it made no sense. None. No one really ever spoke to Ms. Clark, so it was hard to imagine her dating someone so ordinary and down to earth like Lee.

He still claimed to be single, and keeping his options open. But Liz could discern from the pictures that flashed on Lee's computer that this was a real relationship and not some one night love affair. In a state of shock and disbelief she quickly made her way out of the office and the mailroom, out into the dusty hallway.

She couldn't stop thinking about Lee and Ms. Clark's well disguised secret they had been keeping. Most employees at Jackson & Fitz really could not stand Ms. Clark, especially the women on staff. She seemed to be so stuffy and snobbish, nothing like Lee's type at all. Now Liz wanted to know why the secrets, why all this deception? Liz sought after and desired answers to protect her friend from the female executive with the evil reputation.

More importantly to Liz, she also wanted Lee to get back with her sister Simone who would be moving back home in a few weeks. Her mind raced faster than horses in open pasture as she made her way to the in-house cafeteria.

Lee awoke in his chair, looking disheveled and wiping drool from his wet stubble filled chin. He knocked over the bottled water. He opened the bottle and sipped the refreshing fluid rapidly.

He smiled as the delicious images of him and the model like beauty Ms. Clark flashed on his computer monitor. After closing out the pictures, he laid back down to sleep after he finished his balanced lunch of aspirin and water. He was intent on sobering up completely for his time that night when he'd spend time with Rita. Liz had other plans.

Chapter 12

With quickened pace Liz descended downstairs to the cafeteria, so many perplexing thoughts entered her inquiring mind. Why didn't Lee at least convey to her about his relationship with Ms. Clark? Why were they keeping things secret?

This veiled love with Ms. Clark came as an utter shock to Liz. Simone would be moving back home to be close by the family, but in the back of her mind she thought maybe she could work things out with Lee. Right now that prospect looked bleak since Lee and Ms. Clark appeared to be plummeting in the pool of love.

Liz had always been outspoken, and this time would be no different. Liz knew that no matter how risky a move this proved to be she had to go to the Executive Suites upstairs and meet head-on the dreaded Ms. Clark. Liz knew also this would mean getting past all the secretaries that were put in place to hinder the so called regular employees from integrating with the executives in anyway, shape or form. She made the resolution that this is what she would have to do. Her inquisitiveness and her devotion to her sister had gotten the best of her as she altered her plans for lunch.

She figured if need be she could tell Simone to just move on and forget about any plans of a future with Lee. Simone and Lee's on again, off again romance reached a screeching halt over the past few years and there may be no need to continue the charade of hoped reconciliation any longer. As Liz entered the elevator which would take her to the top floor she gathered her thoughts together, quickly rehearsing her lines over and over in her mind.

Rita Clark had purposely built a reputation as a no nonsense executive who did not back down from anyone, man or woman. Liz thought momentarily that her very job may be at risk as she planned to obviously over step her bounds as an employee and dig into someone's personal affairs. But in Liz's mind, this was bigger than that right now, because her family's emotions were involved. Even if her sister never got back with Lee, he still didn't deserve to be played by some high and mighty big shot business woman.

The elevator reached the top floor and as the bell chimed Liz froze. Her heart beat like a bass drum as she moved. After inspecting her unfamiliar surroundings she stepped off the elevator and headed towards the young blond receptionist who was occupied on the phone.

"Can I help you ma'am?" the receptionist asked, smiling.

"Yes, can I please speak with Ms. Clark?" Liz asked.

"Do you have an appointment?" the young lady fired back with a fake smile already knowing the answer to her question.

"No, I don't but it's important that I speak with her."

"Ms. Clark is very busy and you'll need to schedule a time to see her. Let me look at her date book. Your name please?"

Liz explained that she was an employee from downstairs and that she needed to speak with Ms. Clark today and it wouldn't take up too much time.

"Her next available opening is next Wednesday at 10 a.m. I'm so sorry. If this is a complaint issue I can direct you to Mr. Harrison. He is director of HR."

Liz interrupted the receptionist. "Listen, it's not a complaint, it's more personal than anything else."

As she was getting those few words out of her mouth, Frank Harrison stepped out from behind the large frosted glass door looking like he was in a rush. "Where in the world is my chauffeur Cindy? I requested the limo a half hour ago. I have a very important meeting downtown with the insurance group," Frank bellowed. He stomped around in his shiny black wing tips looking down at his gold Movado watch.

"Mr. Harrison," the young receptionist squeezed out.

"Hold your thought," Frank said. He rudely interrupted the receptionist by holding his hand up in her face. He started eye-balling Liz, slowly looking her over. "Well, who do we have here? I don't think we've been properly introduced. I'm Mr. Harrison, head of HR, but you can call me Frank."

His eyes were looking as if he was a starving man and she a perfectly cooked steak. He stroked his black dyed beard, smiling at her with a grin as Liz pulled her hand away from his slimy grip.

"I'm Elizabeth, from the Mailing department and I was here to see Ms. Clark for a brief moment."

"Well Elizabeth, I don't get down to your floor very often but maybe I should. It's really nice to get to know the employees, especially the ones like you." Frank salivated over Liz and her feminine attributes, making sure to flash his gaudy jewelry. If he thought for one minute she was impressed, he was sadly mistaken. Liz raised her left hand exposing her wedding ring as she brushed through her long black hair.

"Is Ms. Clark in?" she asked once more. Her inquiry sounded more like a demand than a question. Her face carried that look of *get out my face* that Frank knew all too well.

"Let me see what I can do for you," Frank said as he cast his shadow over the receptionist desk picking up the phone. Rita's phone rang on her desk, breaking her concentration as she was reviewing the quarterly financial statements.

"Hello, this is Ms. Clark."

"Visitor for you in the lobby Rita," Frank spoke rather gruff. A dial tone greeted his ear on his end of the phone.

"She'll be right out," Frank assured Liz as he looked at the receptionist frowning. "Page me when the driver shows up." With that said he turned and went back through the bulky frosted glass doors.

A few minutes passed by when out came Ms. Rita Clark. Dressed in a black pin striped women's suit and she approached the receptionist about her visitor.

The receptionist pointed over at Liz. She was sitting down, pretending to read a magazine while nervously waiting.

Rita approached her looking bewildered. "How may I help you?

Liz asked herself again, what Lee saw in this stuck up snob. Sure, Rita was an undeniably beautiful woman, but besides that she wondered what their relationship could be based on. Liz instantly didn't care for Rita or the way that she spoke. It seemed to her that Ms. Clark was trying to be so professional and proper that it came off as fake.

Liz stood up. "I need to speak with you, about someone we both know. You might want a little privacy though. You know what? I *know* you do."

Rita raised her hands. "Excuse me. You are in no position to make demands. And furthermore, don't ever come trying to speak with me and tell me what I might want to do. Now, let's begin all over shall we? What is this about *ma'am*?" Rita was stern yet professional in her response to Liz.

"One word...Lee," Liz said and rolled her eyes at Rita.

"Please, step into my office," Rita said, hastily ushering Liz through those same immense frosted glass doors that were only moments ago impregnable.

Chapter 13

After being seated in Ms. Clarks posh office Liz asked her a stunning question. "So, how long have you been dating Lee?"

Rita seemed flabbergasted as she looked around her large well decorated office, shaking her head in disbelief, gasping. Rita turned and stood at the large wall of glass behind her desk which overlooked the busy city below giving way to a breathtaking view.

As she turned robotically to face Liz she asked sarcastically. "What are you going to tell me next? Are we on Cheaters?" Her reference of the scandalous television program gave Liz a small chuckle.

"Ms. Clark, I realize you're wondering who I am and why I'm here so let me start explaining. First off, I'm not crazy. Second, I'm not in love with Lee, in fact I'm married."

"Well then, what do you need?" Rita asked.

"My name is Liz, and I work in the mailing department with Lee. He's like a brother to me. We grew up together."

"What's that have to do with the price of tea in China?" Rita snipped at Liz.

"You need to relax. It's obvious you're all uptight."

Rita interrupted again. "Don't tell me to relax. You barge in here making wild accusations about Lee..."

"Let me finish," Liz snapped back. "I just found out you and Lee are somehow supposed to be together. To be straight up, I'm shocked."

"Shocked? Why?" Rita took offense from the last comment.

"You don't seem like Lee's type, and I know him better than you."

"How would you know what his type is may I ask?"

"He's been with my sister forever that's why, and she's nothing like you. The two of them were together since they were kids. Believe me. I know Lee's type. Like I said, I know him better than you do."

"I beg your pardon," Rita shook her head side to side. Rita wondered why he never mentioned working with Liz or his relationship with her sister. Here he was working side by side with a close family friend and the man never made mention of it.

Lee did however slip up the other night saying that he had been hurt before. Could this woman be telling the truth? Could her sister be the one that hurt Lee so bad before? What reason did Liz have to lie?

Rita was beyond disturbed that Lee would conceal these truths from her, after she'd been so upfront with him all along. She knew she had to get to the heart of the matter and do so that night. She still contemplated taking the position of Vice President in London she had a lot of cataloging of her emotions to do.

She decided that to be fair she'd have to allow Lee to plead guilty to all this information tonight when they met that evening. He would then have a chance to let out all his secrets and clear the gloomy air.

Doubt crept into her mind the same way a fuzzy spider steadily moves to a dark corner of a shadowy basement. All of these months of her willing to settle down with Mr. Lee Johnson and now she surprisingly discovered skeletons falling from his closet.

The past few months Lee was the one who started to have his uncertainties about the length of their relationship and now it seemed a bit of role reversal was taking place. Rita now had strong suspicions herself, realizing that maybe her mother of all people was dead on from day one. Maybe Lee was a player of legendary proportions? Right now she didn't know as Liz kept gabbing, revealing detail after detail about Lee's life.

Liz told her about his connection with Simone, and the real reason his baseball career ended, even his recent DUI. *When was she going to shut up?*

Lee told Rita that he injured his shoulder while diving for a fly ball, tearing the rotator cuff. Rita never even knew he had a DUI, but he showed signs of being a heavy drinker. She sunk deep into her well-built leather seat at her desk and listened as this woman sat before her and described a stranger. She was already becoming concerned over Lee's heavy consumption of alcohol and now she hears about his history of violence and past love affairs. The revelation was almost too much to bear.

Now she fully understood the lyrics by Sade as the news hit her like a slow bullet. Love certainly was a gun. Eight months of dating and Lee never made mention of anyone of these things that were so important when contemplating a lifelong commitment with someone.

Why did he and Simone breakup? They did break up didn't they? She was too scared to ask although the possibility was implied. Rita decided that she would as a minimum give Lee the chance to be a man and fess up. She didn't want to call the whole relationship off after investing so many months into it. If things were ever to be pieced back together, it would take quite some time for Lee to build back the bridge of trust leading to her heart.

Liz sat across from Rita, so confident and convinced in what she spoke, leaving Rita in a complete conundrum. Salty tears were streaming down her oval shaped face once again. The past twenty-four hours were like a violent forearm shiver to the face. How could she have been so blind?

Liz took full command of the conversation, steering it where ever she wanted it to go with reckless abandon, leaving Rita to dangle on her every syllable. In some ways Liz's presence there was somewhat of a godsend. Rita engaged her fully in the discussion; volleying questions like tennis serves. They were returned with the force of one of the William's sisters, sending her unsatisfactory answers in return.

On Liz's end of the bargain she was able say everything on her mind. Maybe Ms. Clark would back off before Lee was hurt, or in too deep? Part of her reasoning for approaching Ms. Clark was for Lee, but the large majority was to open up the door for her sister to get back her man.

Liz felt that she definitely had reason to owe this to her younger sister. Liz was under the perceived notion that she was crazy to be taking this risk by talking with Ms. Clark. Even so, her plan was executed to perfection.

"What kind of relationship is this anyway? Are you embarrassed by Lee because he's not some millionaire?" Liz's question hit Rita like bombs falling over war torn lands. "How do you think Lee feels? You're keeping him all hush-hush like he's some kind of rent-a-date."

"He's the one with all the secrets. I didn't know half of what you're telling me!" Rita rationalized out loud.

"Why should he not keep secrets, he *is* a secret. This whole thing is foul. Wait until I talk to Lee." Liz stood and turned to leave.

"Please, don't. Please...I will tonight. I'll talk with him tonight. We're meeting up later and you're correct in what you said. We need to come clean, and let people know were together, no matter if it looks odd to them." Rita stood while smoothing her blouse and regained her once lost composure. "Let me ask you one thing Elizabeth. What's the real reason you came and spoke to me? Most people wouldn't have bothered. Tell me. Do you care about Lee that much?"

"Yes, I do. I'm willing to stick my neck out for him. He's been through a lot. The real question is... Do you care about him?"

Rita stared blank into space pondering that question, without answering.

"*I didn't think so,*" Liz said with noticed emphasis as she walked to the door leaving Rita to sit in solitude contemplating her deepest emotions.

Chapter 14

As the lunch hour elapsed Lee slept off the damage done to his body by the previous night. His rest was interrupted by Liz rapping lightly on his office door and then stepping inside the shade drawn room looking at him with a small amount of pity.

"You know you gotta slow down Lee, you can't hang like you used to." They both laughed at her unsympathetic statement. Liz was smiling as she usually was and Lee held his head, wincing from the still throbbing headache.

"Did you bring me in some water earlier?" Lee asked her holding up the water bottle he found placed on top of his desk.

The question surprised Liz throwing her off guard. She quickly regained control. "No, I just peeked in and saw you sleeping so I didn't want to bother you."

"Oh, okay that's cool, I've been out of it most the day anyhow." Lee knew he had to pull himself together.

"Hey Lee?"

"What's up Liz?"

"I think it's only fair I let you know."

"What? What's going on?" Lee sensed Liz was about to tell him something serious.

"Simone will be back in town in a couple of weeks. Mom was going to have a little welcome home party for her and Shawn. We were all hoping that maybe you would be there, at least for a minute." Liz seemed nervous as she shifted her weight around to each leg. "It would mean a lot to Dad too, and you could get to know Ray a little." She smiled trying to sway him with the opportunity to meet her husband.

"I'm sorry Liz, I don't think that'll work you know. It's kind of awkward with how it all went down," Lee said, while tapping his fingers against his heart.

"Why can't you give it a chance Lee? Simone told me she wants to make it work, if you would just...you know what? Forget it. I'll leave it alone, I'm sorry." Liz threw her hands up and closed her eyes.

"I know you're just looking out but I'm good. Me and you, we'll always be close, you're my girl. But with me and the rest of the family, it can't be like it used to be. Tell everybody I said hi, and give mom a hug for me," Lee shrugged his broad shoulders as if to say, I don't know what to tell you. He just looked back at Liz while taking sips from the water bottle.

"Let me ask you one last question then. It's not about Simone." Liz assured him by way of a halt signal. She wanted to know if he'd at least be honest with her about his relationship with Ms. Clark that he still thought was a secret or if he would disguise the fact that they had something real.

"Okay, shoot," Lee said, looking up at the ceiling.

"Are you in a relationship right now with anyone special?" Liz stood patiently while awaiting his reply. "I mean, I'm just asking because Simone is ready to make things work with you. She's smart, she's beautiful, she's fun, and she's always been yours."

What she saw next was the face of a desperate man. "She's not mine," Lee said as he rocked back and forth.

"You didn't answer my question. Is there someone else?" Liz demanded an answer out of the man who miraculously turned deaf mute.

Lee looked down at his feet for a moment and then brought his head back up to look at Liz saying, "I'm alright. Right now it's just me. I'm still doing my thing. I've been single, I'll probably stay single."

"Are you sure about that?"

"Yea I'm sure, I need some time for Lee right now," he said as his face answered differently. His demeanor seemed depressed and frustrated.

"Alright then, I'll tell Mom and Dad you said hi." She left the room shaking her head in disbelief. How could he look her in the face and lie to her like that?

Lee followed her to the door and closed it inaudibly behind her. He leaned back and closed his eyes. He rested against the door and stared over at his messy desk realizing just how much of a lie he'd been living.

He'd lied to Rita about his failed baseball career, and about his past, only to slip up last night.

It probably wouldn't even have been a big deal to Rita either but he tried so hard to make a strong impression on her from the first night they met. He lied from the beginning and had to work hard to keep the story consistent over the course of time. Lee thought about how he even lied when she would ask about his drinking issues, which were methodically getting out of hand.

He lied because he didn't want to lose her and if she knew the truth, they never would've gotten together to begin with. He realized how every time he was supposed to go to her place that he would find some excuse to cancel. The few times that he did go over there, he would carry with him an inexplicable attitude. He knew he had to tell her why.

There was a very real reason he detested going to her place so much, one that dug at his emotions, so painful to him. He'd never told a single soul how it affected him inside. But he knew right then that he had to say something and do so that night. If she did leave, Keith and Uncle Charlie would have their riotous voices ringing in his ears non stop, maybe for an eternity. They would be saying continuously, *"I told you. I told you she would leave you."*

At that same moment in time, Rita sat upstairs and sent all her calls to voicemail as she looked out at the busy metropolis spread before her down below. Her office, so lavishly decorated with plush leather and expensive Oriental rugs now felt more like a State penitentiary. Inside that office was a chill, a wintry feeling like December spent in Toronto.

Rita contemplated the ability of Lee to treat her cold as arctic snow. She sat there all afternoon wondering if and how she could tell him it was over. The understanding part of her personality that once dominated her heart was being drained and choked out from Lee's tangled web of lies.

She figured that they could have a discussion that night, and act civilly, giving him opportunity to reveal the truth and remove his mask. It was only fair that after nearly nine months together he could clarify the reason for his dishonesty, yet there could be no justification for it. Whether he was owed even that, was left to be determined later.

Nearly nine months was a long time together she thought, longer than any past love in her life for sure. She loved hard this time, and it seemed to burn her back with wild flames. Over a period of nine months some women brought children into the world filling their life with joy. The past nine months for her had culminated into a hard, ugly birth of unwanted reality, producing more anguish than her aching heart could tolerate.

Rita started to pick up the phone on her desk to call her mother and realized she knew what she would say to her. *"I told you Rita, he's a loser, you should've got rid of him months ago."*

Putting the phone back down Rita pulled her hand back and realized something important. She didn't know Elizabeth from a hole in the wall and maybe this woman was a conniving liar seeking to drive a wedge between her and Lee for reasons unknown. Still something told her all she heard today was probably true. Rita hated to lose and refused to be proved wrong by anyone, especially a stranger.

She reasoned she couldn't carelessly toss away a potentially blissful future due to hearsay. It wouldn't be fair to her heart or to Lee's, whatever was left of it. "Maybe I can be more understanding, maybe this can work," she whispered to herself while cradling her own body in her arms.

Chapter 15

Just before 7:30 that Friday night Lee slowly walked into the coffee shop which sat below Rita's condominium loft complex. He looked particularly dapper as he strolled in wearing his black dress boots, dark jeans, and suede blazer.

Lee quickly spotted Rita sitting in a corner looking divine, her lips pressed against a steaming hot latte. There could be no denying of her good looks he thought as he approached noticing that she had her hair pulled up into a bun. He liked it when she wore her hair that way, exposing her long feminine neckline.

"Hello Ms. Clark, can I sit down?" Lee was doing his best to be smooth, now that he was altogether sober.

"Please do, you look great Lee. I'm glad we could get together tonight and talk."

"The pleasure is mine. You look wonderful baby. I love when you wear your hair up like that."

"I know you do." They both smiled shyly while touching fingertips, and a few strands of hair fell into Rita's forehead. "Listen Lee, I don't know how to really say this so I'll just put everything on the table."

"What's going on? Go ahead."

"It just that lately I've been thinking...It seems like there's some issues in your past that maybe I should know." Lee immediately thought about their phone conversation last night and how he spilled the beans about being in a past serious relationship and being hurt. Little did he know she already knew the details, thanks to her earlier conversation with Liz.

As Lee stirred around uncomfortably in his wooden chair she wondered if he would finally tell her the truth, or call this yet another misunderstanding. The past few months together that's all she heard out of him. Nothing was ever his fault, just one misunderstanding after another.

"Secrets like what? You want to know about that time I said I got hurt?" Lee asked. He was visibly disturbed as he pulled his hands back and then folded them in front of him like he was playing cards. Somehow, it felt very much like a cutthroat game of poker and all the chips were down.

"Yes, I think that would be appropriate for me to know, don't you? Unless of course, you don't care to share it with me. Maybe you don't since you've kept it a secret this long." Rita's tone had gone from civil to intimidating instantly.

What he didn't know about this poker game was Rita was playing with house money. "What's up with all the questions about my past all of a sudden?"

"I don't know Lee, sometimes you think you know a person, and the next minute you find out they were engaged, married, or separated, something like that."

"Engaged? Married? Please! Where are you getting this?" He sat back with one eye closed up. Lee's convincing act could've fooled most people.

"So, you're saying that the relationship you were in wasn't that serious?"

"It was but it wasn't, you know?" Lee waved his hands back and forth like a balancing scale trying to explain.

"If you say so Lee." Rita then cut her eyes at him. She'd given him a opening and occasion to be forthright. She felt if he couldn't even be honest about something like this then how could things last?

She couldn't stand to be lied to and wouldn't be able to trust Lee again. Since he was fixed on continuing to lie, she would have to apply pressure with vice like force. Lee went on explaining how he never got to serious with any one girl just kind of bouncing around.

"I never got serious until I met you. I've treasure our time together baby. I can see forever in your eyes." Lee gave best effort to smooth talk his way out of trouble, trying desperately to salvage his future with Rita, dropping one sappy line after another.

Somehow he could tell something was wrong, when she didn't even respond to his phony act. "How are you doing with your drinking? You know, if you're not careful you could get a *DUI*," Rita said.

Lee rocked his neck back and forth at a slow pace trying to crack it, ending up looking more like a turtle trying to come out its shell.

"I slipped up last night, but overall I'm getting better. Work has lightened up so I'm not so stressed either."

"Really? Good for you Lee." Rita was now fully proficient in sarcasm as she gave him a mocking round of applause. Maybe she was the one full of surprises herself. Lee never could hit a curveball too well and right now she was throwing plenty of them.

"I don't know what your problem is, but I didn't come here to be interrogated."

"No?"

"No."

"Then why'd you come here then?"

"I believe that we can make this work, that's why," Lee reached his hands across the table. Rita's hands felt cold and dead, all the electricity that was once there now vanished.

"I'm not blind. Over these past few months you've been acting differently. And when I bring up commitment, you dodge the subject wanting nothing to do with it. So guess what?" Rita said.

"What's that?" Lee muttered under his breath, his eyes narrowing.

"Maybe you started believing in this too late."

"No, let me..."

"No! Let me finish Lee, all of a sudden you want to get serious. Just last night you weren't ready, you were telling me give it time. You do a complete one hundred eighty degree turn in one night. Give me a break."

"I realized I could've lost you."

"Could've?"

"Listen, I don't know what happened today. But you're tripping. Did you hire a private eye or something? Did you do a background check?"

"What if I did? What would I find?"

"Nothing!"

"Are you sure about that? Because frankly, I'm not sure anymore."

Liz told Rita earlier that Lee had been arrested for attacking and injuring his baseball coach in the minors. The coach pressed charges and sued for medical damages. That was half of the debt he was still paying off. Also there were his legal fees for his DUI that occurred a few months before meeting Rita.

"Yea I'm sure Rita, I think I would know if I had a record."

"I bet you would, you're just a regular pillar of honesty aren't you?"

"I try to be."

"You're a liar Lee. You've been lying for the past half hour about everything. I know the truth Lee. What are you dense? Why do you think I've been asking all these questions...Why?"

Chapter 16

A pale and gothic type looking manager with heavy eyeliner and lip piercings asked the two to settle down, or please leave. The strange looking coffee manager gave them both a stern look, letting them know he was serious.

"Sorry, we'll keep it down," Lee whispered. The purple-haired man walked away satisfied.

"How do you know everything? Are you spying on me?" Lee asked.

"They say God looks after fools and babies, and it seems like I've been playing the fool for you. I'm surprised you even met me here tonight. You're usually too intimidated by my place. Let me guess. You feel more comfortable at Charlie's Lounge?"

"You don't even know the real reason why I hate this place, so chill alright." Lee's bottom lip began to quiver enough to be noticed.

"Why Lee, tell me then, why? If it's not a problem with me, where I live, what I drive, or my money, then why Lee?"

This was the first instance that Rita ever brought up money in anyway.

Over came the coffee house manager again, frowning. "Okay I've asked you two to both politely to quiet down. Now I'm afraid I have to ask you to leave. We encourage our louder customers to take their conversations outside to the seating area."

Lee moved first, standing up and brushing down to the floor some crumbs from a muffin he had been sampling, followed by Rita who was overcome with disappointment that she had caused a disruption.

Once outside the conversation continued. Lee picked right up where they left off. The weather shift brought in rain clouds.

"You wanna know why I don't like it here?" He slammed his fist into his other hand.

"Yes. I want to know. I can't wait to hear this!" Rita said quickly in response, arms folded.

Lee turned around away from her with his hands resting on his neck. "My father died here Rita! *Right here!*" He turned around and pointed at the building behind her.

"What?"

A panic stricken look covered his striking face like a shroud. "You heard me Rita, this is the old furniture factory that caught fire. My Dad was a firefighter and he died in there. I hate this building! I hate it!" Lee began to cry as tears now rolled limp down his cheek as he walked to the nearby seating area and plopped down on a park bench.

Other customers moved aside as they watched the emotional interchange unfold. Some of them wondered if she was in danger, because of his yelling.

"Lee, I didn't know, you said your father died fighting a fire but I didn't..."

"Nobody knows really. I don't talk about it, I never bring it up. I can't." His voice was garbled and his nose in need of tissue. Rita offered him napkins from around her cup of latte while placing her soft fingertips on his neck.

"I played baseball in the park behind her growing up. Looking over here I'd see this old building and get so upset. I played angry, at least that's what the coaches said. It gave me an edge, because the anger made me put everything into my game. I just channeled it into my play on the field, you know? I blew it though...I blew my shot at the major leagues because of that rage. I look at this place and it reminds me of what I've lost." Lee had finally stopped crying and sat back on the bench exhaling heavily, as if a humungous burden was gone.

"I never knew Lee, I'm so sorry. All that pain, you have to let it out, and let go. I would've tried to help you, understood, anything."

"You know, that place took away my Dad, and it took away the sport I loved to play ...in a way. I know I can't blame everything on that building, I mean that doesn't make sense. But in my heart I can't stand the sight of this place, even if it is renovated. That's why I try to avoid it. It's just so ironic that you moved in here."

"I know. I feel bad kind of..."

"It's alright, it's not like you knew. I should've told you everything from the start. The truth about my ex, the DUI. All of it."

After the old building was renovated a few years back Lee stepped inside those dreaded walls for the first time. He visited an open house for a unit in the building because he thought that would help him move on. Instead it gave him such an eerie feeling that he said he would never set foot in that old factory again. Ever.

Lee was now flowing with emotion as Rita softly ran her perfectly manicured fingernails along his muscular neck and shoulders. He went on practically revealing every last detail of his life including his time with Simone, and growing up with her family. This was a monumental occasion, being the first time he'd ever opened up to anyone besides Simone.

"Thank you for listening to my problems. I can't believe I cried," he said covering his face.

"There's nothing to be ashamed of. You're human."

"I'm still embarrassed." Lee held his hands up in disbelief. The rain clouds began pressing in, hiding the last bit of sun as the smell of moisture filled the air. Rita reached over and took Lee's hand.

"If we're going to do this, you're going to need counseling Lee. We can get you the help that you need. You need to talk this out." Lee had always assumed that lying on a couch with a shrink was for rich people. For a second he almost forgot, that's what she was.

Guys like him just worked things out on their own, sometimes drowning sorrows in a bottle, drinking booze until their mind went numb.

"I don't want to loose you Rita, this whole London thing, the distance is crazy."

"We'll cross that bridge when we come to it okay? But right now you need to promise me. Look at me Lee. No more drinking." She was begging, her arms around his neck hoping he'd listen.

"What about London?" he asked sounding worried. His puppy dog eyes were filled with a glimmer of hope.

"They tell me absence makes the heart grow fonder."

Lee laughed and shrugged, "Yea but too much distance and we could drift apart."

Rita smiled. "I'm willing to take my chances."

They got up and began to stroll leisurely through the park where Lee once played youth baseball, and discussed ways to piece things back.

"I'm willing to start fresh, a clean slate. Will that work for you Mr. Johnson? On one condition."

"What's that?"

"No more secrets, not even at work. I can't live this lie anymore. I'm not ashamed of us. I'm sorry I even suggested that we keep it hushed in the first place." Lee hugged her, bringing her in under his arm, causing him to breathe in her sweet perfume.

"Lee, I have a confession too."

"Can't be any worse than mine," he said while smiling and sniffling.

"My father drank. When I was young he used to get drunk after work. Before long, he started hitting my mom. That's why they divorced and why we left. My mother has never really trusted a man since then. I'm just so scared you could spiral into that too. That scares me so much."

"I love you too much to do that."

"I know you love me but, alcoholism is a real disease. I saw it first hand, it makes people act so strange." A few tears rolled beneath her big eyes which were now glossed over. Lee wiped the last of her tears away telling her he could change.

He began to think back to the day he met this perfect stranger, and hoped their love would find a way. The diving sunset behind the clouds caused the night to cool off. The couple had new resolve to start things over again even if that meant the possibility of a move to London to accept the Vice President position.

Their displays of affection continued as they made their way back in front of the building hand in hand. They were greeted by the earsplitting sound of a thundering Harley Davison motorcycle pulling up in the front entrance.

Chapter 17

The Harley Davison motorcycle sputtered and coughed as its hearty idle came to a close. Its rider swung his large legs over the bike, the whole time looking in the direction of Rita and Lee. The two of them felt uncomfortable as the full-size man seemed fixated on them as they stood outside finishing up their conversation. As the leather clad biker pulled off his shadowy helmet his identity was revealed.

Frank Harrison, director of Human Resources at Jackson & Fitz stared a hole through them. This was the same man that Rita filed a sexual harassment complaint against at work earlier that morning. He stood before them looking like he just witnessed a murder, and now he was moving towards them.

"You gotta be kidding me! What's going on here?" Frank asked getting extremely too close, invading all boundaries of personal space. Lee knew exactly who this was and now the pendulum had swung his emotions from love to war within seconds.

"First off, back on up, and if you have a question, you can ask me. Don't talk to her." Lee gestured to himself while creating some room between the two parties.

"I don't talk to low level punks like you. But apparently Ms. Clark here does. It seems like she likes to slum around. Wow, who knew?" Frank spoke with a grotesque look on his face as if he was sickened by that thought.

"Slum? You've got some nerve coming to my home," Rita interjected.

"Relax. I'm here for the bookstore, maybe a coffee. Unlike some people, I can read," Frank said while pointing at Lee and frowning. Then he continued, "Anyways, I'm moving here soon, so get used to me. We can be closer together."

Frank smiled at Rita explaining how he put down his deposit on the condo earlier that week.

The loft property was a hot real estate item at the time. They were brand new units with all the amenities one could want. Plus they were just the right distance from the hectic city life, making it an ideal location.

Frank reached out to touch her hand all the while looking at Lee. Lee knocked his hand away while Rita came between the two men. "Lee don't do it, it's not worth it." She clutched his arm.

Lee's eyes stayed pinned to Frank. "I told you what I would do when I saw this fool."

As Frank stepped back he laughed. "I just can't believe you two are together. I saw you walking up the hill and standing there looking like a couple of lovebirds. This is crazy, I mean what is this? A charity case?"

"Lee and I are just private people, that's all," Rita explained.

"Who are you talking to old man?" Lee asked stepping into Frank. Rita sensed trouble on the horizon as she tugged on Lee's shirt.

"I think she's ashamed of you tough guy." Frank flipped his hand towards Rita while shaking his head in disillusionment at Lee. Then Frank changed the subject, "I *know* you don't live here mailman. You couldn't get in the door on your salary, believe me I know. I set your pay scale little man."

"That's enough Frank," Rita said and moved back between them.

"Why don't you get on your bike and get out of here man," Lee said.

"I'm going to be her neighbor, so get used to me mail boy."

"The name is Lee."

"I don't care what your name is, but if you get out of line. I'll fire you! We'll get a new manager in there so fast, you won't believe it." Frank winked at both of them.

"You'll do no such thing Frank, no such thing." Rita irritably waved her finger back and forth.

"Try and stop me cutie." Frank leaned in Rita's face. Lee had just about enough as his body temperature reached a feverish level.

The coffee shop manager stood in the front window, fretfully praying for the argument to blow over.

The upscale section of town was not used to any sort of physical confrontation what so ever. Patrons who were once sitting outside now scurried about, moving to their cars, other's went inside to get away from the storm that was brewing between them.

"You know, on second thought. I have an idea," Frank raised his head like he received some kind of premonition. "Mailman here can buy the unit inside where that firefighter died back in the day. My realtor said they can't give that one away. She calls it a fire sale."

As Frank laughed emphatically he put his arm out to mockingly pat Lee on the back. Lee clutched Frank's left arm which was extended and forced it behind Frank's back, then hurled him into his motorcycle which went toppling over in a crashing heap on the pavement.

The manager inside saw what transpired, alerting fellow employees to call 911, and telling patrons to stay inside. There was a panic among some customers, not knowing where this would end.

"You shouldn't have done that," Frank said while maneuvering himself up off the Harley Davison Road King Custom bike. The new motorcycle was now scratched significantly by the asphalt.

"Done what? This?" Lee asked while kicking the motorcycle back over again spilling onto the pavement.

Frank howled as he lunged past Rita. Lee took a swift step back. Rita moved herself out of the way, standing behind a parked Audi A4, and begging Lee to stop. He couldn't hear her, no matter how loud she screamed. Frank clumsily tried to grab Lee but was greeted by a rapid left hook. The punch landed squarely on Frank's right ear leaving it ringing. Lee followed that up with a sharp right jab to the cheek that cracked Lee's knuckles, while he then sent the cumbersome man flying to the ground with a vicious combination of punches that would make any boxer cringe.

"Enough!" Rita shrieked, "What are you doing?" At this point Lee wasn't listening as Frank squirmed around on the ground distraughtly clawing at Lee's knees. Lee brushed him off by kicking his legs, connecting a few times with his upper torso. Frank was now visibly incoherent and grasping for breath, lumbering about.

"Stop Lee. Stop!" Rita cried out repetitively as the two continued to scuffle with Lee time after time having the upper hand, using his opponent as no more than a punching bag. Lee never heard Rita those three to four minutes that they were fighting, but his eyes functioned fine as the blue and red sirens glimmered as police vehicles pulled into the parking lot in haste.

Before Lee turned away from the beaten man below him, he did his best camel impression and spit on him.

"Why?" Rita asked evidently traumatized. "Why?" she asked again.

"He dissed you, he dissed me, and he dissed my father that's why. This guy put his hands on you Rita! You want to defend him?" Lee was in disbelief. She didn't want to defend Frank but she also didn't want this night that was moments ago filled with hope to be forever tarnished by this act of violence.

There was no time for her response as officers backed her away. The other officer's ordered Lee to lean against the car that was next to him at the time. He knew this routine. He'd been there before as he placed his hands behind his back, waiting to be cuffed.

Frank was sitting like a child with his legs folded explaining to officers that the attack was unprovoked. One of the officers handed Frank an ice pack for his noticeably bruised face, as he attempted to remove the salty blood taste from his mouth. Onlookers inside the coffee house and lofts pressed their noses against glass like children staring at the season's first snow. Raindrops fell in slow motion for Lee as he was escorted to the police car and placed inside, to take the long ride of shame.

"He'll be at the station here in town ma'am," an officer explained to Rita as she stared over at the man she had just resolved to work things out with. She had never seen anyone so upset, or anyone act like this for that matter.

She glanced over at Frank and the other officer blurting out, "He's lying. He started it. He started it!" she shouted out while nearly stumbling.

"Calm down," the police woman encouraged. She proceeded to confirm with Rita that she lived on location suggesting she go inside to cool off. Rita had never been so scared and embarrassed in her entire life. She had never experienced the spectacle of two men fighting before, except on movies or television. This looked so different than it did on the screen. It really wasn't even like a fight, as Lee appeared further practiced in this sort of behavior.

Rita side stepped down the freshly burgundy stained sidewalk, past the overturned and scuffed up motorcycle and a bruised and battered Frank Harrison. Her head was soon buried in her hands, covering her flush cheeks as she made a mad dash to the elevator leading to her floor.

Once there at her door, she went inside to gather a few things and intended to meet Lee at the police station. The red light indicating a new message on her answering machine was flashing, so she decided to check it in the event that it was Lee. Criminals always had one phone call to make on the TV crime shows she thought.

Unfortunately, this wasn't television, it was real life. In fact, the message was far from being Lee's voice. It was a message from Jackson & Fitz International Division, confirming that her presence was being requested in London, two weeks from the following day.

Chapter 18

As Lee was sitting on the cold dirty backseat of the police car he knew he'd made a gargantuan mistake that would put a titanic blemish on the complexion of the already rocky love affair. Not so much as a half hour passed since Rita suggested he needed counseling for his anger issues when this brawl happens.

The car stopped and an officer looked back at him. "We're going to get out now. You'll be put in a holding cell for a while until we sort this mess out. The other unit is on the scene sifting through several accounts of eyewitness testimony." Lee was brought in the station and fingerprinted, just the standard booking procedure. He wondered if Rita would understand this time around, or if it was all over like credits rolling at the end of a movie.

After a snail like period of forty-five minutes filled with counting the stains on the grimy concrete cell walls he heard the greatest words ever uttered. "Mr. Johnson you're getting out."

Lee stood trying to adjust his now tattered clothing, doing his best to look mildly presentable. He made his way out of the small holding cell, leaving behind the awful lingering smell of old urine and vomit. It was the undistinguishing smell of hopelessness and sorrow. One he'd never erase from memory. As he was escorted to the front of the police station he was debriefed and received explanation on what happened.

"Well Mr. Johnson, after eye witness testimony was taken it seems you were correct in claiming self-defense. It appears Mr. Harrison did attack you, and it was your right to protect yourself and your lady friend."

The officer pointed across the hectic room which was filled with commotion and over in the corner was Rita. She sat uneasily placed on a bench patiently waiting for him.

A huge sigh of relief came over him as he thought about just how wonderful she was to support him, after he acted like an animal. "Mr. Harrison will not be pressing charges against you." the officer said.

"Okay good," Lee said with a smile.

"However Mr. Johnson, you can wipe that ridiculous grin off your face. You will be paying a city fine for disorderly conduct."

"Come on? Are you kidding me? What was I supposed to do, stand around dodging punches until you all showed up?"

"No Mr. Johnson, but from what we saw on the scene and from testimony, you had that man beaten. Defense is one thing, you serving an old fashioned butt kicking is borderline vigilante justice. Understood?"

"Yea I got it."

"Good. Besides that, you have a history with these sort of things, so cool it." The officer was no longer speaking casually.

"Yes sir," Lee said, realizing he had gotten off light. After filling out some paperwork and signing a few documents Lee was released and he hurried up to Rita with outstretched arms.

"Come on so we can get you to your car." She marched out of the city precinct in silence. Lee still had his arms extended appearing to be a mime holding a boulder.

"Rita, Rita," Lee pleaded, skipping behind her.

"Get in if you want a ride," she responded while getting in the drivers side of the car. As she slammed the door, Lee took her suggestion got in and buckled up. He gazed at her lovely profile the whole time. He resembled a puppy that had done wrong by tearing up its owner's carpet.

"What? Rita I'm out. It's all good," he said while patting her on the thigh.

Rita flinched, still shook up over his violent display. Those were the same hands capable of so much damage, enough to bring a mountain of a man like Frank Harrison to his knees. Lee felt backed into a corner, after having enough of being verbally murdered by the overpaid bully.

The ride back to Rita's condo was deathly quiet as Lee got the hint. She didn't feel like talking. My Funny Valentine played from the speakers in the car on the jazz radio station she chose to listen to. The night had now grown dark, like insides of eye lids and the clouds began to cry matching the tears Rita shed as she drove.

"Baby, don't cry, I'm sorry," Lee said.

"You're always sorry Lee, that's all I hear lately."

"He had it coming."

"Okay Rambo, whatever." Rita smacked her glossy lips together. "Please, you could've killed him."

"I don't care! He fronted on me."

"That's no reason to act the way you did. He was down on the ground, you started going at him like some kind of maniac thug."

"Come on..."

"No, you come on. Grow up! We just talked about change, and you just revert back to your old habits, maybe worse."

Lee didn't even bother to respond as they finished the night drive in the summer rain. He glanced out the window watching the steam evaporate off the hot asphalt which reminded him of his own relationship, disappearing before his very eyes. As the car came to a halt Lee unbuckled and thanked her for the ride, again apologizing for his actions.

"I've got to live here you know. All my neighbors saw you acting a fool out here." Rita reminded him of that before he got out the car, sliding out the plush black leather seat.

"Sorry," he said again while staring over at the building complex. Rita began walking towards the front door and Lee lagged behind.

"Goodnight Lee," she turned and said politely, asking him to leave.

"I don't want to lose your love," Lee said. The numbness set in. He could still taste the tear drops from earlier that evening. He inched forward. "Would it be out of place if I just?"

"Tonight is not a good night Lee. I need some space."

"Hopefully not too much..."

"We'll see."

"Hey Rita," he stepped closer as she grabbed the door handle to head inside.

"Yes?"

"I knew the first time I saw you, I knew you were special." He did his best to try to get her to smile, even a little. It wasn't working. Her face was made of stone as she relayed to him the message she received on her answering machine.

"Two weeks? But I thought you said a few months?" Lee was now the one upset.

"I did too, but they are saying now, I'm needed as soon as possible. Mr. Sander the VP wants to speed up this process, so he can step down sooner."

"So it's like that huh?"

"Like what?"

"You're out then? Two weeks, and it's just goodbye?"

"It's not goodbye, it's see you later. We'll work on this but I need my space right now."

"So are we through or what Rita?"

"Do you want us to be?"

"No."

"Well okay then. We'll just deal with the long distance and take it one day at a time. You can come visit me, and who knows, maybe you'll like London."

"I doubt it."

"Well I don't know what to tell you. What am I supposed to do? Quit my job for a man who doesn't want to commit, and in the next breath he does?" The sad reality was, at one point in time she may have done just that, but not now. Lee had a lot of trust to build back up and prove that this was genuine love.

This would be a huge test for their love. In her eyes, it would be a final exam.

"Rita, will I ever see you again?" Lee was nearly whining.

"Do you really love me, or is that your male ego talking?" she asked him as she stepped inside the building, and out of the light rain. "Goodnight Lee." Rita walked away feeling sadness run through her veins. Lee stood outside alone in the rain just staring at the bare doorway with no one to blame but himself.

Chapter 19

As Lee drove down the streets he kept thinking about what Rita said before she went inside the condo. The words "we'll see" stuck out like a bellybutton. At best he figured now he only had half a chance of making things work. The past twenty-four hours had been so turbulent that it was taxing on them both.

He'd almost made it home when he decided to call Rita to see how she was holding up. Her cell phone rang without her picking up, so he left a voicemail. "Yea Rita, it's me. Look, I want to apologize for tonight. I know I hurt you, I messed up. I would feel so much better if I could tell you face to face, and look in your pretty brown eyes. This is like a bad dream, I love you."

After hanging up he decided to try her home phone, again no answer. Lee left a similar message. A few minutes later his cell phone began ringing inside his sports coat. Without even looking at the caller ID he answered the phone in a hurried fashion.

"Yea Rita, I'm so sorry baby."

"What you do now?" It was Keith on the other end laughing hysterically.

"You done laughing?"

Keith sensed something serious was going down. "What happened man? You sound like ya'll broke up or something."

"I don't know. It's up in the air right now."

"For real?" Keith sounded disappointed and excited all at once.

"Yea for real, but look... I don't know what to do."

"Come to Charlie's... let's talk."

"I don't know man," Lee said.

"Lee...Come on. We'll talk."

"Alright."

"See you in a minute."

"Cool."

Lee called Keith back as he pulled up to the Lounge. "Hey, I'm outside. It looks packed up in there."

"The Marion Meadows show got cancelled but it's still filled up."

"I almost forgot that show was tonight."

"Get in here man, come on," Keith said. He was anxious to see what transpired.

"Can I park?" Lee joked as he hung up the phone. As he got out his new black Durango he thought about how he was back to where he started. Another Friday night spent with Keith, chilling at Charlie's Lounge. I guess it's true what they say he thought the more things change the more they stay the same. With that in mind he popped a couple green tic tacs in his stale mouth and entered the front door.

Like a once caged wild animal put back in his natural habitat, he was right at home. Though his clothes were noticeably wrinkled, and his shirt stained, he still danced his way through the capacity crowd. Once through, he discovered Keith and Charlie in the back of the lounge plopped down in their usual booth.

"I don't even know how you made it to work today," Charlie said with a blank look, referencing the previous night of drinking while giving his nephew a pound on the hand.

"So what happened? Why ya'll breaking up, and you look all crazy?" Keith hurled the words out of his mouth, sitting up vertically out of his slumped position. Lee explained the scenario being sure to leave out the details about Frank. He just said that some guy disrespected Rita while they were out.

"So what you do? I know you didn't stand there like no punk," Uncle Charlie unsympathetically questioned.

Lee was forced to put on a performance as he stood up throwing a couple fist jabs into the air and saying, "You know how I get down."

"That's the Lee I know! Fools step up and get beat down!" Keith stood up and bumped into Lee giving his distinct sign of approval. He was the type of guy never to back out of an altercation, and he was proud of that fact.

"Oh yea, you know that." Lee laughed as he started to loosen up clapping hands with Uncle Charlie, pulling his hands back and snapping his bruised fingers. Lee went on to explain how he beat Frank Harrison like a hostage and related his brief time in jail that night.

On the exterior he was looking like a regular tough guy, but his inside was crying out for Rita. Still, Lee demonstrated the combination of punches he used to breakdown Frank Harrison as Keith began dancing around in a small circle.

The group of three began to laugh and joke around with the excitation of Lee's fight gradually taking a backseat to the recollection of the vast female patrons in the Lounge that night.

"Ex to the next boy. Time to move on." Keith pounded on Lee's shoulders like he had football shoulder pads on. "Ex to the next," Keith reminded him again.

Lee half smiled, frightened Rita would somehow overhear. "Drink up. It's on me tonight," Keith said. He almost sent Lee into cardiac arrest. Keith was always broke and never offered to buy drinks. Most times he was trying to get something for free from Uncle Charlie.

"Hold up. You gonna buy drinks tonight?" Lee wobbled and rocked around placing his hand over his heart like he was going to pass out at any minute.

"Yea, I said drink up. I got a nice deal going with this dude that can get me bootleg DVDs to sell. I told all those barbershop cats in town and they said come through, they wanna buy like crazy. They've all been calling me all day asking when I'm coming through. I might even get some business cards made up." Keith's feel good mood was infectious as he spoke, almost leaping off the ground.

Lee paused and remembered what Rita said earlier that night about his drinking habits, and trying to work things out. "What up? What you want?" Keith was asking as he was getting the hard-working bar tender's attention.

"Let me chill tonight Keith, appreciate it though," Lee said.

"What? Let me guess, you can't hang cause of last night?"

Reality was Lee wanted to change and show Rita he was about his business of trying to mend their relationship. Uncle Charlie overhearing the conversation made his way to the bar, bellying up, and roaring at the bartender to get his nephew a draught beer.

"Here Lee," he said seconds later, sliding the frosty mug overflowing with frothy bubbles in Lee's direction.

"Come on man, after the night you had, you gotta kick back." Keith reminded him by holding up his fists and posing, then acting like he'd just been knocked out. Lee and Uncle Charlie laughed like hyenas as Keith acted up, pushing the ice cold mug even closer to Lee.

The cell phone in Lee's jacket jostled around against his chest, which reminded him of how he tried to call Rita but obviously she was still too upset to talk to him. If that was so, he didn't owe her any explanation for what he chose to do.

"Maybe just one," Lee accepted the drink, gave his thanks and took a minute sip.

"He's back playa," Charlie punched Keith good-humouredly on the arm. Their hours of foolishness spent at the Lounge was just getting underway.

Chapter 20

After the evening approached its final act, Lee said his final goodbyes and made it out to the dark parking lot. Before getting in the SUV he checked his cell phone again. Still no call from Rita. It was now after 2:00 in the morning and regrettably too late to give her a call. Lee reminded himself to stay optimistic, but now began to feel like their love was built on sands of time.

As he slowly put the cell phone back into its home, he sloshed around in a puddle from the earlier heavy rainfall, dampening his pants. Great. His night was now truly complete as he got inside the SUV and fired up the engine. With a few nods and waves to other stumbling regulars leaving the popular lounge he was out of the parking lot, to make his journey homeward.

Realizing that in a few months he'd be moving to his old house across town and that commute would be exceptionally farther. Tonight he had the luxury of winding through back roads and side streets to maneuver home. He'd taken this route enough times over the years to drive it blindfolded.

Everything changed. Within seconds he was wide awake as a police car pulled behind him seemingly materializing out of thin air. Now he questioned if he'd make it home at all, or if he should've attempted to drive. He used that late night at Uncle Charlie's to escape the madness of that wild day.

His 'one drink', snowballed into two, three, four, and so on, placing him in this arduous predicament. Beads of sweat began to trickle one by one down his forehead as he gradually dropped his speed, making sure to obey all known traffic laws. How could he be so stupid?

The officer stayed close following Lee's every turn. Now, only four blocks from home Lee began to wonder if he'd ever make it, or if this cop would stop him at any minute. This would be his second DUI in a year, which would come with stiffer penalties and maybe jail time. More than likely his license would be suspended all together. Rita would never forgive him for this.

He was only two blocks from home when he saw it. Sirens. Flashing blue and red lights indicating him to pull over to the side of the road. As he slowed the vehicle down, he observed that he was the only car out on the road. Not exactly the conclusion to the night he envisioned. As the officer stepped out and approached the driver side window, there wasn't a good vibe.

"License and registration," the officer said.

"Yea no problem." Lee nervously took the required documents out of his brown leather wallet.

"You're out pretty late huh?"

"Yea, a little," Lee chuckled, again seeming nervous.

"Been drinking?"

"Had a couple brews, you know? The playoffs were on." Lee was doing his all to remain composed.

"Johnson, Lee Johnson?" the officer repeated his name like he knew who he was.

"Yea." Lee confirmed his identity with his hands still gripping the steering wheel, while facing straight ahead.

"Hey, didn't you play baseball in high school around here?" he asked.

"Yea, all state three years in a row," Lee smiled, turning to answer the officer.

"I thought you were going pro for sure. I really did. I played for Piedmont High, you guys beat us senior year to take the state title. You were unbelievable out there."

"Get outa here," Lee said as he tried to sound friendly. At this point it would take extreme good fortune to get out of this situation, and maybe this was the break he needed.

"Tell you what, let me run this," the officer shook the license. "Just procedure, I'll be right back."

"Alright, no problem." Lee was feeling decent about his chances for once. He watched through his driver side mirror as the officer got back in his car. As minutes began to pile up Lee felt less and less confident. What was taking so long?

Now mentally fatigued he ever so gently rested his head back against the head rest and closed his worried eyes. The water formed a wet rainy abstract on his window while he grappled with a kaleidoscope of emotions.

"Mr. Johnson?"

He sat up at once, his heart beating faster than a runaway train through his chest. His breaths were short.

"Yes." He barely got the word out of his mouth which was parched and full of spittle.

"It seems like you've had a busy night."

"Kinda," Lee winced.

"I tell you what. I see you live around the corner. I'll just tail you home, but you gotta straighten up guy."

"Thanks so much," Lee sighed in relief.

"I'm only doing this because I feel sorry for you. Everybody thought you were going pro. *What happened?* You were unreal on the field." The officer squinted in confusion as he spoke.

Lee stayed unvoiced, just wiggling in his seat.

The officer continued, "Listen whatever happened, you already blew your dreams. Do yourself a favor, don't hit rock bottom."

Lee wasn't in the mood for a lecture from some guy he didn't even know. "I didn't blow nothing," he argued.

"Please," the officer laughed interrupting Lee's outburst. "You had more skills than anybody I've seen play on the field. Now look at you. You've been arrested once already tonight and it could be twice. Be glad I have a soft spot in my heart for a washed up has been. Besides my shifts about done, and I want to get home to my wife and kids. You got a break tonight, so don't talk back to me. I can change my mind. I smell the beer on your breath from here."

"Thanks," Lee muttered faintly while shoving the license and registration back into his wallet. Just like that, it was settled and the officer kept his word, following Lee the two blocks home. Lee stood at his front door fidgeting with his keys and lock, finally getting inside his home. He shed the stained shirt immediately and walked through the living room.

He entered the kitchen and poured a glass of water into a plastic cup, then opening the aspirin bottle from the cupboard, he swallowed three of them. The whole time he recalled the officer's statement to him. Who was he kidding? He did blow his chances, and could've spent the rest of night in jail if not for the officer's mercy. He continued to stand over the dented and water stained aluminum sink thinking about his life and where it was headed. *Rock bottom*? Whatever.

He had a good job, and a great woman by his side, well kind of. It appeared that Rita was steadily slipping away from his grasp. Maybe? Stopping to check his cell phone, he realized there were still no new calls. Another night went by, ending with another unresolved argument. Lee mulled over what it would be like to have a wife and kids of his own to go home to. Unfortunately, all he had was Keith and Uncle Charlie which wasn't anything to brag about.

His focus quickly turned to Rita and developing a scheme to win her back. An hour disappeared without his awareness as he came to the realization that in two weeks she would be gone, and maybe for good. The officer was absolutely right. He had blown chances in the past. He told himself he wouldn't make the same mistake again.

Chapter 21

A sluggish journey up the stairs placed Lee inside his bedroom. He belly-flopped onto the old bed and laid there for a few minutes staring at his reflection on the mirrored closet. Blowing chances was what Lee was best at. Even after all these years. Part of his body wanted to cry after realizing how foolish he had behaved tonight with Rita and later at the lounge, narrowly dodging his second DUI in a year.

He lay there alone, half sleeping as the sound of her laughter resonated in his dreams. His deep thoughts were abruptly ended by his cell phone ringing, the vibration from inside his coat jumpstarted his slow beating heart.

It was 3:45 and any news at this time of night was never good. He reluctantly took the phone out of his pocket while sitting up on the unmade bed. "Hello?" He spoke nervous with his eyes closed, and his arm rubbing the back of his now sore neck.

"Lee, it's me."

"Rita?"

"I'm sorry it's so late."

"Its okay babe, I mean…is everything alright?"

"Yea, I'm okay. I've been doing a lot of thinking you know, I couldn't sleep."

Lee swallowed stiff as a silence came over the phone. "Rita, you still there?" Lee asked her being careful with his tone of voice. His ears took in the sound of tears. The sound that makes a man want to cry himself because he knew he was the cause of them. "I need you in my life Rita. I need you. Listen, I'll do anything. Whatever it takes, I promise."

"How many times can we keep doing this Lee?" Rita's words were given in a whisper.

"I'm just saying. Look, I'm only human. Can't a man make a

mistake once in a while?"

"A mistake is one thing, but on top of all that, you..."

"I what baby?"

"Don't baby me. You can't even commit to me. The fact that you had all those secrets, that worries me. You don't trust me. I don't know if I can trust you."

"You can."

"How do I know?"

"I'm telling you, you can."

"Just like you told me about your old girlfriend, for goodness sakes you were practically married. Plus, the assaults, the DUI..."

"Hold on, that's not fair."

"No. You're not fair."

"I was scared you know? I thought if you knew, you'd bounce."

"I've always been understanding haven't I?"

"Well yea."

"Ok then, you've got to learn to trust me."

"I do."

"Apparently, not fully." Again, the silence took hold of the phone lines. He checked to see if she was still there.

"Rita?"

"What?" she blurted out.

"Why'd you call me?"

"I still love you... Don't ask me why. You have a lot of good qualities but we've got to start all over again, from day one."

"So, does that mean you're not leaving?"

"No... I'm leaving in two weeks and maybe the space will do some good."

"That's crazy! London is so far away."

"Calm down, first of all." Rita began to regain control of her emotions, setting her box of tissue down gently next to her on the bed. She was now controlling the relationship, and setting up ground rules. "I'm not passing up an opportunity for a man who's not sure about our future together."

"I am sure," Lee insisted.

He placed his head in his hands.

"You're sure now. Now that you know I'm leaving. That's the only reason."

The truth hurt. He grimaced as she inflicted the verbal slap to his face. "Two months right?" he asked.

"Yes. I'll be gone two months and we'll see how it goes. At the end of my assignment I will have to decide whether or not to accept the Vice President position. I'm hoping we can make that decision as a couple."

This was the best deal he would be able to strike at this time, considering the damage he'd caused. He understood the terms given. He kicked the air in silent frustration. "I hope we can make this work."

"Me too," Rita said.

The relationship now began to travel down the long path of redemption, with Lee carrying the brunt of the load. "Hey. I called you earlier tonight. Where were you?" Lee was still rather alert. It was closing in on 5:00 a.m.

"I was taking along hot bath, just sitting back thinking about life."

"I was worried about you," Lee said.

"Really?"

"Yea."

"Well you never called back, if you were so worried. Let me guess. You went over to Charlie's and hung out all night didn't you? That's probably why you were still up when I called." Rita never ceased to amaze. She never missed a detail.

"Well...I mean. Yea, I did go by there for a minute."

"You see Lee? This is what I'm talking about. I'm supposed to put my career on hold *for this*? You can't even be straight with me. Plus we just talked about your drinking." She was understandably disappointed again, her feelings punched through the phone. For some reason she gave Lee chance after chance. He possessed what many optimists would call potential. Even so, most women would have given up on his shenanigans months ago.

She continued disclosing how she felt. "My dreams were so close to coming true I could almost reach out and touch them."

"They still can come true," Lee said.

"You know. I've been a fool for lesser things than love. This time around I thought I'd take my chances. Everyone told me not to, but I thought you were different." Her feelings so filled with love and emotion placed him back face to face with the shame he'd come to be familiar with.

"You've got to believe in love," he reassured her.

"I'll try, listen it's late. Let's get some sleep alright?" she said.

"Yea, what is it almost 6:00?" he asked.

"We haven't talked on the phone this long since that first call almost nine months ago," Rita said.

"I remember that."

"Me too." Rita smiled and it penetrated through the phone illuminating his drab bedroom.

"Goodnight baby."

"Goodnight."

"Rita?"

"Yes."

"Call you tomorrow okay?"

"Sounds good."

The call ended, leaving Lee in his room, still in his blood stained wrinkled pants, staring out the window. The new day was commencing to dawn along with the love in his heart as well. He knew there couldn't be too many more occasions to mess up, if any at all.

Chapter 22

That Saturday went by with several brief phone conversations between Lee and Rita as they discussed how they would proceed in their relationship. Also the unavoidable subject of Frank Harrison came into play. As the police officers had indicated to him, Frank would not be pressing charges for the damage done to his motorcycle. Still, many questions remained unanswered.

By the time Sunday arrived he was worried about the possibility of Frank having the gall to confront him at work, and maybe find a bogus reason to fire him. He was still skeptical even though Rita did threaten to have Frank terminated if he caused a stir.

Unfortunately, their once secret relationship would be out in the open, exposed, and not on their terms. Undoubtedly Frank would tell other employees that he spotted them out together displaying various forms of affection. Surely it was a mistake to try and conceal what they had to begin with. A mistake that now reaped unwanted consequences.

The decision was made that they would both acknowledge their status as a couple but reaffirm their desire for privacy. If only they were able to go back and change the decision to hide the fact that they were in love, there wouldn't be need to face embarrassment which laid ahead this week at work.

One sure change was that in a matter of weeks Rita would be off to London and the office scandal would surely die down. His resolve was to keep his cool and not give in to Frank's prodding and pressure. He agreed to keep level head, knowing beyond a shadow of a doubt that if he acted in a violent manner while on Jackson & Fitz premises, he was sure to be out of work, or worse. Maybe he'd be reduced to crawling back on his hands and knees to Home Towne Mailers and beg for his management position back, overseeing their cast of misfits and social rejects.

The entire day Sunday was spent in the house, just cleaning up and also in the beginning stages of packing for his move back into his mother's house that Uncle Charlie had recently purchased. There was six weeks left on his lease at the duplex before he'd take possession of the four bedroom home across town in a nice family neighborhood. The worst thing going on over there was squirrels fighting.

Before long, guilty feelings swept over Lee when he realized his friend Liz would discover the news about his hidden love affair at work the next day. What he wasn't privy to was the fact that Liz already unearthed his buried secret regarding his dating status, thanks to his carelessness on his work computer. Liz had already given her preeminent attempt to back Ms. Clark away from Lee. Her knowledge of Lee's romance was well guarded as she didn't even clue her family or sister in on Lee's status yet.

Lee began to feel unnerved about confessing to Liz that he'd been deceitful the whole time she would query his availability. Deciding to call Liz was the final verdict. He wanted her to know the truth from his lips, not some sloppy second rate depiction given by nosy women folk at the office. After all, like they always said, she was all but family.

The phone began to ring.

"Hey Liz, what's up?"

"Hey what's going on boy?"

"Bad time to talk?" he asked.

"No, go ahead, what's going on?" She had an idea what he wanted.

"Listen, I want to make a confession. I want you to hear it from me before anyone else told you."

Liz was quiet already suspecting she knew the information he was going to state. "Go ahead, I'm listening."

"I've been lying about the real reason I don't wanna get back with Simone. The real reason is I've got a serious relationship going with someone special. Someone we work with."

"You talking about Sharon? Ha, ha." Liz played off any knowledge of Lee's personal life to perfection by referencing the homely older woman who worked in their department at work.

"Yea, you caught me. Me and Sharon have been kicking it for weeks now…just kidding. Seriously though."

"You crazy Lee. Who is it? Tell me, I'll be cool."

"It's Ms. Clark, from upstairs." Liz began to act flabbergasted. "Hold up, you talking about the executive Ms. Clark. The COO?" She deserved an Oscar for her riveting performance. Best surprised friend and coworker.

"Yea, that's the one, Rita Clark. We've kept it on the low. We met at Charlie's Lounge back before I even started working there. We just hit it off, it was crazy but once I started at J and F we kept it low key. Anyway, something went down on Friday and it's probably gonna be all over work tomorrow."

"Well I gotta be honest with you…. I'm shocked. She doesn't seem like your type. You know how people talk about her at work." Liz was wrapped in a ball of confusion, trying to figure out how they were still together after she exposed his faults to Ms. Clark on Friday afternoon.

"Yea I know people say she's mean and acts stuck up and all that. But, for real. She's real cool when you get to know her. That tough act must just be for work, so people take her seriously."

"Whatever."

"Don't trip Liz. I just thought you should know that's all. You're my girl, I felt bad for lying to you."

"That's cool, hold on a second someone's beeping in."

"Alright."

Liz clicked over her phone, and to her surprise it was Simone on the other end. "Hey," Simone said.

"You not gonna believe who's on the phone with me right now," Liz said.

"Who?"

"Lee."

"What?" Simone sounded excited and pleased to hear his name. So close, yet so far away.

"For real."

"Tell him I said hi for me."

"You know I will," Liz agreed.

"Liz. Don't be exaggerating what I said, I just said hi. Oh, but let him know I'll be home in two weeks and he better come to Mom and Dad's to see me. Shawn has been asking about him constantly. I'll probably text him later. We haven't talked in at least six months."

"Alright. I'll call you back in a second."

"Okay, bye."

Liz commenced into a silly little victory dance as she clicked back over to Lee. "Hello."

"Yea I'm here."

"Guess who that was."

"I don't know."

"That was Simone. She said hello and that she'll be home in two weeks, and that you better come visit."

Silence had again taken control of Lee as he went numb all over. He finally picked up his dialogue. "Two weeks?"

"Yea two weeks, why?"

"Uh, nothing. I just have something going on in two weeks that's all. Never mind."

The sheer irony of Rita leaving and Simone moving home on the same day was mind-boggling.

"Whatever Lee. You know my sister is a lot more fun than that stiff Ms. Clark. You know in your heart you need to be with Simone. You know that."

Lee didn't respond.

"Besides ya'll got history."

"Yup, that's what it is too...History..."

"Well okay then. I'm not going to argue with you. I'm glad you told me about your secret woman, but I give your little fling another month. When you break up don't try to come running back to Simone either. She's not about to be a second option for nobody. She doesn't need you. You oughta be glad she held out waiting for you this long. But, you're blowing it."

"Chill Liz. I'm not trying to disrespect her. It's just that Rita came along."

"All you and Simone's off and on drama was crazy. I'll admit that. But, really, it was mostly you, and now you want to settle down?"

"Yea, I do. Besides your right, Simone deserves better than me. I haven't treated her right. Her or Shawn. So why do you even want us to get back?"

"Because deep down, you're made for each other. She's forgiven you."

"Yea right," he scoffed.

"She has. She knows the situation was sensitive and touchy. She understands. Why don't you?"

"The timing is messed up," Lee said. He was growing frustrated.

"Skip Ms. Clark," Liz said.

"What? Just throw her to the side?"

"She'd do it to you."

"No she wouldn't," he said, doubting that possibility.

"You sure about that?" she asked.

"You sound like Keith."

"Keith? You still hang out with that fool? Wasn't he in jail?"

"No, that's his dad."

"Anyway, he's crazy too," she said.

"He's my boy though. Always been there. Oh, and he told me to tell you hi too. He said if Ray messes up, he'll be there for you."

"You must be sick, I'll see you tomorrow," Liz said, laughing as they hung up the phone.

Lee took a seat on the couch as he shook his head smiling. Liz was something else. He wondered if she would ever give up on getting him back together with her sister Simone. Probably not.

Chapter 23

The next week and a half flew by in a blur. Neither Lee nor Rita could comprehend that her departure was in mere days. It was Wednesday and her flight was Saturday at 4:00 a.m. Rita was occupied in preparation for her trip, staying late at the Jackson & Fitz office almost everyday, leaving little time to socialize.

There were nights where she wouldn't leave until 8:00, which concerned Lee greatly. Unpredictably to both, not a word had been spoken at work about the fight with Frank Harrison, or to the fact they were an item. Frank had taken off a full week giving his injuries and ego ample time for recovery.

Even the always chatty Liz made up her mind to back out of Lee's personal life. It was almost like calm before a violent tropical storm the way things had miraculously worked themselves out since the chaotic weekend. Lee was even staying in the house, and avoiding unnecessary contact with Keith and Charlie while he prepared to move as well.

Unfortunately for Lee, Rita was now in the habit of keeping secrets. Big secrets. She had been staying late at her office, packing up every item, for a permanent exodus. She was now certain that she would accept with pride the distinctive position of Vice President of International Banking. Once she arrived home it was more of the same, only this packing was of personal items. Jackson & Fitz would be assuming her mortgage, and selling the highly sought after loft condominium. They would also cover her moving expenses, and ship her belongings to her a few weeks after assimilating to life in the United Kingdom.

Upon arrival she would be staying at the Renaissance Chancery Court Hotel in an executive level suite for at least three weeks. Currently she had to decide how to reveal this life altering news to Lee. He was under the impression that she would return inside of two months, and things could return to normal. That wasn't the case.

Far from it in fact.

Their relationship was doomed to be tremendously distant, possibly in more than one way. Rita elected to believe if the strength of their love was great enough, things could work out. Meaning; Lee moving to London to support her career evolution. That still hinged upon his ability to regain her full trust and somehow resemble the man she once fell in love with. Nothing was certain.

She prompted him daily to cease in his drinking alcohol and to seek out help for his anger issues. So far, after a week and a half, he did neither. No counseling to be sure, and at the minimum a couple of beers every other night, in his eyes a significant advancement and a sign of improvement. He reassured her that 'everything was under control.'

Purposely avoiding long conversations with Lee was her best defense in the days leading up to her departure. They chatted like strangers sitting at a diner counter about trivial subjects. No longer did they sound like life long companions. Keeping true to her word, the romance was reduced to a halt, as they tried to forge a friendship like they captured several months beforehand.

She deliberated over the proper time and place to lay out her thought process and plan to Lee. She became so tense each time she was about to tell him, and the moment never seemed fitting. In the recesses of her mind she recounted his blazing anger, and the way he struck Frank Harrison with brutal impact. It made her flash back to the one occasion she saw her father strike her mothers beautiful face. He scared her. He was never aggressive towards her in any form. But he scared her.

They planned to meet for dinner on Friday one last time before she departed for London. Dining arrangements had been made at the magnificent Chateau Le Blanc, where they once celebrated their six month anniversary. Rita prized the posh French Bistro giving Lee reason to believe that location would be the perfect site to express what was on his mind. Lee had plans of his own. Big plans.

His involved the idea of her returning in a short time and settling down with him in the house he grew up in. The home he would be moving into while she was gone overseas. He was finally sure he reached the level with Rita that caused him to want to settle down and commit to love everlasting.

Each day that passed he grew more anxious in anticipation of celebrating a new chapter in his life with this admirable woman. It was nearly 9:00 in the evening and she would surely have a bit of time to talk by now. He decided to talk just to iron out plans for Friday's dinner, as well as arranging plans to drop her off at the airport. As he dialed the familiar seven digits he thought of how much she'd be missed and how far they'd come since their chance meeting at Charlie's Lounge.

"Hey Rita what's going on?"

"Oh hi, nothing much. I'm just about packed for my trip."

Rita lied. This was much more than a trip. A trip means you will return. This was specifically a move that would take her across the Atlantic Ocean, and into England. She had to tell the truth and soon, as the days were dwindling down like the last sands slipping through the bottom of a hour glass. Friday at dinner. That settled it. She would tell him there. That would be the last chance to talk face to face so she would be forced to confess.

That night at Chateau Le Blanc she would bring to light her acceptance of the permanent Vice President position. Still a rather young woman, a chance to become a VP of a publicly traded company was a chance of a lifetime. Lee most certainly had to understand that fact, the same way she understood and forgave so much about his life. It was only fair. Convincing herself the distance would bring a longing for one another, and Lee would be moved to join her side within a year.

"You ready for the flight?" he asked.

"I'm prepared as well as I can be. I'll probably just try to sleep most of the way."

"I'll be thinking of you every minute you're gone baby." Lee was planning to pull out all the stops at dinner.

"I'll miss you too." Her words were soft and sincere. With each part of her body, she questioned her final decision to accept the weighty assignment. But, as she explained to him the night of his horrific fighting incident, she wanted a man who was ready to commit, which he wasn't at that point.

She had known and heard rumblings of a possibility of this opportunity months ago but had been weighing her options, dependent on his feelings towards marriage. Each time that word came into play, he wanted no part of it, sometimes becoming upset.

The conversation drifted on for a few more minutes as they agreed Lee would drop her off at the airport and discussing how they would spend their last night together.

"Two months, I'm gonna miss you girl," Lee said.

Rita smiled sitting up against her headboard on the bed, wiggling her feet around. "You don't have to miss me."

"What do you mean?"

"I'm saying, I could take the VP job, and you could move to London with me and we'd be together everyday."

"I thought you said you weren't taking that position." Lee now seemed confused. Unknown to Lee she had already accepted the offer. There could be no turning back now after the corporate wheels were in motion.

Her contract with Jackson & Fitz was worth over $170,000 annually. Rita was now doing her best to convince Lee to come with her and try things out.

"No Lee, I said I wasn't sure, remember? We agreed to see how things were going."

"Things are going good, what's the problem?" he asked, while standing over his sink, washing dishes.

"Things are going good, but it hasn't even been two weeks from the conversation we had."

He stopped washing and dried his hands. "Yea, but come, on let's be real. We've been together for nine months, I love you."

"Nine months, I know, calm down."

"No, I don't wanna calm down, I need you Rita. I need you and you're just going to throw this away?"

He threw the dish towel on to the counter, shaking his head in disgust.

"I'm not throwing anything away. This is a golden opportunity for me. I didn't go to school eight years for nothing. Do you know how hard it is for a woman to get where I am? Do you have any idea?"

Rita now sat up, swinging her legs off the bed.

She had acquired her B.A. in Accounting as well as two Master Degrees, one in International Business and another in Business Management.

Lee stayed silent on the other end of the phone, pouting like a fat little boy told no more cake.

Rita sat up on the bed. "This success means nothing if I have no one to share it with. I need someone to laugh and to cry with. Someone to share my secrets, and my love."

Half of Lee knew she couldn't turn down a chance like this, but his selfish half wanted her for himself, and on his terms. "No, you're right. I've got to look at this from every angle. It is a good opportunity. I know."

"So does that mean you're coming with me?" she stood and slipped her pedicured toes into some pink fuzzy slippers.

"Maybe, who knows? Like you said, we'll see." Lee leaned against the counter, opened the fridge, looking for nothing, only fidgeting.

It was the first time he'd even entertained the thought which made Rita happy to know there was a slight chance. But really in the corners of his mind he knew for this to work, she'd have to stay. His mother was already in Mexico and Uncle Charlie was all the family he had left. This town was all he knew, he couldn't leave. Plus he was about to move into his old house where he grew up, and he couldn't wait. Lee began to inflict a bit of self-pity.

"What are you even doing with a guy like me? Compared to you I'm a failure. Just a washed up, never was baseball player," Lee said while quietly opening a bottle of Miller Lite.

"Don't you ever say that again. I'm so sick of hearing that garbage. You're not a failure. You're a really nice guy, you make me laugh, you're handsome, a great listener. I can go on. Plus you have a great job yourself,

Mr. Manager. Don't let your self doubt and insecurities get in the way of our love. Do you hear me? I love you, for you. I don't care about the amount of money you make. I've dated wealthy men before...I need you, for you."

She placed her hand on her hip as she walked the hall to the living room where she took in the park view.

Lee had heard this speech more than once before, but each time he could hardly believe it was real. There was no doubt Rita was sincere in what she said, every bit of it was true. She really didn't care.

"I'm sorry Rita. You're just so sweet; I just can't believe it sometimes. I can't believe this is real being with you. You could have any man that you want-"

"But I want you."

"I want you too," he said. Pulling the phone away from his head he took a quick sip of the malted refreshment.

The conversation continued for another hour, reminiscing over the past nine months, the good moments and the bad.

"Goodnight Mr. Johnson," Rita whispered soothingly to end the phone call.

"Goodnight, but before you hang up... I've got something really special planned for Friday okay?"

"What is it? You know I can't stand surprises," she said.

"Sorry. I can't tell you just yet. But you'll see....you'll see."

Chapter 24

It was Friday morning, and Rita's last day on the job as COO. At midmorning she was interrupted by a knock at her office door. As she opened the door she was greeted by a delivery man, bearing not one, but two vases, one in each hand full of the most beautiful red roses she had ever seen in her life. The two dozen long stem roses were promptly placed on her desk as her face beamed forth an expression of ecstasy, smiling ear to ear.

She neatly opened the attached note that read: *"I want you to know how I feel about you. I'll put you high on a pedestal. I'll handle you with care, because you're fragile. There are so many things I want to say. I know you could have any man that you wanted to. I'm taking this chance, to offer you my love. I will miss you. Love, Lee."*

Rita fell back in her chair, and turned around gazing out her window like she so often did. Staring out at the cityscape below, she realized this man of hers was truly unique. She next dialed his extension to reach him at his desk, expectant to hear his melodic voice.

He sounded like one of those smooth morning drive radio DJ's. Instead of his voice she heard a recorded message. "Lee Johnson is out of the office today, if you need immediate assistance please dial 219. Thank you." That was peculiar. Lee didn't say he wasn't coming in today. Where could he be?

She quickly dialed his cell phone to see what was going on.

"Hey baby, thank you so much for the beautiful flowers. I love them. They smell so good. You're the best," she said. Her face was aglow with excitement.

"You know you deserve it. I'm so proud of you. I'll miss you while you're gone and I wanted you to know that."

"Thank you so much. Hey. Where are you? I called your office phone and it said you're out today."

"Yea, I took the day off, I had some last minute runs to make for tonight."

"What are you talking about?"

He peaked her curiosity.

"Oh, you'll see baby. It's all good."

She sometimes wondered what was going on inside his head.

"*Heaven must be like this!*"

Loud crackling voice singing came across the phone, causing Rita to jump back, jerking the phone away from her ear. "What in the world was that?" she asked looking unquestionably confused.

"I'm sorry, that was Uncle Charlie trying to sing. He's with me, we're in the car."

"What are you two doing?" Rita asked.

"I can't tell you that," Lee said.

"I hope you didn't blow off work to hang out with your uncle."

"Baby, you gotta trust me okay?"

"Okay Lee," she sighed, masking her frustration.

"Alright Ms. Clark, I'm gonna let you go. I'll see you tonight. I love you."

"Love you too, thanks again for the flowers. I'll see you tonight. Oh, I almost forgot. Mr. Sander and some of the other exec's are in town. Well all be flying back together tonight, well tomorrow morning technically. Anyway you know what I mean."

"Yea four in the morning is a crazy time," Lee said. He remembered her odd flight time.

"Yes I know. But it's an eight hour flight so we'll touch down around five in the evening London time."

"That's like a five hour difference between us then."

"Correct. But don't forget there doesn't have to be a difference in time at all, if you move over there with me." Rita looked at the cars below out her window, wondering where he was exactly.

"We'll see. But after tonight you might want to stay here."

"Really?" Rita asked.

The conversation came to an abrupt ending as her secretary blared through the intercom.

"Ms. Clark. Mr. Donald Sander is here to see you."

"I've got to go Lee, love you," Rita blurted out and with that said she was gone.

Lee was now used to being hurried off the phone so Rita could conduct her business. Sometimes he would empathize, other times he felt kind of belittled. Today wasn't one of those times since there was so much on his mind.

"You know she isn't coming back, you know that right?" Uncle Charlie finally spoke up after he finished singing.

"After tonight, she'll be back. I know she will." Lee sat back at ease, not even glancing over at Charlie.

"I don't know about that man. But look, you wanna go through with this. I'll support you. You're my nephew. I got your back." Uncle Charlie was at least being honest as he playfully pushed Lee in the back of the head.

"Thanks for rolling with me, and for the hook up," Lee said while driving.

"Oh yea, you know I got the hook up on everything. My man Mazan, he's from overseas, he's got this little jewelry shop. He said he could find something real nice for you and take that old ring in on trade."

"Cool."

"You sure you wanna trade in that ring playa? That's a two karat and it's flawless. Mazan's cool and all, but he isn't going to give you no deal like this," Charlie pulled out the engagement ring Lee had once purchased for Simone and held it up to the light.

"I can't give Rita this ring man. That was for Simone. It doesn't feel right, you know?"

"No, I don't know. You're about to spend more and it won't even be as nice. You got this in New York, in the diamond district, you can't beat that deal. Plus, it's paid for."

"It's not about the money," Lee said.

"Oh, so you got it like that now? Can *I* get a job at Jackson & Fitz?"

Charlie rocked around in his seat. The big man shook the SUV while laughing hysterically.

This was the first time the two of them had hung out in quite some time, and Lee was having a great time.

"I gotta tell you, I don't know how you pulled your girl Rita. Honestly I didn't think it would last but look at you." Charlie shook the ring around in his hand, looking at it and smiling.

"Yea it's crazy, we're so different but the same too, you know?"

"I know me and Keith always pick with you about how much money she's bringing in, but if you can handle it, more power to you. I couldn't do it. I'm telling you though. She's gonna want you to move over there. Watch."

"Who knows, maybe I will." Lee smiled.

"Please boy, what you know about England?"

"What you talking about, I've seen Austin Powers....*yea baby*!" Lee fired back playfully, doing his greatest impression, triggering their laughter yet again.

Shortly thereafter, they arrived at Uncle Charlie's hook up spot for jewelry. Just like he said Mazan was inside and ready to wheel and deal. He had on navy blue dress pants, slip on loafers, and a blue paisley print silk button up shirt, unbuttoned halfway down his chest exposing a plethora of gold chains.

The conversation was broken up a bit, due to the calls incoming on Mazan's bluetooth earpieces. Yes....earpieces. This was one of the rare individuals that had an earpiece in each ear, truly a sight to behold. Either this guy was really, really important, or he had a multitude of transactions going. You couldn't tell.

Either way, an hour went by and no deals were being made. At least no deals that didn't involve Lee being completely ripped off. An hour passed, and agreeing to disagree Lee departed from the jewelry shop still owning the two karat ring once bought for Simone.

"Look man, hook ups don't always pan out. That's my bad." Uncle Charlie was embarrassed by the lack of deals offered.

"Hey we tried. No big deal. I wanted to swing a deal but..."

"Listen. I don't see nothing wrong with using that ring tonight Lee. That's a nice ring." With each of the last four words he poked Lee in the chest.

"Yea, you know, you're right. Besides it's three o'clock now. I'm not gonna just trade this thing in all last minute. I've got to do this tonight, before she leaves. I'm not letting her get away." Lee was clearly nervous as he shifted his weight from one leg to another.

"Yea. That Simone thing got crazy. She was a nice girl too though. That really could have worked."

As they ascended back inside the SUV Lee explained, "Yea Simone was great. She really was....She's moving back to town too. Something like this weekend, I'm not sure."

"Who?" Charlie leaned back.

"Simone," Lee said.

"What?" Charlie expanded that word for at least a good five seconds, then asked. "You gonna holla at her?"

"Come on man, I'm about to propose to Rita tonight. How's that look?"

"You aint married yet playboy. Simone was all that! Keep her on the back burner, at least. Low heat."

They both burst open, laughing at Charlie's unorthodox logic, though only partially kidding.

"Yea, we had some good times together....and she was fine." Lee agreed with his Uncle as they clapped hands and continued their laughing all the way home. It was now almost four o'clock and Lee had to get himself primed for dinner, which was at 7:00 p.m. sharp.

Chapter 25

The couple planned to meet at Chateau Le Blanc at seven in the evening. Lee made reservations for the dinner. He arrived first and waited for her in the reception area. He was beginning to become severely nervous as he was preparing to ask her this life altering question. Even though he had purchased an engagement ring before, this would be his first attempt at a marriage proposal.

7:00 slipped into 7:15 with the concierge raising the question to Lee of when his date would arrive, also informing him that in fifteen minutes the table would be given to the next available patrons. The eatery was extraordinarily popular and very challenging to get a seat, especially on a Friday night.

He continuously checked his pocket, to see if the ring was still there. Where was she? Jackson & Fitz was only about seven city blocks away from the restaurant, and she planned on taking a cab there from the office. The limo driver would take her luggage along with the other executives that would be flying back to London. These highly esteemed men would be spending the rest of their night, passing time at stuffy cigar clubs, sipping brandy, and later be dropped off at the airport. Rita told them she arranged to be dropped off and she'd meet them in the executive quarters at the airport later that night.

The dilemma was at 7:15 she was still finishing up her last order of business at the office. The meeting ran over its scheduled time by at least an hour. Mr. Sander proved himself to be exceptionally long winded and slow in tongue. His heavy British accent made him impossible to listen to without having a large amount of sleep come over you.

"Excuse me sir, I must be going. I have an engagement I'm late in arrival for as we speak." Rita stood, clutching her purse under her arm.

"Young lady, as a Vice President now, Jackson & Fitz is your top priority. Your other....engagement as you say, can be placed at bay. At least until we're finished. Agreed?" It was more of an order, rather than a question. Mr. Sander spoke with his droopy bagged eyes half open.

"Sir I understand, it's just that. I've made a promise and I need to keep it."

"Understood, but we've made a commitment to you Ms. Clark. You must fully commit to our company. We're almost completed here, you'll be late but I'm sure you'll explain." The old man made turtles look fast as he reached for his glass of water.

"Sir I feel we could talk at length on our flight. I really must be going," Rita said.

Mr. Sander sipped his glass, frowned and folded his arms across his chest, resting them on his potbelly. "I sleep on airplanes. Don't think of troubling me then my dear."

"Sir," Rita stepped towards the door.

"Ma'am?" he responded.

"Yes?"

Mr. Sander let out a king sized sigh. "Be on your way if you must go, hurry on. Very well then."

Heading towards the door and past the other men in the room she uttered, "Thank you sir."

Mr. Sander stood and called her. "Rita."

"Yes Mr. Sander sir."

"That's why we chose you, you know?"

"Why's that sir?" she asked.

"You're not afraid to stand up for yourself. You will have no fear in representing our company's interests. Most of these men here would never think of questioning me. You have no dread! We appreciate that quality in you. Keep up the good work and we'll see you tonight. *Don't be late.*"

Mr. Sander smiled showing his well stained teeth as he pounded the desk in a show of approval.

"I won't, see you then."

"Have a jolly good time."

"Indeed." Rita nodded her head while exiting the door. As it closed firmly behind her, she began to run down the hall, straight through the large frosted glass doors and towards the elevators that would carry her to the lobby.

Reaching the front steps she whipped out her cell phone to call Lee.

"Rita, where are you baby?"

"I'm so sorry Lee. Mr. Sander was impossible. He kept talking and talking. I was supposed to be out of there an hour ago."

"It's seven-twenty-five, they're going to give away our table."

"Tell them I'll be right there," Rita said.

"Please, they don't care. This place is packed."

His eyes scanned the busy waiting area, as the restaurant began shrinking as more couples filed inside.

"I'm sorry baby. I ruined our night." She flagged down a taxi cab while talking. "It's not ruined. Just call me when you get close, and we'll go from there."

Lee hid his disappointment well. The last thing he wanted to accomplish was to seem upset. In actuality his plan was crushed, the mood wouldn't be desirable if they settled for some everyday chain restaurant.

This was his last chance to propose to Rita, to save this relationship, and to persuade her to come back home from London.

Great. The concierge was headed his way.

"Sir, I'm sorry we have no choice but to give up your table." The news was given to Lee by way of a discreet whisper. But it felt like he had just been screamed at.

"I understand," he replied, standing up and sighing. He then commenced to wriggling through the crowd of young and trendy diners, out into the bustling city sidewalk. Pacing on for about a block he stopped and took a seat on a bench that was occupied only by unidentified stains and grime. Old newspaper and random garbage swirled around his feet forming miniature cyclones.

His phone rang. He answered and to his surprise it wasn't Rita.

Liz blurted out, "Well I thought I'd let you know ...she's here."

"Who's where?" Lee asked and frowned.

"Simone. Her flight came in this afternoon. I would've told you earlier but you weren't at work. What's up? Were you drunk again?"

"No I wasn't drunk. I had some business to take care of that's all."

"Well, they made an announcement at work about your girl leaving. They said she was moving to London to be the new VP."

Lee shook his head. "No. That's still up in the air."

"Uh-uh, they made it sound like it was a done deal. They said she was gone for good," Liz argued.

He wasn't in the mood for a debate. "I think I would know," he said.

"You hope so....."

"Come on, like she'd lie to me."

"I don't know, really don't care. Just thought I'd let you know your girl was officially in town."

"She's not my girl."

She used to be. She used to be his everything. He felt ashamed things had unraveled so far between them over the past few years.

"That's not what she said," Liz laughed.

"I gotta go, for real."

"I'll let you go," Liz said. They hung up.

Lee began feeling somewhat bitter realizing, if this was a sample of life with a Vice President, he didn't like the taste of it.

His phone rang again in his tightly clenched in his hands. He was interrupted from people gazing, watching the interesting characters pass by on the street. He looked on inquisitively, wondering if their night was going as well as his.

He answered the phone. "Hello."

"Lee you're not going to believe this."

"Now what?"

"There's a police blockade and I'm only four blocks away."

"Get out and walk, I'll walk to you. Where are you? This is our last night together." His statement was made as if she didn't realize that fact.

"I can't, the police won't let anyone out, or near here."

"What?" he shouted.

"I don't know why, hold on....Excuse me sir?"

Rita stuck her head out the grimy cab window asking a nearby police officer what was happening.

"It's a bomb threat at the school. Stay calm ma'am and stay in the vehicle." The officer explained and quickly moved on to direct traffic.

Rita turned her attention back to Lee. "They said there's a bomb threat at the college, and they're closing the block."

"I'm headed there now, alright." Lee began jogging up two blocks with the commotion coming into view. "I see what's going on now, hold on okay." Lee was fast approaching the police blockade. "I'll call you right back," he assured her approaching the officer and beginning to plead his case.

"I gotta get through there ...my fiancé ...my girl is in there." Lee was emphatically pointing to the traffic jam.

"I don't care if your Grandma's in there. We can't let you in the perimeter. Everyone will be cleared out in about an hour, tops."

Lee in a last ditch effort flashed the engagement ring, explaining how he had to take care of this at that moment.

"Sorry kid." The officer with the overgrown stomach wouldn't budge a muscle.

Lee quickly called Rita back just like he promised her. "I can't get through. They said you'll be out of there in less than an hour. I'll just wait here for you."

"I'm sorry Lee. I ruined our night together," she mumbled.

Even though it was true Lee had no choice but to understand, the same way Rita always did. A few minutes dwindled away as he kept peering over to get a glimpse of the commotion going on down the street. Police were still blocking people off and assuring everyone that there was no real imminent danger, just a precaution. Lee's phone rang again.

This time he checked the caller ID. Liz again. What does she want now he thought already having heard enough about Simone for one day. He let the call go to voicemail. Instantly, she called back again. He reluctantly answered the phone, hearing her voice sounding frantic. She began to speedily explain that her father wanted her to get a hold of him immediately.

As a firefighter he was with the first responding unit to a horrendous accident that just occurred in town, near Uncle Charlie's Lounge. Liz was crying chaotically. Lee knew grim news waited.

"What's wrong?" he asked, fearing devastation on the horizon.

"Lee...," she grasp for breath.

"Come on Liz, what's wrong?" he asked again, this time with urgency in his voice.

"It's your uncle. He was in a car accident. Daddy called me and said to tell you right away. Momma's calling your Mom right now. Get down to County Regional, I'll meet you there."

Lee nearly dropped the phone as his mouth went bone dry within a split second. "Is he alright?" he asked.

Liz's continued crying answered that question.

Without thinking he broke into a complete sprint, heading towards the parking garage where his SUV was located. Just as he thought the night couldn't digress any more, he received a call like that.

Lee prayed continuously as he penetrated inside of the parking ramp shadows. Firing the V8 engine he floored the 4x4 vehicle, heading towards the hospital, without delay.

Chapter 26

Rita finally emerged from the police blockade after the determination was made by authorities that there was no bomb at the college building. As she paid the cab fare and stepped out in front of Chateau Le Blanc she ran her hands through her hair, and checked the time on her watch. It was 8:45. Certainly Lee would be upset about the events unfolding on their last night together.

She felt a horrible sense of guilt about not telling him yet of her acceptance of the Vice President position. It worked in her favor that he missed work that day, since they held a building wide conference call to announce she would be leaving to accept the position overseas. Rita's head was on a swivel as her eyes skimmed around frantically trying to locate the familiar handsome face of Lee Johnson. He told her fifteen minutes ago that he'd meet her right there where she was standing. Where could he be?

Lee moved down the interstate highway at speeds exceeding ninety miles per hour, weaving dangerously in and out of traffic on his way to County Regional Hospital back in town. It was usually a half an hour commute if you had a early morning start, bumped up to forty-five minutes with rush hour traffic. This was a Friday night which made the road congested with travelers entering and exiting the city.

He had been driving for nearly fifteen minutes and despite the heavy traffic he was half way to the hospital. Too edgy to call Liz for an update, he focused on bobbing and weaving through the pile of cars lining the highway.

His cell phone began to ring, knocking off his concentration. He flipped it open seeing Rita's number, only then realizing his blunder of not calling her to let her know what transpired. His attention switched over to concern for the health of his uncle, maybe even his life.

"Rita, oh my goodness, I'm so sorry, listen." Lee spoke a mile a minute, leaving her mystified.

"Lee slow down. Where are you? What's going on?" Rita knew him well enough to know something happened.

"It's Charlie. Liz called me. He's been in an accident, a bad one back in town."

"Where are you?" she asked. At the same time she loathed hearing the name Liz.

"I'm so sorry babe, I just panicked and ran to the truck, I forgot about everything else. Why is this happening?" he screamed banging his closed fist on the dashboard.

"Lee, stay calm."

"My uncle might not make it, this is crazy." Lee's voice began to shudder.

"I'll go with you, where are you now?" Rita said.

"I'm like ten minutes from the hospital. I got outa downtown. I just left as fast as I could," Lee said.

"Why didn't you call me?" she asked.

"I don't know, I wasn't thinking...," he explained.

"Okay, okay...lets just make sure your uncle is alright."

"This night has been a nightmare. What's next? I can't believe this!" he shouted louder while pulling off the exit ramp.

"I wanted to see you before you had to leave," he explained. Lee began yelling at the elderly couple in front of him on the road. "Get out of my way. Move! Move!"

"Calm down Lee," she suggested.

He ignored the advice, continuing to lay on the horn.

"What time is it?" he asked.

Rita checked her watch again. "Nine."

"I need you Rita, you're all I've got. I'm at County Regional. Can you get here?"

"It's at least forty-five minutes in this traffic," she explained. She looked around at the city, still in shock of the night's turn of events. "I have to be back at the airport by two at the latest to check in and so on."

"What? You're still going?" His forehead wrinkled in disgust.

"I don't have a choice," Rita said.

"My uncle's laying up in the hospital half-dead and you're leaving me alone?"

"Lee? What am I supposed to do?"

"Tell those fools you have an emergency."

"I...I....," she said and paused.

"I can't believe you!" he screamed back.

She now felt torn in a way she'd never experienced before, as she was now the one ashamed. There was no way to explain to him right now that she wouldn't be returning, except for a visit. "I'll be there, see you in about an hour," she said.

"Alright, County Regional, Emergency. I love you."

"Love you too," Rita sighed while hanging up the phone.

This time she was the one being rushed off the line.

After a few quick turns Lee veered into County Regional Hospital parking lot, jumping the curb he found an open parking spot. It was 9:15 as he rushed inside the hospital's emergency room, while at the same time Rita sat inside a cab, on her way to town.

"Please hurry, this is an emergency," she coerced the driver. He only ignored her, and pushed another button on the box that indicated cab fare. Talk radio chattered on softly in the background. If the cab driver made good time he'd arrive at the hospital by ten, enough time only to check on Charlie and say a quick goodbye before getting to Metro Airport.

Mr. Sander's words of punctuality were still fixed in her head, stuck there like quicksand.

The group of executives were expecting her arrival at the airport around midnight, enough time to sign a few documents and prepare for their flight back to London.

Lee scrambled inside the emergency department at the hospital. As he turned the corner he saw a sight he hadn't seen in such a long time. The entire Hart family was huddled in a corner at the waiting area, some pacing, some praying, and one looking at him directly in the eyes.

"You made it," Liz said. She was the first to jog over to him and throw her arms around him. Her husband Ray who he had heard so much about came next, patting him on the shoulder, nodding his head with respect. Lee did the same in return.

Mr. and Mrs. Hart began approaching Lee slow and cautious, as if he were a dangerous creature or rabid beast. Mr. Hart had on his fireman's gear, explaining how he arrived at the scene. Mrs. Hart tenderly kissed Lee on the cheek and squeezed his hand in support.

"I called your Mom and Aunt. They know about the accident. They're trying to get a flight out tonight. Okay baby," Mrs. Hart explained to him.

Lee was completely engulfed with affection, from a couple on each side. They encouraged him and gave him all the updates about his uncle's condition. Still, there was one set of ebony eyes that was staring at Lee in a nervous manner.

After a few moments Shawn approached him, holding a portable video game in one hand, waving hello with the other. Lee squatted down to his level and shook his hand while fixing the brim of his baseball cap.

As he stood up, Simone was right there, face to face. She leaned in hugging him tenderly. She whispered delicately in his ear, "I'm sorry." Her voice was velvety, just like he remembered. Her skins softness rivaled fine satin, while her hair and neck emitted a sweet aroma of coconut and orchids.

"Thank you," he whispered back as with teary eyes he let her go and looked around at those once familiar faces. Those faces were now being blurred by the tears that could no longer be contained. He now deeply regretted all the times he ducked and hid from the Hart's when seeing them around town. Here now, at this moment of tragedy, in need of a shoulder, he had many to lean on.

He was grateful to the utmost sense of that word as they all took seats in anticipation of an update. Shawn was at his right side and Liz to his left, the rest of the group sat across from him. One of them gazed upon him as if she'd never seen anyone so precious.

As they all sat there mute Lee realized, none of them had to show up to support him. Sure, they knew Charlie, everybody in town did. But they were much closer to his mother than Charlie. But right now, it was clearly evident that they were there to support him.

The time was 9:45 and Rita was still stuck in traffic, about twenty minutes away from the hospital. Lee's cell phone was unable to receive service inside the busy hospital emergency department as she tried resiliently to contact him. Frustrated and frazzled, she kicked the seat in front of her, not hard, but enough to hurt her toe and scuff her pumps.

"Please remain calm or I can let you out of here," the cab driver spoke by way of a thick accent she was unable to decipher. With that said he pushed another button on the box indicating cab fare, as it instantly jumped $3.00.

Mr. Hart explained that a drunk driver in an old pickup truck ran a red light while speeding and broadsided Uncle Charlie's Cadillac CTS. The impact forced Charlie's head into the side window causing injury to the face and closed head trauma. He was also suffering from internal bleeding from the steering wheel, since he was not wearing his safety belt.

Mr. Hart stabilized Charlie before he was placed in the ambulance and rushed to the emergency room. The veteran firefighter went on to explain to Lee about his unconscious state, and also the fact that the biggest threat was internal bleeding. Lee grew quite agitated, not with Mr. Hart, but with the hospital staff's lack of new information. The admitting nurse assured everyone that everything possible was being done to treat his uncle.

Lee couldn't believe the tragedy happened only a block away from the Lounge that served as a second home. The general feeling was clear, and he could tell from Mr. Hart's face that the outcome didn't look promising for Charlie.

After a few minutes of silence a doctor emerged from inside the emergency room department and asked to speak with the family of Mr. Charles Lynch.

Mr. Hart spoke up. "We're his family over here, this is his nephew," he said, extending his hand towards Lee.

"Can I speak with you privately?" the doctor asked moving to a more secluded waiting area. Tension gripped the air like a vice as Lee began to shake like a ninety year old man. Everyone had seen those scenes played out on television and no one ever wanted to have the role in real life. It was happening to Lee right now, and on a night he had planned to be memorable for other reasons.

"Is he gonna be alright? How's he holding up?" Lee asked questions, trying to be optimistic and convince himself it would be okay. The doctor looked like this was the worst part of his job, and looked Lee in the eyes with sorrow, shaking his head from side to side.

"We couldn't stop the bleeding internally. We tried so hard, we just couldn't stop..." He shook his head again. Then the doctor whispered the two words one never wants to hear inside a hospital, "I'm sorry."

Lee went blank. He stared at the physician, then turning away in disbelief, almost pushing his way past the Harts who stood behind him. He rushed out into the hallway to be alone. Slamming his back against the wall he stood there silent, shocked and angry all at once. He stared blankly, with a stoic look on his face.

Mrs. Hart and Liz began crying themselves, holding one another. Ray did his best to distract Shawn from the emotion by walking him down the hallway towards the cafeteria for a snack. Mr. Hart slowly began pursuit of Lee, as Simone grabbed her father's wrist, shaking her head.

"Let me talk to him," Simone said.

Mr. Hart agreed as he put both of his hands behind his neck, looking up towards the ceiling. He'd seen this scene so many times over the years, but could never get used to it. The tall man sat down, overcome with emotion from the news, and the memory of the loss of his friend. As Simone ran into the hall she spotted Lee standing there alone in a daze.

Simone hurried to him, grabbing him, pulling his arms around her and placing hers around him. A few seconds passed as they began to cradle one another in the confines of their arms, nestled in close as birds in a nest.

They were both crying, holding each other for the first time in years. In some strange way it felt so natural, as he relished the serenity in Simone's warm embrace. She stood there with him, holding him close and wiping away tears for the next ten minutes.

The two stood intertwined like a sculptured piece of art.

Simone whispered in his ear. "Don't be afraid. Let it go." He began to weep heavily. Lee felt comfort in those familiar arms of hers, and could now feel her heart beating against his chest. She gazed ever so lovingly into his sad eyes, and he into hers. This time, both of them now looking at each other as someone that was very precious. Realizing they were holding one another once again, neither let go. Instead he pulled her ever closer. Her head nestled into his neck.

The silence was interrupted by the faint sound of high heel shoes clicking against the tile floor in the distance as Rita rushed inside the hospital searching for the emergency department. The two of them stood in a trance, oblivious to the world surrounding them, still freshly mourning the news of Charlie's death.

Rita first was greeted by Liz and her frowning face. Liz rolled her eyes as she saw Ms. Rita Clark. If facial expressions could hurt, hers did enough to strike Rita down. "Where's Lee?" Rita asked, almost demanding.

"Around the corner," Liz told her then said under her breath, "About time you showed up."

"Who's that?" Mrs. Hart inquired, between sniffles.

"Nobody," Liz said frowning and wiping her weeping eyes.

Rita had a habit of being so poised and under control. But no amount of schooling could prepare her for what she saw next.

Chapter 27

As Rita turned the corner, there was Lee pressed against a wall with another woman blanketed in his arms. She gasped, as she asked herself. Why?

This particular woman needed no introduction at all. Rita knew exactly who it was. The question instantly switched to something else. What was she to Lee? By the way they were snuggled up, it was clear they were more than comfortable with one another. So much so they didn't even notice her presence as she stood only a few feet from them both.

"Lee...Lee...Baby. I made it what's going on? How's Charlie?" Rita asked. She reached her hand out towards Lee, as if to pull him away from his past love. Now realizing how close he and Simone were holding each other he slowly created some space between them and took Rita's hand. This was beyond awkward, already being difficult with the news that the doctor had dispersed.

"He didn't make it," Lee said in disbelief. "He didn't make it," he said a second time as Rita then wrapped her arms around him and lovingly caressed his neck. He stood there now holding on to her, feeling more uncomfortable each passing minute. The time was ten-thirty when Rita explained her turbulent taxi ride and how they were stuck in traffic, and got lost since the driver wasn't familiar with the town, or the hospital.

The whole while Simone was still standing next to the two of them. She was standing off to the side kind of hugging herself as if she had the shivers. The remainder of the Hart family gathered just around the corner of the hall, occasionally one of them would peek around to see what was happening. Suddenly, the situation became stranger as Lee started to cry again, realizing his uncle, who was also his friend was really gone.

Rita began rubbing on his hand as he cried out his pain. As his head slumped south Simone approached, putting her arm around him and standing on his opposite side. This was no time to be bidding for Lee's attention, but she attempted to hold his arm next to her. All three stood silent, in respect, until he calmed back down considerably and regained control over his emotions.

"Oh my goodness," Rita broke the silence, while glancing at her watch.

"What is it?" Lee asked.

"It's eleven, I almost forgot. I've got to get back to the airport, oh my goodness." Rita was now panicked stricken, wide eyed looking at her phone and checking for messages.

"You mean, you're still leaving?" Lee was shocked, not to mention offended by her statement. You could hear the disappointment coming from his soul.

"What do you mean? You know I have to be in London. You know that." Rita tried her best to logically explain.

"My uncle just *died* and you're telling me you're leaving? You've gotta go tonight? You can't postpone the flight? Reschedule? Anything?" Lee was now upset with the fact that his Uncle was gone, as well as her momentary departure.

"What do you want me to do Lee? What? Just tell Mr. Sander I'm not going?"

"Yes!" he screamed, startling himself.

Simone squeezed him tighter, rubbing his back with her left hand. He didn't pull away. In fact he didn't even notice he began to hold her close with his right arm and emphatically gesturing to Rita only with his lone free hand.

"Lee don't be impossible. I broke my neck to get here...to see you. For support."

"Some support, you show up here for five minutes then tell me you gotta go. Because of *some job*? I thought I knew you better than that."

"What's that supposed to mean?"

"You're putting the company before me."

He was visibly disgruntled as he still was hugged up next to Simone who stood perfectly still and silent looking at Rita. Rita noticing their stance became more upset with each passing second. Rita noticed Lee presently holding his past, causing her to contemplate their future.

"So you're telling me you can't call, or see if you can get a different flight? Or leave in a week or two? I don't see the big deal." His head was shaking in disbelief as to what he was hearing. He didn't want to hear anymore.

"It's not that simple Lee," Rita said as she reached for his hand.

He was too busy, holding it to his chin, looking at her with a scathing expression. "It's never that simple is it Rita?"

"Look the cab driver is outside waiting for me. I don't have a choice, my hands are tied." Rita was speaking sheepishly, now ashamed of herself.

"Then go then. I'll get through this," Lee said, playing his famous confident role.

"I'll help you through," Simone interjected, looking up at Lee.

"Get your filthy hands off my man," Rita pointed towards Simone with her emotions on a rapid decline.

"He's not *your* man. If he wanted me off of him, he would tell me himself," Simone reminded her.

Lee said nothing.

He again realized his embrace with Simone.

"This is not how this night was supposed to go," Rita said then sighed heavily in exasperation.

"Sorry my uncle ruined your night," Lee said. He was fuming. His voice emphatic. Outraged.

"I didn't mean it like that," Rita explained.

"You don't even know what I had planned," Lee hollered.

"What?" Rita asked.

Lee shook his head while recalling how excited he was earlier, ready to propose to her. He was thankful he hadn't. He never fathomed he'd be standing in a hospital hallway arguing with her, while holding onto Simone and mourning his uncle's death.

"Listen, I'll call you as soon as I can," Rita offered while looking shifting her weight around and fidgeting. She ran her hands through her hair then clutched them behind her neck.

Lee shook his head, saying nothing.

Silence was the only sound heard. Rita leaned forward, gently kissed his cheek then backed away. "I love you," she whispered softly.

Lee continued his vow of silence as he watched her turn the corner out of view and head out into the night and back into the smelly yellow cab with the rude driver.

"Where to now?" the cab driver asked.

"Metro airport," Rita said, barely getting those words out as she broke down and cried. Her last memories of Lee were of him in a saddened state, holding the beautiful woman he once loved. Rita kept pondering over the image of Lee never letting Simone go, and all the things Liz revealed to her a few weeks earlier. Rita blamed herself. Part of this was her fault. She never even had a chance to explain to Lee that she had taken the job in London.

This job had already done catastrophic damage by making her late for dinner earlier that night. If she had at least been on time, they would've been together when he heard the tragic news about Uncle Charlie. Upset with herself she continued to weep as the yellow cab drove through the dark of night to the airport.

Lee had been less than honest before she thought, trying to reassure herself. Maybe he would understand? Surely he'd forgive her error, and her leaving that night. Maybe?

At the hospital, the Hart's assisted Lee with the arrangements for Charlie, and filling out paperwork. Mr. and Mrs. Hart took charge, easing his pain and discomfort. He'd never had to handle business like this before. Simone never left his side. She stayed right next to him through it all. After all the final arrangements were made at the hospital it was late into the night.

Mr. Hart extended the invitation to Lee so that he wouldn't be alone.

"Lee come on over, you're family son. You shouldn't be alone tonight. Liz and Ray are staying over too. You can stay as long as you need to, there's plenty of room."

"That's alright, I'm okay," Lee said. His tough guy act wouldn't fly.

"Lee please... for me then," Mrs. Hart pleaded. She always had a way with him, as she rubbed his arm.

"Alright. Let me grab some things from home and I'll be over," Lee agreed, realizing it would be best not to be alone during this emotional time.

"I talked to your Mom. She'll be here tomorrow afternoon. She's doing as well as can be expected," Mrs. Hart said as she was smiling at Lee. The exact same way she always had.

"Okay," Lee said, happy to hear that bit of news. It was the first positive bit of news he'd heard all day.

As the group entered the parking lot Mr. and Mrs. Hart, along with Shawn got in Mr. Hart's mud stained white F150 extended cab pick up truck. It was parked next to Ray's Grand Prix which the rest of the group entered.

"See you in a minute," Liz reminded him as he walked away into the night in search of his SUV. He had altogether forgotten where he parked.

Inside the car Ray spoke up. "Is he gonna be alright?"

He looked at Liz and then to Simone, who was in the back seat.

Without a second thought, Simone opened her door, pulling one leg out as she looked up at Liz. "I'm going with him."

Liz smiled, and looked over at Ray.

Simone walked quickly over towards Lee and called out. "Lee wait... I'm riding with you."

Lee said nothing verbally in response, but his actions spoke up clearly as he calmly walked to the passenger door of his Durango and opened up the door, helping her inside his vehicle.

Chapter 28

As Lee made the short commute across town from the hospital the ride was completely silent, with neither he or Simone saying a word. It was as if they were afraid to speak, and thought about speaking only because they were scared. He honestly couldn't believe the night he had just endured.

The pain swelling inside was overwhelming. His plan to propose to Rita was nixed. Even the chance of spending time with her before she left for London was ruined. In his mind she would return in two months, but after her abrupt exit he feared even that might not be true.

Liz had no reason to lie about the announcement that was made at work. He would find out when he returned to the job if that was true or not. Somehow at the hospital Rita seemed to be holding something back behind those exquisite mocha eyes of hers. Reality began to set in. His uncle was dead, his life ending so sudden. Now, in some sick twist of events he was driving with Simone, her first day back in town.

She was the girl he grew up adoring and the one he originally planned to spend his life with.. *What were the odds?* Even with those quirky happenstances he was still carrying on him the engagement ring, which bumped against his chest as he made turns en route to his house, driving over the pothole infested path.

Simone was sitting quietly, half gazing out her window, starting to speak then stopping again. The moonlight seeped through the sunroof, giving her a glowing appearance that made her breathtaking. He was now feeling slightly agitated for holding her so tight while they were at the hospital. He assured himself that he didn't realize that it was her and that his emotions temporarily blurred his eyes along with his judgment.

He'd managed to avoid having any real conversations with Simone for over a year. Sure, they would talk, text, or email each other every other month or so, but nothing serious at all. Ever since Rita came along, he'd cut off all communication with Simone. He really never even thought about her until he took the job at Jackson & Fitz and started working with Liz. She was the one who pumped the idea of getting back with Simone into his head daily.

Lee broke the silence. He sighed quietly and released a frustrated laugh as they pulled into his driveway, where he'd go inside and get an overnight bag, so he could spend the night at the Hart's.

"What is it?" Simone asked while folding her hands in her lap.

Lee cut the engine, leaving the battery power on for the radio to play and inched closer to her lowering his voice. "I just can't believe you're here with me. Especially after all we've been through, that's all."

"I'm always going to support you, no matter what. Besides, I know how close you were to your uncle. I'm so sorry." Simone was still shook up by the loss herself.

"I know we've been so off and on, about a year ago I kind of shut you out of my life. I felt bad but I was ashamed for all my back and forth. I didn't want to hurt you anymore. You or Shawn."

"So we couldn't work it out after all we had together? But you could settle down with that chick I saw at the hospital? The one that left for London and didn't even tell you?"

"She's coming back," Lee said rolling his eyes in defiance.

"Liz said they announced it at your job. Your girl played you. I would never do that. Just look at me and tell me you have a future with her. That's what you think?"

"I did," Lee said.

"You *did*? Listen to yourself."

"I mean, I do."

"Really?"

"Yea."

"Then why are we sitting in your car, holding each others hands?"

Lee looked down, only to be surprised once again, not realizing his undeniable physical connection to her.

It seemed to happen so naturally for the two. They fit like the last puzzle piece. He saw their intertwined hands, but didn't let go.

The conversation continued.

"I used to cry my heart out every night thinking about you and how we fell apart," Simone explained while looking down at their hands.

"I'm sorry. It's just that the situation just ate away at me over time. I needed that time to just be out there. Next thing I know I met Rita and things looked up."

"Does she make you smile like I used to?"

Lee looked at her. Something in his eyes gave away the answer. No.

Simone continued. "Why can't we just leave the past behind? We have a chance to start over now. We can write our own happy ending."

She looked up slowly, smiling some, and trying to stay positive. Her smile was like an ever addicting drug, that he couldn't get enough of no matter how hard he tried.

"I gotta be real," Lee said, "In my dreams we've gotten back together so many times. But I was scared to let it be real. Scared of the commitment, the responsibility."

"It can be real baby, I'm right here. Let me be the rainbow after the storm." She slid closer to him, caressing his stressed out face.

The word baby she used was one he'd gotten used to only hearing from Rita's lips. But it sounded good to hear Simone call him that, just like so many other times.

"I wanted to tell you so bad how I felt inside. But every time I hesitated," Lee said. He started to contemplate his next move.

"If you let me. I'll be there for you. Before you can call me I'll come running. Why do you think I moved back home?"

"To be with your family," he answered.

"I've been in Atlanta since college. I came back home to be with you. I want us to be a family."

The words of his Uncle Charlie from a few weeks ago when they had a heart to heart talk came to mind.

"Family-That's what's important."

Those were the words Uncle Charlie told him. His uncle urged him to settle down in his old house and start his family there and ditch all the love games.

"What am I supposed to do? You think I should just throw away nine months with Rita?"

"I don't care about Rita. I care about you. I'm right here. I haven't left your side all night and I never will. You have to decide if you want me next to you."

An undersized tear began to run down her alluring face.

"Hey don't cry," he said, while wiping her tears away.

"I can't help it Lee. It's like you're right here, but you're still so far away. Ever since I was ten years old I wanted to be yours. You're the only man I've ever loved. I never stopped. What happened?"

Silence once again reared its ugly head bringing everything to a stand still. She was slowly crying while the two sat hand in hand, struggling to fight off the past. He now had watery eyes as he reached into his pocket, locating the box that housed the engagement ring. His entire relationship with Rita flashed before his eyes, as if it was dying from a swift execution.

He thought about their good times, as well as the bad. He remembered how he had been so insecure and doubting of her on numerous occasions. Through it all she was empathetic, forgiving of his faults and deceptions. Even when Rita found out that he lied to her she still gave him another chance for redemption.

He slowly let go of the jewelry box in his pocket. He lifted Simone's head up and looked her in the eyes for the first time in years.

"I never stopped loving you either. Never," he said, whispering the last word, for emphasis as the two fell in each others arms.

Even Lee didn't know what that statement meant for their status. Right now, at this particular moment he had two very special ladies in his life to choose from. They were different in countless ways, but also enormously similar.

Both women were striking in appearance, but had different attributes. Both had hearts of gold. Looking at either one of them for extended periods of time and you would see femininity personified. He knew he would quickly have to decide what to do. Which one could he love permanently? His long time love, or his recent flame?

There would be no way to carry on a serious relationship with both at once, even if Rita was halfway around the world, and Simone living in his back yard. Literally. His childhood home which he would occupy soon backed up to the Hart's home where she would stay until getting acclimated again in town.

Rita was understanding from the second they met. He had to be the same. But was it even possible if she secretly accepted the position in London? He wasn't sure he could be that understanding of her. Maybe that wasn't fair. Maybe it was?

There, in his vehicle sat Simone, the girl of his young dreams in every way and his first true love. She longed to be with him in the worst way but there was the tumultuous past that went along with her commitment. He knew he'd have to iron out all the pain from the former days.

There were so many times he seemed to lead her emotions on. All his wavering exploits aside and she still waited for him patiently to return. He would tell her he was finally ready to settle down and a few months down the road when talk of marriage surfaced he'd crush her again. Simone was truly understanding as well, overlooking all his mistakes, and for so many years at that.

He now sat amidst a misunderstanding of monstrous proportions that involved two extremely delicate hearts that were exhausted by his lack of decision making. This was a complicated game of risk for Lee as he planned on juggling both women, briefly, before deciding on which one to give his all to. He knew he'd have to decide quickly if he was not to be caught playing this dangerous game.

Somewhere over the Atlantic Ocean on her way to the land of fog and warm pints of beer, Rita was looking intently out her window with her head rested on a tear soaked pillow, wondering where Lee was now and what he was doing.

He sat in his SUV with Simone, they were still holding on to one another and to memories of a once lost love. He was now beside himself, holding onto Simone, falling back in love with her by the seconds.

The precious moment was interrupted by a cell phone ringing from inside Simone's purse. They gradually let go of one another so she could take the call. "Hello," Simone said.

"Where are you two?" Liz asked. She called to see what was taking so long.

Hours had disappeared and the two were still at Lee's duplex, sitting in the driveway.

"We're at Lee's. He's finishing up getting his things. We'll be home in a minute or two."

"Everything okay?" Liz asked.

She answered her sister with a smile, "Yea, everything's fine." She sighed in relief and began to tell Liz the exciting highlights from her conversation with Lee.

Chapter 29

It was fast approaching noon when Lee finally awoke from his sleep. As he yawned and looked around, he almost forgot where he was. The Hart's home was both familiar and new all at the same time. He hadn't spent time there in years.

There was a spacious family room in the basement along with a finished bath. Also downstairs was a guest bedroom and Mr. Hart's office. Shawn would now be occupying the guest bedroom since he and his mother Simone would be staying there until they found a place of their own.

Lee was stationed on the pull out couch in the family room, when he awoke to find a stack of neatly folded towels and wash cloth laid next to him. Attached was a note that read; *"If you need me. I'll be there for you. Love, Simone."* Lee appreciated the way she stayed close by, and realized how nice it was to have her support.

Simone was always supportive throughout the years. This time was no different. Lee sauntered over towards the bathroom with his duffel bag stuffed with a change of clothes in tow. He walked past the stairs that lead to the home's main level. As he passed by he could hear a multitude of voices that were now beginning to gather at the Hart residence. Everyone was anticipating the arrival of his mother and aunt who would be arriving that afternoon from their flight.

No matter how hard he tried, Lee couldn't grasp the concept that his uncle was gone. He kept feeling like any minute he'd be receiving a phone call from Charlie telling him about some new hookup he'd found in the city. What he wouldn't give to hear his uncle's loud annoying laugh just one more time.

Lee finished showering, got dressed, and headed upstairs into the busy kitchen. There was an over showering of love and support.

Various members of the community and family friends consoled him. The wounds of death were still fresh yet Lee hid his pain like dark cloud mass, masking the suns resilient glow. He was determined to be strong. He had to.

That afternoon Simone continued being a pillar of support he could lean on. She fixed him plate after plate of food and did whatever else was needed to make him comfortable. Mrs. Hart showered Lee with hugs and kisses constantly, so pleased that he accepted the invitation to spend the night.

"You can stay as long as you need to," she assured him.

Mr. Hart was in the backyard lighting the old faithful charcoal grill he was famous for. Shawn was in the yard as well with his baseball and glove. He was busy tossing the ball high into the air, pretending to signal for a fair catch, and then making the catch. He repeated the motion several times, perfecting his catch while looking into the glare from the golden yellow sun.

Lee's childhood home could be seen clearly in the distance of the deep lot. He recollected all the days gone by as a boy, doing the same thing as Shawn, practicing in the backyard for hours. He would dream of one day playing before thousands of adoring fans at a professional stadium. Lee must have been watching so hard he could've burned a hole through the window.

Ray approached him with a suggestion. "Go on out there man. The kid won't bite. I heard you used to play ball."

Lee laughed feeling embarrassed. One part ashamed. One part guilty for abandoning Shawn the past few years. It was wrong the way he bounced in and out the young child's life.

"I haven't played ball in so long. Really, not since the minor's."

"Oh come on. You know you've still got the skills in you. It's just like riding a bike."

"Yea...but I don't have a glove."

"Dad's got a whole bunch of old gloves in the garage. Come on man, go ahead out there. It might take your mind off things." Ray patted him on the shoulder and nodded, looking out towards Shawn.

Finally out of any real excuses Lee walked out to the garage, digging out a nicely broken in glove from a dusty crate in a corner.

Lee stepped out into the back yard and asked, "Can I play?"

He was nervous.

Shawn answered back enthusiastically, "Yes." He was thrilled and excited. It was obvious, he had missed Lee.

The two commence to tossing the ball back and forth, each time with more velocity until the ball began to whiz across the yard. Each catch was being made with the sound of a crisp popping noise as the round white ball with red stitching entered the worn leather of the baseball glove. Ray was correct; it was like riding a bike all over again. It felt better than that, it felt peaceful.

Mr. Hart was satisfied now with the burning of the coals as they turned gray and went inside to collect the meat that had been marinating.

"Where have you been?" Shawn broke the silence. He innocently posed the question towards Lee.

"What do you mean?" Lee tried to play dumb. It wasn't working.

"I haven't seen you since I was eight, I'm ten now. I missed you." Shawn explained his position the best way any child could. Honestly.

"Well, your Mom and I...um, listen." Lee's delivery was sloppy and hard to follow. He was all over the place, and none of what he expressed made sense. It didn't feel right discussing this right now.

Mr. Hart came back and sensed the tension in the summer air, noticing the ball had ceased from flight. Lee's conscience ate away at his heart like someone forced him to swallow a gallon of battery acid. Mr. Hart intervened and called for Shawn to go inside.

"But I wanna finish playing catch," Shawn said.

"You can come back out. Your Grandma needs you inside for a second or two."

"Alright," Shawn agreed.

Mr. Hart approached Lee trying to appear nonchalant. "Lee, let me talk to Shawn okay? About everything."

Lee knew what that meant, and agreed it might be easier having Grandpa explain Lee's errors. It certainly would trump Lee's stumbling and bumbling effort.

"I'm a bum," Lee said catching Mr. Hart's ear. He was kicking at the grass beneath his tennis shoes.

"We'll talk later son. Everything will be okay. It'll be alright." Mr. Hart assured him and nudged his elbow into Lee's side.

That afternoon before his Mom arrived in town Lee decided that he would never drink and drive again. After experiencing all this pain caused by a drunk driver, he couldn't violate that personal pact with a clean conscience. That statement he made to himself was not a threat. It was a promise, and one he would keep.

His mom and aunt arrived in town late that afternoon with himself, Mrs. Hart and Simone there to greet them at the airport. After a long series of hugs and kisses, the sad entourage journeyed through a sea of cars in the parking lot to begin voyage back home. It was a deafeningly quiet ride home that offered few words, but occasional soft whimpering as one in the group cried silently.

Lee sat in the backseat, next to his mother. It was a blessing to have her around, though the circumstances were atrocious. His mother informed him that they would have to meet with Charlie's estate attorney on Monday to review his business affairs. Neither of the two were in the mood to tackle that task, but Simone and Mrs. Hart agreed to join them for moral support. That offer was readily accepted, as well as appreciated.

Simone had a week off prior to starting her new job as an Account Manager for Rockstone Industries, a regional manufacturing plant. When the group arrived at the Hart home they were once again smothered by longtime friends and completely showered with support.

Laid out before them was a smorgasbord of foods, ready for the sampling. Ribs, chicken, macaroni and cheese, and collard greens. The list was endless as every bit of soul food imaginable covered counters and tables. The night passed unhurried as people told great stories of Charlie, doing their best to stay positive and cheer each other up. They pursued that goal in the best way they knew how. Through laughter.

Lee spent a great deal of time that night playing video games in the family room with Shawn. Simone stayed close by, watching the two together again. She hoped this time it would last. Late in the night Lee's phone began buzzing, alerting him to a new text message which read; *"So sorry. I've been busy since I arrived. Call you tomorrow. Get some rest."*

Simone couldn't help but notice Lee reading the message, with a slight frown. She leaned over him while he sat on the floor.

"Who was that?" she asked.

They both very well knew the answer to her simple question. To her surprise and pleasure he simply tossed the cell phone a few feet, where it landed near his overnight bag.

He looked up at her and smiled. "Nobody important," he said. With that moment quickly departed he patted the floor next to him, inviting her to sit down.

Chapter 30

Lee decided to spend not only Friday, but also Saturday and Sunday night at the Hart's. He was really feeling comfortable there just like the old days. He was surrounded by all the people who he loved and those that loved him. The support was what he needed to get through the tough transition of losing a loved one in death. He began to realize just what his uncle meant when he told him the value of family, because for the first time in a long while, he had one to call his own.

Over the weekend Lee spoke briefly with Rita, but jet lag took its toll reducing the length of the conversation drastically. When they did speak Lee told everyone he needed to take a walk alone, but he could be seen halfway down the block talking on his cell phone.

People knew who he was talking to, including Simone. She told herself that maybe he was breaking things off, and realized that sometimes that took time. She was willing to wait, but not too long. Lee was obviously interested in being once again romantically involved with her. That fact was observable to all.

His actions were noticed by Mr. Hart as well. He was in no way interested in seeing his youngest daughter or grandson hurt again. He wasn't impressed with Lee's decision making skills. He planned on talking to him man-to-man, just as soon as the sting from Charlie's death wore off.

Monday morning was the time Lee and his mother would meet with the lawyer. As they entered the law office of Richard Bloomsfield. Lee felt nervous to the point of it upsetting his stomach. Noticing his discomfort Simone grabbed his hand as they entered the building. The two mothers exchanged excited nudges back and forth while pretending not to notice the display of affection by their adult children.

The receptionist ushered Lee in the office, along with his mother and Simone. She was still hand in hand with Lee as they entered the private office. Once settled in, Mr. Bloomsfield shuffled through some preliminary paperwork..

"I'm sorry Mr. Johnson," Mr. Bloomsfield said.

"Yes," Lee said.

"The information we're about to discuss is of a sensitive financial nature. Our records indicate that you are a single male. Due to the confidentiality of what we are going to discuss, you may want to ask your lady friend to step out of the office…just until we're finished here." Mr. Bloomsfield spoke with his eyes pointing towards the door, looking at Simone.

By the embarrassing silence and appearance of everyone's faces he continued to explain the scenario. "We will be discussing specifics about assets and properties Charles allotted to both of you," he explained. This time he was looking at Lee and his mother. "I'm sorry if I spoke out of context, if you wish to have your fiancé present, that's fine."

He said the word fiancé as if it were a question that needed to be answered. "Let me remind you, this is personal business of highly sensitive nature. It is intended for your ears only, or that of a spouse. If this young lady fits that description I apologize sincerely. But I will have to excuse you while I discuss your mother's benefits, etcetera."

Lee stood up. "Just call us when you're ready for us."

Emphasis was placed on the tiny word, us. Us?

Mrs. Johnson smiled shyly as her son exited the room, still hand in hand with Simone Hart.

"You all are done already?" Mrs. Hart seemed stunned since they were in the office for mere minutes.

"No, he's going to talk to Mom first, then us," Lee answered.

There was that word again. Us.

His explanation puzzled Mrs. Hart but she shrugged it off saying nothing, proceeding to read her magazine. Lee and Simone walked down the hallway to speak privately.

Once out of earshot Simone spoke first. "What are you doing? I'm not your fiancé, or your wife. You don't have to do this. I'll understand."

She folded her arms slowly awaiting his response.

"I want you to be there," he said rubbing her arms.

"Why? You heard the lawyer, we're not engaged or married. That's private information."

"You don't know what I have planned." Lee spoke to her smoothly, his hands now holding onto her waist. As they stood face to face Lee smiled. He watched her face take on a matchstick glow.

Why did he say that? He had nothing planned. He was caught up in trying to be debonair, which he was successful in doing. The bad news was he was now playing Russian roulette with her heart. There could be no doubt she would be thinking of a grandiose ending to his charming advances. She was prepared to take the front row in his life. Any proposal he made, she would accept.

It had only been two days since she reappeared in his life, like a comet, causing him to choose between the two women that played a vicious game of tug of war in the blood pumping vessel in his chest. At that point, Simone had the advantage.

For starters, she wasn't in London. Secondly, she was Simone. Third, she had always been sunshine for his cold soul, warming him up on cloudless days. She held a special place in his heart that was undeniable. Simone was stealing away his affections with the cunning of a bandit. She looked back at him with eyes full of wonder, having no fear that he'd ever massacre her dreams of happiness.

The two stood quietly together, until the receptionist resurfaced.

"Lee?" Simone said in an undertone.

"Yea, what is it baby?" he said, leaning still closer.

"I love you," she mouthed.

He could've melted right there into a puddle on the floor, but instead he dug deep staying calm. He possessed the rare ability to play it cool as the other side of a pillow.

He kissed her tenderly on the forehead. "I love you too."

Was it reflex? Did he mean it? What was he saying? Just three days prior he sent two dozen red roses to Rita, planning to propose to her, until this outlandish twist of events unfolded. Leaving him there with Simone verbally telling her I love you and speaking with a lawyer regarding deep financial business. One word, careless. The word described perfectly his irrational thinking. Simple carelessness.

The lawyer was now under the impression that Simone was his fiancé and his mother and Mrs. Hart no doubt would draw similar conclusions. What other conclusion was there to draw? The biggest question around was, what was Lee thinking? Better yet, did he ever think at all?

They entered the office ready to hear the news. "Have a seat you two," the lawyer said with outstretched arms.

"Thank you," Lee replied.

"As you know, I handled all of your uncle's personal affairs and business interests." Mr. Bloomsfield sat up straight adjusting papers and lowering his eye glasses.

"Yes," Lee said, waiting to hear more.

Mr. Bloomsfield explained to Lee and Simone what Uncle Charlie had done for Lee. They both sat back in their chairs in disbelief.

"It's obvious your uncle cared about you greatly. Please...whatever you do, get yourselves a good professional financial advisor to help you with managing this. I've seen too many times people come into wealth and blow it by poor decision making. Your Uncle has your future set up for you, if you handle this correctly. I'd be happy to assist you with anything you need. It would be my pleasure. I'm sorry for your loss. Your uncle was a great man. I viewed him as a friend. You know, I'm sorry...I didn't get your fiancé's name earlier." He reached his hand across the large oak desk.

They shook hands as she answered. "Simone."

"Beautiful name, beautiful lady..." Mr. Bloomsfield stood up and smiled as if to say he had no more to tell. "You take care of this lady Mr. Johnson. Nice to meet you both. Please, be in touch."

"Yes, thank you again," Lee said as they turned to exit.

"Remember, I served your uncle for twenty years. I'd be more than happy to assist you," Mr. Bloomsfield reminded him.

As Lee walked out of the office his entire financial landscape was totally different from when he walked in. Uncle Charlie had left him as a beneficiary on his life insurance policy totaling $750,000. That was more savings than some people accrue in a lifetime. In addition to that he assumed sole ownership of Charlie's Lounge, which was a turnkey operation. As long as he kept a competent staff the popular nightclub that Charlie expressed was doing really well would continue to generate income. He also owned the warehouse Charlie purchased that was located in the city.

There was more. When Charlie purchased Lee's mother's home he made provision that upon his death, Lee would take over the mortgage. He would still be able to live in the home. Even with all this overwhelming news, he realized something even more important. Simone was still there, clutching his arm as they left the law office together. He looked over at her, knowing for certain that she always had loved him, even when he had nothing.

Chapter 31

Over the span of a week, Lee's life took numerous changes. Uncle Charlie's funeral was Thursday and Lee began to move into the house he grew up with his mother on that Saturday. Keith was struggling to cope with the loss of his running buddy. He along with the Hart's helped Lee achieve his cross-town move.

His mother left early Saturday morning to catch their flight back home to Cancun. Lee decided it would be best to take another week leave of absence from work in order to have time off to become settled in his new environment. He also planned on taking Mr. Bloomsfield's advice and consulting with a financial advisor when he received his new found acquisitions over the next few weeks. It was going to be very precarious living behind the Hart's, especially with Simone and Shawn living there for the unforeseeable future.

Lee was still casually exchanging "I love you" back and forth like a seesaw with Simone, at random no less, even in the presence of Liz and others that happened to be around. Falling back in love with Simone was second nature, like breathing out and breathing in.

Those actions were absurd, considering how he was still in the habit of sneaking to speak with Rita on his cell phone. Those conversations were going decent, but the intensity nonexistent.

No mention was made by her regarding the acceptance of the new position in London. That frustrated Lee. Just as Liz stated, a company wide email was sent out that confirmed Rita's acceptance of the job in London. He told himself that he'd wait for her to bring it up, and discuss it then. The problem was his personality was totally unsuited for sustaining that level of patience. Each day would pass and he'd grow more irritated by her high level of deception. It would take intestinal fortitude on his part not to lose control once she revealed the truth.

On a beautiful sunny June day with the perfect temperature for a move Ray and Keith lugged in the heavier pieces of furniture, Mr. Hart pulled Lee to the side for a quick chat. He could wait no longer.

"Hey Lee, after we get you settled in, I want to talk. Man to man." Mr. Hart's demeanor was changed and instantaneously he was dead serious as his large powerful hand gripped Lee's shoulder.

"What's wrong?" Lee asked.

"Nothing's wrong...I hope."

"What do you mean?"

"Listen. Here's the deal. My daughter's not some toy. I love you like a son, but that's my baby girl you're playing with. You hurt her again, and I'll....Look. Just don't be playing no games."

"I'm not," Lee said. He fibbed.

"You sure about that? Hey, look at me son, you sure?" Mr. Hart shook Lee a little, not violently, just enough to get his full attention.

Lee deeply respected Mr. Hart and finally answered honestly. "I just gotta end this old thing I've got going."

"Man, that should've been handled before you started telling Simone you love her. *Are you crazy?*"

"I don't know what I am," Lee said, falling back against the van.

"You better figure it out quick Lee. I'm not playing with you. Last night Simone, Liz, and Mom were sitting around the table talking about wedding plans...you hear me...wedding plans." Mr. Hart did the perfect loud whisper, while surveying the area like a spy in enemy territory.

"I know, I know, but my ex, my girl, whatever she is...in London."

"Hey. I don't want to get in your business. But you made it my business when you told my daughter you loved her, parading her around that lawyer's office and all that like something's about to happen."

"Yea, you're right. I'm sorry. I let this get out of hand."

"It isn't just about Simone either. Think about Shawn. He worships you. The boy asked me what he should call you. Dad? Lee? What? How am I supposed to answer that question...huh?"

Lee didn't respond, only sulked as Mr. Hart poked him in the chest.

"It's time to grow up. Step up to the plate. If you want to be a husband and a father, then do it. If not, then keep hanging with that friend of yours. This can be your little bachelor pad for all I care. Just don't bring your garbage into my family."

"Yea I know."

"You know huh? I can't tell. Can you step up Lee? Can you be a real man? You know, when your father died I was crushed. For myself, but more for you and your Mom. He was my best friend, we grew up together, right here in town. I'd do anything for him, and in turn for you. Remember how I took you in back in the day? I raised you like one of my own. I hope I had a positive impact on your life. But I can't sit back and let you walk all over my baby. I can't watch this and not say something."

Mr. Hart frowned at Lee, then calmly walked around the side of the van, and began unloading boxes like nothing was even said.

Five seconds later Keith came bouncing around the side of the moving van drinking a Heineken and offering one to Lee.

"No thanks," Lee said.

"What's wrong? You're looking like you just caught a beat down."

"Naw I'm cool."

"Just checking Playa."

"Hey Keith...don't call me that alright?"

"I'm sorry but that's what you are. *International* playa! I'm talking about broads in different area codes. Two girls. Both of them are fine too! I swear I'd cut off a pinky toe for either one of them. Rita still wants you, now you got Simone back in town. They'll never know. Plus Simone's inside talking about decorating in there. She's gonna hook the place up." Keith was pointing towards the house.

"I have got to cut one of these girls loose man."

"You crazy!" Keith playfully slapped Lee across the face.

"I'm for real," Lee said folding his hands behind his neck.

"You're crazy. If you drop Rita you'll see me in London like...Bonjour," Keith said, holding out his hand to high five.

"What are you saying, that's *French*."

"Whatever. I'm just saying," Keith said, unfazed by his miscue.

"You don't make sense," Lee said.

"No. You don't make sense. Both of these girls are fine. I'd keep them both...flat out." Keith began laughing and dancing around as usual, his antics were completely ridiculous.

"You'd just better get down to the college on Monday. For real."

"Oh, you know I am. I'll be there," Keith said.

"Cool. I'm counting on you man. Uncle C is too."

"I appreciate it. I just can't believe I'm going back to school. My mom almost passed out when I told her. I still have like thirty credits from back in the day before I dropped out like a dummy."

"Just take care of business, and one day you'll be the manager."

"I'm gonna do this, besides I can't stay with Grandma forever."

Lee had arrangements made for Keith to be hired as assistant manager at the lounge, only if he agreed to go back to school for restaurant management at the local community college. They both agreed that was more than fair.

This would be Keith's first real job in years but would also allow for him to be at the place he loved the most. Charlie's Lounge. Upon completion of his degree and earning valuable on the job experience he could one day assume the role as manager. The position would be Keith's to lose. Lee strongly desired to keep the Lounge in the family and Keith was the closest thing he had to a brother.

Lee just hoped he hadn't made a huge mistake as Keith walked away heading to the front door of the large white two story colonial house with black shutters, that sat on a quiet street in one of the town's nicer neighborhoods. Lee eyed the handsome home.

He could now see Simone through the large front window, she was directing people and telling them where to set various items. The look on her face was one of excitement, and with good reason.

She accompanied Lee upon his return to that attorney's office to pick up the keys to the home. Mr. Bloomsfield even handed them directly to her, as Lee watched. She was so thrilled and he loved to watch that smile of hers. It lit up his heart, the same way it had for so many years.

He prayed he wouldn't cause her pain...

Chapter 32

After everything was finally moved inside the home, one and all crashed in the family room. That was an addition Lee's mother put on the home back when he was in middle school. From that room you could walk out onto a deck and into the backyard, which flowed into the Hart's yard. There was a fence between the properties, but years ago Mr. Hart made a doorway in the fence so you could walk through to the other yard, instead of hopping over the fence or walking around the block.

Lee looked at his watch, realizing the time. He had to hurry and get the moving truck back before he would be charged for another day's rental. That would be a waste of money since the move was already completed.

"I gotta get this truck back before eight. I'll be right back." Lee jumped up immediately and walked to the kitchen to retrieve the keys. Liz and Simone both walked into the kitchen after him, emptying everyone's plates in the trash.

"I'll go with you," Liz spoke up, "I gotta run by the store anyway real quick on the way back." She had already decided earlier that day in her mind that she absolutely needed to speak with him privately.

"Can I go too?" Shawn came running in the kitchen. "I want some ice cream."

Liz spoke up again. "No baby, you stay here with Uncle Ray. He wanted to play catch with you. I'll bring some back. What kind do you want?"

"Bubble gum."

"Okay."

Shawn was satisfied with that arrangement and ran off to fetch his baseball glove and ball. Keith and Mrs. Hart were having fun playing cards in the family room and watching a movie on television. Mr. Hart came in the room next and cleverly made eye contact with Liz, then asked Simone for some help measuring windows upstairs. Simone agreed and gave Lee a quick peck on the cheek before heading upstairs to assist her father.

"You ready Liz?" Lee asked, now standing at the front door, with one foot on the steps and one inside.

"Here I come," she said.

As they walked out to the van the cool breeze blew through Lee's tee shirt cooling him off. Little did he suspect that his night was about to heat up.

"Lee we gotta talk."

"What's up?"

"About Simone, Shawn, everything."

"Everything's all good."

"No, it's not all good. I know why you've been afraid to take the next step with Simone all these years."

He wasn't afraid. It was something else...something hard to describe. Lee was quiet as sweat ducts began functioning allowing perspiration to instantly appear across his brow.

"Lee listen, you gotta trust in her. She would never hurt you."

"I know," he said, never taking his eyes off the road.

"Then what's wrong?" Liz asked.

"It's just that sometimes I can't get it out of my mind."

"It wasn't her fault."

"I know."

"Do you really? Or do you think she'd make all this up? Do you think she'd lie to everybody?"

"No."

"I was down there when it happened. I was visiting her at graduation time. We went out to that party together. Simone wanted to go out to eat with her roommate and chill. I was the one who dragged her to that frat party. *Me!* How do you think that makes me feel?" Liz began bawling, and trying to communicate.

"It's all my fault! It's all my fault you never got together," she said between cries.

Lee felt sick to his stomach as he drove down the road. His speed was decreasing, and the lump in his throat was growing. It was now the size of Texas, and it was choking him, making it harder to swallow. How many knots can fit into one mans stomach he wondered? He wasn't sure, but he knew he had to be close to setting a new world record.

The truck rental business was across town near his old duplex, giving them ample time to talk. His SUV was still parked there, and he'd planned to pick it up there and drive it back home.

"I never knew that," Lee said.

"You think I wanted to tell people I screwed my sister's life up? I'm just so glad she forgave me, after all that went down. She never blamed me."

"I still gotta clear things up with Rita."

"*Who?* The woman who used you? Are you crazy? She took that job in London and never looked back. She didn't even consult with you. Together what, nine months? And she didn't even see how you felt before moving halfway around the world? You've got Simone right here and you still want to play."

"No. I'm just saying..."

"Saying what?" she asked.

"I'll handle it, trust me," he assured her.

"Forget her, I'm not talking about what's her face."

"Rita," he reminded her.

"Whatever her name is, I don't care."

"You alright?" he asked as he noticed her pain.

Liz was slowing down on her crying, but still distressed, still holding on to the crumpled up tissue in her hand. "No, I'm not alright. You can't do this to Shawn either. You're the only father he knows."

"Yea, but he's not even my real kid."

"He doesn't know that. All he knows is that you come and go every six months to a year, he's hurt." Liz began her crying again.

"Ya'll never told him?" Lee asked.

"No. Why would we? He's been calling you daddy since the day he was born. You were even at the hospital for the delivery. It's weird; he's just like you in so many ways too..."

"Yea," Lee whispered out, his mind overrunning with memories.

"There's something else I've gotta tell you too."

"What is it?"

"You know the guy who put that date rape drug in her drink?"

"Yea, I know," he mumbled while closing his eyes as if it would block out the horrible thought.

His hands gripped the steering wheel.

"He died in prison a couple months back."

"*What?* Are you serious?"

"Serious. He was convicted for all his attacks. He attacked something like six or seven girls on campuses down there. Maybe even more."

"Yea I heard about that, but..."

"Yea, he got jumped by some inmates that found out what he had done to all those college girls. By the time the guards got to them, it was over. Some people think the prison guards let it happen."

"That's wild. I can't even think right now Liz, this is crazy."

"She's been through so much Lee...so much. It wasn't her fault. I should've kept a closer eye on her, instead of out on the floor dancing. You know Simone never went out drinking or clubbing like that. She didn't even know what was going on. Me and a couple of her friends found her in the room upstairs. We saw the dude go out the window. We barely even saw what he looked like, until they caught him. It took Simone years to overcome the emotional scars caused by that. It's still a struggle sometimes but she feels comfortable with you."

"I never even wanted to see that guy. I know I would've killed him on the spot for putting his hands on my girl."

Lee began to cry now too as he wheeled the moving truck onto the shoulder of the road. He was unable to steady the vehicle. Cars whizzed by as the two sat recounting the horrible sequence of events, reliving the heartbreaking ordeal.

Lee started up again, "I remember when ya'll called me that night. I had been home about a month after being kicked off the team. I just got in my car and drove. My life was falling apart. I was still worried she'd leave me since I wasn't going pro."

"She would never leave you, she loved you for you. Not because you were going to be a professional athlete."

"It's just when we found out she was pregnant, I was so mad...so helpless and confused."

"I know, we all were. It was devastating to everybody. Imagine how Simone felt."

"I just don't know why she stayed down there so long, she could've moved back here," Lee said.

"Come on Lee. One minute you wanted to be with her, the next you didn't. She stayed down there for Shawn, so you wouldn't be bouncing in and out his life so much."

"Yea, but I still did. I went down there so much, he's probably all confused. I wouldn't be surprised if the kid hates me."

"No...he adores you. We always told him that his Dad had a real important job to do and was real busy. But we told him you loved him."

"I do love Shawn, he's a great kid. But that lie is gonna get old quick. He's not buying that sorry story."

"It doesn't have to be a lie anymore if you get back together. You'd be a family again."

"Again?"

"Simone never forgot how you showed up for Shawn's delivery. That had to be the hardest thing you've ever done. Your support meant the world to her, to all of us."

"It was hard... real hard," Lee said repeatedly, slamming his fist into his hand.

"Simone feels like she let you down somehow."

"She didn't, how could she?"

"How is she supposed to know that?"

"I don't know....I just need to make this right."

"Look. She doesn't want you to marry her out of pity. She doesn't want people to feel sorry for her, or to even bring up what happened. She would only marry you, because you want to."

"I do want to, but I gotta handle something first."

"It's not a rush, but please...don't play with her heart."

"I'm not."

"She's never been with another man Lee. I'm serious. Believe me, I would know, she tells me everything. The past few years have been rough with you not around though."

"I just had to find myself, just kind of pull it together."

"It seems like you got a little sidetracked," she said.

"I did, but I think I'm ready now."

"I know ya'll have talked a million times on this, but I just wanted to let you know the role I played in it. I'm sorry too."

"It's okay Liz."

"No it's not...Simone was big enough and understanding enough to forgive me. This is the least I could do for her, trying to get ya'll back together after all these years. I wanted you to know the details she never told you."

"I understand."

"She's ready to move towards the future, and for once it looks like things might work out."

"I want the same thing too. Just give me a little more time. It's gonna be alright."

"I'm so happy for you two."

"Thank you. For real Liz. Thank you."

Liz sniffled. "We better get this truck back before they close."

Lee started the moving truck back up, and pulled onto the road. After dropping the truck off, they got in his SUV headed back home, after a quick stop for Shawn's ice cream. Lee realized as he drove, that he had one more task to complete before that night was through. He still had a long distance phone call he needed to make.

Chapter 33

Around midnight everyone went home, except Keith who decided to crash at Lee's house. Hugs were exchanged as all the Hart's including Simone walked across the yard and through the fence. Lee watched them from the deck the whole time until the lights came on inside their home. The stars were out in all their splendor that night, and flashed before a full moon. The air was damp as Lee breathed in deeply, working up the gumption needed to make his dreaded phone call.

He turned around and entered into the living room where Keith was sprawled out across the carpet, flipping channels aimlessly on the large screen television. He had finally finished hooking up the surround sound.

"Keith, you good?" Lee asked, seeing if his friend needed anything.

"Yea man, thanks for letting me crash," he responded. Keith held up a beer bottle, his own way of letting Lee know he was content.

"Thanks for helping me move, especially the heavy stuff."

"No problem, you know I got your back."

"Thanks again," Lee said, while patting Keith on the arm in a gesture of gratitude.

"Hey Lee?"

"What's up."

"That Ray dude is alright."

"Yea he's cool."

"He said he used to play in a band back in the day ...drums. I told him get something together, and we'll let him play at Charlie's."

"Oh for sure."

The two talked leisurely for a few more minutes until Lee could stall no more. Keith walked into the kitchen, looking in cabinets for some aspirin.

"My back is killing me. You got some Motrin? Vicatin? Some

Hennessey?" Keith asked holding his lower lumbar.

"You crazy, look up in the cabinets over the fridge. I don't know where she put everything," Lee laughed.

"Hey, ya'll gonna hook up for real or what? Simone's acting like she's moving in here Playa."

"I told you, I'm not a player."

Keith and Uncle Charlie both used that word, playa, so much it had become a virtual chant.

"That's what I always call you. Besides, how you not a player with two girls?"

"I'm about to handle that right now," Lee explained while walking through the kitchen and into the spacious empty living room. He didn't have any furniture in there just yet, since he put his leather couch and love seat in the family room.

"Where are you going?" Keith asked.

"I gotta call Rita."

"Now?"

"It's what, twelve-thirty here?"

"Yea. So, it's five-thirty in the morning there. I hate to do this on Sunday morning, so early...but this can't wait."

Keith came bounding into the living room, jumping around like a baby kangaroo.

"Let me listen in," Keith pleaded.

"Come on...this is serious. I'll be upstairs. It might be late when I'm done. If you're sleep, I'll holla at you in the morning," Lee told him.

"So it's Simone then?"

"Always has been."

Lee reached out, clapping hands with Keith and bringing it in to a quick hug. As he began the slow trek upstairs Keith yelled up behind him. "Do your thing baby!"

Lee shouted back. "You know how I do."

Lee was great at putting on a show, especially the role of confident ladies man, when in actuality he loathed the thought of confrontation. Right now inside he was as nervous as a prisoner on death row, hoping for a last minute presidential pardon. He dialed the number, and as the phone began to ring, he paced back and forth.

"Hello." It was a familiar voice, speaking in a groggy tone.

"Rita it's me."

"Lee? What's wrong?"

"I just had a lot on my mind."

He couldn't believe he was ending this, after the way he felt only a little over a week ago, when he was ready to propose. But that was before she lied to him and accepted the Vice President position.

"What is it? It's five-thirty in the morning. What's going on?"

"Like I said. I had a lot on my mind."

Rita sensed instantly that something was wrong. Something was horribly wrong. She was wide awake, sitting up in hotel bed, bracing for what would inevitably come next. The strong smell of bad news had arisen out of her one whiff of suspicion.

"Rita look, I gotta be honest with you." Lee was being subtle. "I gotta say what's on my mind."

"Lee you're stalling."

"I'm just gonna come right out with it then. This isn't gonna work out. You. Me. Us. None of it."

Rita threw the sheets back, hurling herself out of bed, hurrying towards the window and pulling back the shades. The grey clouds seemed to be in a hurry as the new day dawned over the famously foggy city. "What?" she asked.

"It's too complicated. This is crazy," Lee said.

"I've been gone a week," she said in both question and statement form. She couldn't believe what she was hearing, especially after overlooking all his faults. She began to slowly fall to pieces, fighting back tears filled with disbelief.

"Yea but I don't even know if you're coming back."

There was an elongated pause. "You still there?" he asked.

"You told me you'd never leave," she whimpered out.

"I'm sorry. Right now I don't see how this can work out."

"Okay listen, okay…"

"I'm listening," he said.

Rita pulled her heavy robe around her, tightening the belt vigorously while pacing. "I confess, okay, I confess," Rita said, blinking rapidly.

"Confess what?" He already knew.

"I took the VP position. I thought I'd be able to convince you to come with me. I was planning to tell you that night at Chateau Le Blanc but that fell through."

"Guess what?" Lee was a chameleon that transformed back into his cold blooded attitude.

"What baby?" she asked.

"You can drop all that baby stuff. *I knew.* You lied to me. You tried to play me." Lee was still stomping around upstairs in his sweat pants and wife beater tee shirt.

"No I did not. I wanted you here," Rita said speaking softly with weeping eyes.

"You never even asked me, you tried to play me like a puppet."

"You've got a lot of nerve talking about lying Mister."

The thought of him accusing someone of dishonesty was absurd.

"What about your lies. Mr. No Serious Relationship. Lying about your DUI. Why you got out of baseball. Your drinking. Etcetera..."

"I'm not perfect, but this is different," he said.

"How?" she asked.

"It just is!"

"Why are you yelling at me?"

"Why do you care?"

Lee was rattled and wanting to just get off the phone as quickly as he could. He still couldn't believe she would lie to him about moving across the globe. He had to find out through a work email. How pitiful.

"I've invested nine months in this. In us, and now you call me up at five in the morning dumping me?"

"Look. I'm never moving over there. End of story,...end of us."

"Why can't you give it a chance?"

"I just moved into my old house, I finally have a decent job...I'm happy here, this is home."

All of their unrealistic expectations were coming to an abrupt end, right before their eyes. Rita was on the verge of breaking apart.

"I thought you loved me?" she cried out in misery.

He was the first man that actually seemed to love her for her, and not for what they could receive from her.

He answered her question, "I did."

"Did?" she asked appalled, stroking her messy morning hair. "I've been sitting here trying to figure out where we went wrong," she continued while dabbing at her leaky eyes.

There was a time not long ago when Lee would worship the ground she walked over. But that time had passed like a forgotten memory, and was hastened along by the arrival of Simone back into his divided heart.

"I think this all has to do with that girl...the one at the hospital."

"Please," he denied.

"I saw how you were holding her, even when I was there. Who knows what's been going on since I left town. You never even let her go while I was standing there. I could've thrown a fit about that."

"You're probably feeling guilty for leaving."

"Why should I? It's obvious now, your uncle was right. You're nothing but a *player*."

"Don't even let his name come out your mouth. You didn't have the decency to support me. Look, all the lies I told, all the drama I put you through...we shouldn't have lasted this long."

"But I forgave you, can't you forgive me? I understood your reasons, can't you understand mine." Rita was trying to strike a nerve, looking for some way to cling on to love.

"Even if I could, you're there. I'm here," Lee said.

"I could come back, I could resign," she stated with optimism.

"Like you'd do that for me." He laughed.

"You can't see what's in my heart. You're just a coward. I was real from the day we met. You never fully believed in us."

"I didn't move," he said calmly.

"That's not fair, you know that."

"Life's not fair...don't they teach you that at UCLA?"

"This is going nowhere," she said in exasperation. The conversation turned in circles, both parties only pointing fingers.

"That's what I've been trying to tell you. We're going nowhere."

"Fine then. So it's goodbye, just like that?"

Next came the classic break up line.

"I'll always care about you, just live your life and I'll live mine."

"Lee wait...What if I gave it all up?"

"What if I was President of the United States? We both know its not gonna happen...is it?"

Her silence answered his inquiry as she contemplated her answer, no longer sure of anything anymore.

"Take care of yourself girl. It was good while it lasted. You taught me a lot about love. You made me believe in it again."

"It's her isn't it? It's Simone. That's her name right? You never stopped loving her did you? That's why you couldn't give your heart to me."

He refused to answer.

"Goodbye Ms. Clark," Lee whispered.

"Tell me the truth Lee. I deserve that much. Is it her?" she pleaded.

"Like I said... if you were here maybe it'd be different. But you're not, you're in London and you're staying. News flash, I'm not moving to London, so enjoy your fancy life as Vice President or whatever."

The mental fatigue and frustration of nine months filled with doubt resurfaced. Too many lies had been spoken, and too many half-truths told.

"You always did amaze me," Rita said. She had regained her composure, just like always. The way she made that statement it wasn't meant to be a compliment.

"I'll never forget you," Lee whispered as he hung up.

The abrupt ending left Rita in a state of shock. It woke her up like a kick in the teeth, despite the time of 6:00 a.m. Rita stood at her window facing the thick fog, now crying desperately and wondering how it could end so fast and wondering if it was really her fault. Any trace of happiness dissolved from her eyes.

Chapter 34

Sunday morning came quickly. The sun shined consistently and brightly through the bedroom window splashing against Lee's face. As he gazed out the window he saw Shawn out in the Hart's yard, playing already.

"Keith!" he shouted downstairs, "You up?" Lee's yelling startled Keith causing him to jump up off the couch.

"I am now," he shouted back woozily.

"It's over man," Lee said lowering his voice as he entered the first floor, rounding the corner towards the kitchen.

"You're serious then huh?" Keith said, rubbing his head from back to front, standing there in nothing but boxer shorts and a single sock.

"Put some clothes on," Lee said while getting some water. As Keith dressed, Lee explained the details, the how's and why's of his conversation with Ms. Rita Clark. They were soon interrupted by a knock at the back sliding glass door.

Shawn stood there with his baseball glove in his hand. Lee opened the door telling him to come in.

"You just now getting up?" Shawn asked sounding disappointed.

"Yea, but I'll be around in a second. I just gotta shower up first. You wanna play catch or something after?"

"Yea, that's why I came over," Shawn said.

"Alright, gimmee about a half hour okay?"

"Okay," the little guy agreed.

Lee walked outside and out into the morning fresh air with Shawn. The ground was still wet with dew. Lee looked behind him and shut the door slowly then took a seat on the deck next to Shawn, putting his arm around him. The smell of summertime spent outdoors was in full bloom.

"Shawn listen, I want to apologize to you."

"For what?"

"I know I've been gone a lot, especially the past few years."

"Mom said it's your job. She said you're really busy."

"Well yea," Lee said. He bent the truth just a little. Okay, technically, he lied. He was hoping to make the conversation brief and move right to the point. "Anyway Shawn, I want you to know that I love you and that I'm your Dad. I'm always gonna be here from now on. No more disappearing out of me."

"Really?" Shawn was overly excited as he hugged Lee tight as any ten year old could.

"Yea really, there's going to be some changes soon too. I wanted you to know that. I apologize for not being there so much."

"It's okay," Shawn said.

"No, it's not okay. I plan on making it up to you, okay son?"

"Okay... Dad." Shawn hesitated saying Dad, but it was obvious he was excited about the news.

Shawn always referred to Lee as dad but was confused over the past few years since Lee had been absent in his life. He was the only father Shawn had ever known, and everyone told him that Lee was his Dad. Perhaps not biologically, but he was in every other way. He was there at Shawn's birth, the first few years of his life, and in and out of it over the past few. True to Mr. Hart's suggestion, Lee would have to step up to the plate. Shawn went skipping back across the yard, in ecstatic fashion as Lee went back inside the house.

Keith noticed that Lee had said something of a serious nature to Shawn.

"What was all that about?" Keith asked, referencing the discussion outside.

"Just trying to right my wrongs," Lee said.

"What you mean?"

"I'm about to tell you something that I never said to you before, something I'm not proud of. That's my son, and it's time I take responsibility for that."

Keith was floored and in total disarray. "What! I thought that she-"

"It wasn't even like that. I just wasn't trying to put our business out there."

Keith was always under the impression that Simone cheated on Lee, and that's why he never could settle down with her. Only Lee, his Mom, and the Hart's knew the real truth about the painstaking situation that occurred. It was no one else's business, not even Keith's. Uncle Charlie never knew either. He always thought the same way as Keith did.

"So we been friends all these years, and you never told me you were his Dad? I know he used to call you Daddy and stuff, but I thought you were just being nice to little man." Keith seemed offended and frustrated with the fact that Lee had hid this from him. Lee knew he would get over it in time.

"That's my bad," Lee said as he patted his chest.

"You've been paying child support? Is that why you never have any money?" Keith asked.

Lee just laughed as Keith returned to his jovial self. Nothing ever seemed to bother Keith. Life was always one big party that never stopped for him. Lee never told him about the large insurance policy that Uncle Charlie left in his name. Lee was now far from broke. With the $750,000 policy, plus the house, ownership of the Lounge, and the warehouse downtown he was worth well over a million dollars in personal assets and net worth.

"All I know is, I want to be with my kid, and with Simone."

"Do your thing ...*family man.*" Keith swayed around looking at Lee giving a sign of approval as only he could, with so much flair.

After a shower and changing the two crossed the yard and went over to the Hart's. As they walked over they could already get a whiff of the BBQ grill that was kicking out mouth watering smells of well seasoned meat that Mr. Hart was famous for. Mr. Hart began showing the two of them the tricks of the trade when it came to working a grill, as they stared at the mouth watering spread of jerk chicken and pork that sizzled below.

Ray came walking around the garage and into the backyard coming over and joining the other three men.

"What up big Ray," Keith shouted out as Ray joined the group.

Lee thanked them collectively once again for the help with the previous day's move.

"No big deal. That's what family is for," Ray said.

Lee realized just how much he'd become part of the family unit again and how sudden it all took place. His thought was interrupted when Mr. Hart spoke up.

"Hey Lee, help me get some lawn chairs out the garage." He passed the tongs used for flipping meat to Ray.

"Don't burn that," Mr. Hart said playfully, as he walked to the garage door.

It was another perfect June day, and everyone was in high spirits for the first time since Uncle Charlie died. Lee followed behind Mr. Hart and assisted with the retrieval of lawn chairs from the overhead storage.

"Shawn told me what you said to him this morning." Mr. Hart closed the door to the garage, so no one could hear them talking.

"Yea. I took care of my past business last night. Now I'm thinking about my future. I know that I want to ask Simone to marry me. Soon."

"Are you asking me, or you telling me?" Mr. Hart smiled.

"Asking," Lee smiled nervously back.

"Listen Lee, this isn't some fly by night decision I hope. Being a father is a life long commitment, and so is being a husband. It takes work...you'll see."

"I just want to make sure it's fine with you first."

"If you're serious...I'm good with it. All I want is for my daughter to be happy, and for Shawn to have a good role model. If you can do that, you have my blessing."

"I can do that."

"You sure?" Mr. Hart asked.

"Yes sir."

"All of that off and on stuff ends here. I can't tell you how many times you broke her heart."

Lee was genuinely remorseful that he had put her through so much pain. She was always so kind, and willing to take him back each time he had a change of heart.

"That's not going to happen again...ever. Before Uncle Charlie died we talked and he told me it was time to settle down. He was right."

"Just make sure you understand what love is." Mr. Hart next extended his big right hand and they shook as Lee looked him squarely in the eyes, knowing this was crucially serious. As they opened the garage door to head back to the yard, Mr. Hart turned and looked at him. "Take your time okay? I can keep a secret. I would tell you welcome to the family, but you've always been family." They both got a kick out of that as they carried the folding lawn chairs into the backyard.

Everyone was now outside, taking in the beautiful day that was given. Lee gazed at Simone. She was standing there looking so breathtaking, as the wind blew through her shoulder length hair and she smiled back at him. Right then and there he knew he made the right decision in his heart. No more doubt lived in his once troubled mind.

Chapter 35

Monday arrived and Simone started her new job, while Lee took the week off from work to settle in the new house. He cleaned up, unpacked boxes, the usual tasks associated with the inescapable pain of moving. Simone proudly selected the paint colors for each room and Lee was more than welcoming in terms of complying with her requests.

Two days of unpacking brought Lee to Wednesday, hump day, the halfway point of the week. For him, it was painting day, nothing more. He began early in the morning and was making progress covering the living room walls a soft sage green color that Simone was crazy about. His cell phone began to ring, breaching his concentration. It was probably Simone just calling briefly to say hello. So far her job was wonderful, as she enjoyed dealing with clients from around the country.

"Hey LJ," Simone said. She was the only one that still called him by that childhood nickname.

"Hey Simone, what's up baby?"

"Oh, I was just calling to check on my man. You working hard?"

"Yea. I'm in the living room right now. This green is gonna look alright."

"Oh good, I can't wait to see it."

"Hey, don't forget we're supposed to go out tonight and look for some furniture to go in here."

"I can't wait. I think I already know what might look good."

"Like I said, I'm gonna let you handle this. You have good taste."

"I chose you didn't I?" she teased bringing down her sugary voice.

"I thought I chose you," he asked back lightheartedly.

"We chose each other then," she agreed.

They both laughed, joyful to finally be together again.

Simone asked, "What's Shawn doing?"

"He's with Mom, they went to the movies a little while ago."

"What they go see?" Simone asked.

"I don't know."

"Oh."

"Hey baby somebody's beeping in on the phone. I'll call you back alright."

"Alright."

"Love you."

"Love you too."

Lee had plans to ask Simone to marry him on Friday night, but he was still deciding how he wanted to propose. He wanted to do something memorable and romantic, something legends were made of. But all he came up with were ordinary unoriginal ideas.

As he clicked over to accept the call, he couldn't believe what he heard. "Hi Lee, can we talk?" Rita was on the phone trying to clear the dense gloomy air. Lee found it strangely fascinating that through this whole ordeal, she would still call him.

"What are you doing?" he asked.

"Trying to make this work," she answered.

"I already told you, it's over."

"Why? Because of her?" she posed.

"Don't worry about it," he said.

"I don't deserve this. Not after all we've been through. I'm sorry I wasn't at Charlie's funeral. I'm sorry I took this job, I'm sorry. Can't you see that?"

She was nearly in tears again. What once would've touched his heart now infuriated him. He had been running for years with no finish line in view, and now he was closing in on happiness with Simone.

"Kill all that noise Rita," he insisted.

"You don't need to speak with me like I'm some street bum."

He wasn't trying to be insulting. Lee just wanted her to go away, disappear, and let things between them become finality.

Rita was born into a family that could give her anything she wished, and she wasn't accustomed to begging for anything. Especially for a man. But for some unfounded reason Mr. Lee Johnson had burned a permanent stain in her heart that wasn't going away easily.

He once again explained his position. "I feel bad that I hurt you, but I've moved on."

"In *two weeks*? Give me a break. We were together nine months and you couldn't fully commit."

"That oughta tell you something," Lee reasoned.

He had a point.

"Let me ask you, do you get some kind of sick pleasure out of watching me suffer like this?" she sniffled.

"I'm not trying to do anything. I just feel like we're on two different wavelengths. Just do you," he said as he exhaled.

"What? Is this about my money, my job title?"

"It aint about none of that. For real, what do you want? You moved...not me."

"Can't you forgive me?" she asked.

"Seriously Rita, I gotta go. What's the use in talking?"

"So I have no chance?"

"I'm sorry," he answered her.

Rita began to cry as the evening slowly hung over London, turning it a dark shade of blue. Lee wasn't interested in reconciliation, their time together ran its course in his eyes. He was a lot of things, but melodramatic wasn't one of them. He was for the most part hot or cold, off or on, all in or all out. In his made up mind, Rita was out and Simone was in. End of discussion. Besides, he had given his word to Shawn, Mr. Hart, and most importantly of all, Simone. In just two days he planned to add what he'd already given her verbally by way of an engagement ring, to be shortly followed by a new last name.

"Rita I'm so sorry. I hope things work out for you over there, I really do. But it's over, it just is....right or wrong, it's over."

He could hear her cries over the phone as he pulled the phone away from his ear not wanting to perceive the sound of her sorrow. The clammy smell of wet paint filled the room as she spoke again.

"I gave my all to you Lee."

"I did too, it just didn't work out. Look, I gotta go. I'm sorry."

"I am too," Rita said while sluggishly hanging up the phone.

Lee lethargically resumed his routine of painting again, his conscience bothered him like a resilient school bully. He felt horrible for blowing off Rita and dismissing any notion she had of compromise. The woman he once viewed as worldly perfection had now become nothing more than a painful thorn dug into his tender flesh. No more than five minutes passed by as the phone began ringing again. Now what?

This time it was Simone, calling him back. Her woman's intuition had been working overtime as she asked him a question.

"I was wondering. Who was that who called you?"

Lee's heart began pounding like Sasquatch feet. His mind hurried in pursuit of words to say. No time for lying, the truth spilled out of his mouth overflowing as if it were a backed up toilet.

"You're not gonna believe this, ha..." He laughed nervously knowing Simone would find no humor in his contact with Rita. "That was Rita, she's tripping..."

"She's tripping, or are you?" Simone was annoyed, and with fair reason. Her words were sharp and cut deep like Ginsu knives.

"What do you mean?" he asked her.

"Why are you still talking to her if we're supposed to be back together? You have me decorating the house and picking out furniture like something's in the works."

"Simone listen."

"No, you listen! I'm sick of your games Lee. You hang up on me to talk to her."

"Naw look-"

"No, you look LJ. You told me you handled that situation, but it sure doesn't look like it. I'm not going to let you hurt me, or Shawn again. Why don't you go furniture shopping by yourself tonight. I don't feel like going."

"Simone wait."

"I have waited. I waited ten years for you to grow up, and I really thought this time would be different."

"It is!"

"Well you got a funny way of showing it...and don't *ever* yell at me."

"Simone I can explain."

"Talk to me after you make up your mind. I have to go."

The phone slammed down. Lee's emotions were sent on a carnival ride, up and down, sideways and otherwise as he took a seat on the steps. For the first time, maybe ever, he knew what he wanted. He wanted Simone in the worst way, despite the last nine months spent with Rita. Rita had proved herself empathetic and understanding for nine months, Simone had done so for ten years. A complete decade of patience. That was simple math. His resolve was to call Rita and squash what he viewed as harassment once and for all.

After taking a few deep breaths his emotions became leveled. Instead of calling Rita, he opted for drastic measures. He called the cell phone provider and requested a change in phone number so he wouldn't be bothered again by her persistence. Somehow it seemed appropriate to do this, even though it was to some extent over the top. A simple phone call, and a few minutes later and it was over. No more unwanted phone calls.

All the back and forth bickering with Rita had turn out to be taxing, and now threatened the ecstasy blossoming with Simone. There was a time when he was the lone individual bargaining in the relationship, pleading with Rita to carry on. Those days were passed on like pages of a calendar The tables turned in his favor.

He resumed painting the living room and thought about waiting another week, if not two before proposing to Simone. He wanted to show her he was serious and had no tribulations as far as commitment was concerned. He was optimistic that he would be able to substantiate this to her, and dispel any doubts stationed in Simone's fragile psyche.

Rita was doing contemplation of her own, trying to scheme up a way to recuperate the man she fell in love with. If there would be any probability of getting him back she knew what she would have to assemble the courage to do. At her lowest point, she was almost willing to do anything, despite what her prestigious colleagues would assume of her judgment.

Chapter 36

The remaining days in the week flew by along with the weekend leaving everything blurred. Lee opted not to propose too soon and suddenly. It was Sunday night and Lee would be going to work for the first time in a two week period. Four days had passed since he changed his cell phone number and there had been no calls from Rita, which satisfied Simone's doubts and at the same time gave him peace of mind, knowing there would be no more quarrelling with her. It was now a clean break from the recent past and an open book lay ahead for a life with Simone Hart.

Monday morning arrived with Lee entering into the office around 7:50 a.m. ready to begin his normal routine. The lobby was saturated with employees in suits moving about, imitating good little worker bees, giving their all to be truly productive members of a chaotic society. Lee weaved through the thick crowd as perfume and aftershave permeated in the air.

A little over a month ago he stood in that very lobby of Jackson & Fitz completely hung over, arguing with Rita about why he never called that night after Frank Harrison touched her inappropriately. After their dispute and altercation the tyrant known as Frank took a week off work, and only a week later Uncle Charlie died so unexpectedly.

Weeks since that tragedy and Lee's pain was still fresh, though somewhat soothed by Simone's caring smile and actions that defined her personality. The elevator chimed, indicating all who took the vertical ride to the third floor that they had arrived. Lee exited the cramped elevator and out into the dusty tiled hall of the third floor.

He stepped out and grabbed firm hold of the cold steel handles of the mailroom door and swung it open, giving way to a pleasant surprise.

The mailroom staff, including Liz had arrived early with coffee and donuts giving Lee a hero's welcome on his first day back to work. Lee had won over the staff's approval a few months back because of his laid back demeanor and nice guy attitude.

An hour or so passed when Liz came over to him to see how he was doing. "Are you okay?" she asked.

"Everything's going alright," he said.

"How are things with you and Simone?"

"I've never been happier. Actually…no, let me be quiet."

"What is it, tell me," she asked sensing good news.

"I'm doing it this weekend. I'm going to propose."

"Ahhh!" Liz shrieked quietly in excitement.

"Don't tell anybody Liz. For real." Lee's face had a stern look.

"Okay, okay," she reluctantly agreed.

"For real," he said leaning in to her, one eyebrow raised.

"Alright. Well how are you going to do it?"

"I'm not sure yet, but, I'm not trying to be engaged long. I'm hoping we can just get married real soon, something small."

"I can't believe this. I'm so happy for you both," Liz said while hugging Lee.

"Thanks. I'm glad you never gave up on us getting together. You were right."

"I know," Liz said confidently. "So do you have the ring?" she asked.

Lee stopped and smiled, laughing shyly.

"I've had the ring. I've never told anybody this except Uncle Charlie. I've had that ring for ten years now. I bought it when I played in the minor leagues. I just can't believe after all this she's finally going to wear it."

"Are you serious?"

"Yea for real, I can't tell you how many times I wanted to give it to her and then backed out."

"Well don't back out this time, she loves you," she said.

"I'm not backing out of this for nothing. I know that for sure. Hey, my phone's ringing, we'll talk later."

"Let me be the first to say congratulations."

"Thanks," Lee said as he ran into his office to grab the phone before it went to voicemail.

"Hello," Lee said out of breath, breathing slightly heavy.

"Mr. Johnson?"

"Yes, this is he."

"Lee it's me."

"Rita? What the..."

"Hold on," she appealed.

"You stalking me now?"

"Calm down baby."

"I'm not your baby, we're through!" Lee's voice was escalating by the second, causing him to put the phone down and jog to his office door, closing it promptly. This verbal exchange required privacy.

Rita interceded, "I've been trying to reach you on your cell for days. What's going on?"

"Can't you see I'm trying to avoid you?" he explained bluntly.

"Why?"

"Because," he said. That word wasn't enough explanation for a toddler, let alone a woman like her.

"Lee, I know I haven't been perfect. I can't even sleep since we talked last."

"I can't keep doing this. You have to chill."

"Let me ask you a question."

"Look..."

"Please, you owe me that," she spoke humble and sweet nectar-like words. Her voice became seductive, and he remembered how she used to whisper gently, tickling his ear with her melodic breath tone.

"Do you remember when we first met? When we fell in love? Remember how we'd talk for hours on end? Those were special times I can't get out of my head no matter how hard I try." She explained desperately, sounding so engaging with a flowing misty voice.

Lee was dancing along the fine line of succumbing to her advances, from the way she pleaded. She told him how she needed him, as he struggled to remove himself from the phone.

"Honestly, I know we had a good thing."

"We still can," she rebutted.

This was now almost an obsessive challenge to her, and she abhorred losing, even in the game called love. She'd come so far with Lee, farther than any relationship she'd previously been in. Now, the bottom had fallen out beneath her, and it hurt like shoes a size to small. He was the first unfeigned love of her life.

"Lee somehow our bond loosened up along the way, things went wrong, I know. All of our arguments, our disagreements. Part of it was my fault, I admit that. I let the job get in the way of our time together...our love. I won't do that again." She sounded sincere. So much so that he began feeling sorrow.

"Hey, I wasn't perfect either you know," he conceded.

"I know, but I forgave you. Can't you forgive me?" A fair question.

"I just think our time ran its course."

"What if I was there? My condo hasn't sold. I could come back?"

He could tell she was serious, and it scared him. "Are you serious?" he asked, each word exiting his vocal cords bit by bit.

Why did he even open up that door of opportunity?

"Yes...I'm serious sweetheart." Rita was pouting. He could hear it through the phone. He envisioned what she looked like when she made those heartbreaking faces. She was so adorable, puppies were jealous. He never learned to resist when she tried her hardest to persuade him into something. She knew what he liked and pulled out all the stops as the conversations tone softened. Twenty minutes passed and his once hostile tone was replaced by a tamer and gentile speech pattern.

"Baby listen. I'm thinking about coming home. I don't care if they fire me, or let me go. I have to be with you." Lee was speechless.

He had recently made up in his mind that he would propose to Simone that weekend and now Rita threatened to crash the party by returning home from London. This was almost too much to handle for any man. He was falling to pieces.

"Rita, I'm glad we talked but..."

"But what baby?"

He didn't prevent her from referring to him in that way.

"I don't know. I'm just so confused," he said. Lee sighed and jostled uncomfortably in his chair.

Rita once again spoke delicately into the phone. "Let me end the confusion. Let me love you."

Lee sat back in his chair with one hand on his head, then he sat up with strong resolve. "No, I can't do this. I'm sorry."

"Just think about it, it would be like old times...remember?" She seductively giggled trying to encourage him to loosen up. His memory was operating; it was his mouth that now malfunctioned. He was silent, like art galleries, and sleeping babies.

"Yea I remember," Lee said.

"I knew you did," she whispered, "Just give us a chance Lee. The way we met, so a chance meeting...this is meant to be." Rita was convincing, a master of persuasion, and Lee was steadily weakening.

"I gotta go, for real," he said. He had to hang up.

"Can we talk again?"

"I don't think so."

"That's not a no," she prompted.

"Seriously, Rita please, I'm begging you. Don't keep calling."

"I'll never give up. *Never.* I know you want to be with me. It just seems like you're hiding something. I want to know what your secret is."

"I gotta go."

"I love you," Rita said again.

Lee remained mute, but didn't hang up until at least thirty seconds passed.

"I know," Lee said back, finally ending the conversation.

It was lunchtime, and he needed fresh air in the worst way. He'd so foolishly left the conversation open ended with Rita believing that a move home and a forfeiture of the Vice President position would draw them back together tight as a gorilla's fist. She was faced with major decision making, but first she had to run analysis on how genuine Lee was on his end of the bargain.

Chapter 37

Lee decided to head outside at lunch for fresh air. The Jackson & Fitz building had a large parking lot attached to the property that spilled over into one of the many city parks where people would go to enjoy lunch, and take in nature's splendor at the same time.

The soft easy summer breeze was refreshing as he walked through the crowded parking lot in route to the park. Once there he would buy a hot dog from one of the many vendors selling food in the area. His stroll was interrupted by someone he never wanted to see again.

Frank Harrison stood before him, determined not to let bygones be bygones. "Well if it isn't the mailman. Finally decided to come back to work huh?" Frank spouted out; acknowledging the fact Lee had been absent two weeks for personal reasons.

Lee attempted to side step him and avoid any contact.

"You don't walk away when I'm talking to you. I'm head of HR, don't ever forget that. Just be glad I tripped that night at the condo."

Lee couldn't help but break out into laughter. "Oh you tripped huh? So that's what happened? All this time I was thinking your face was trying to beat up my hands," he said sarcastically.

"Very funny...I see your lady Ms. Clark moved out just in time. I move in to my unit this weekend. If she was still there, there's no telling what would be going on behind your back while you're across town in your run down shack, or wherever it is you live."

"Just back off," Lee warned.

Frank was getting closer and closer, as his large head shook side to side looking down on Lee. His head was so massive that he resembled a St. Bernard. All that was missing was a waterfall of slobber and a barrel under his neck. "Hit me punk," Frank barked out, "You'll be fired on the spot. Come on, hit me now. You're not so tough now that we're at work."

Lee bit down on his lip knowing that as much as he'd like to, he had to exercise self control for once in his life and walk away. The loose stones and gravel beneath his shoes sifted around aimlessly as he contemplated.

Frank continued egging him on, "Ms. Clark's gone now. She can't save your sorry little job this time."

"I said back up. You keep talking and I'll beat you down again."

"What's wrong? Are you sensitive? Did she leave you without saying goodbye?" Frank asked, ignoring the warning.

"I don't need this," Lee said as he turned to evacuate the area.

Next he felt the huge mitt of Frank Harrison on his shoulder, turning him back around. "Hit me so I can fire you," Frank snarled.

"What's your problem man? You mad because Rita didn't want you?" Lee said, backing away.

"Oh, she wanted me. I saw it in her eyes that day when I grabbed her. She loved every minute of it, believe me. I know women..."

There was a brief pause as Lee balled his fists tightly, having now heard enough insults for one afternoon. Frank had manipulated just the right buttons to set him off. The surveillance cameras in the parking lot would catch everything on tape. It would look like an unprovoked attack by Lee on a superior. Security would be there within minutes to escort him off the premises. Acts of violence would not be tolerated in the workplace.

He was well within striking distance when he heard a familiar voice.

"Don't do it Lee, stay right there!" Mr. Flannigan crawled out from behind a parked van, flailing his spaghetti arms, his bifocals bouncing up and down on his stress worn face. "Frank! Back it up, and Lee calm down." Lee took the advice and retreated several paces, forcing himself to be calm.

"What do you want Flannigan?" Frank questioned the odd little man, who seemed to materialize out of nowhere.

"I heard everything. I was in my car eating lunch, when I overheard you start in on Mr. Johnson here. Listen, I don't know what went on between the two of you outside of work, but that stuff doesn't fly here. You should know that."

Mr. Flannigan's abundance of gestures were directed to Frank.

"He started it," Lee explained like a third grader on a playground.

"I know Lee, just relax," Mr. Flannigan acknowledged the obvious facts. "Frank. I'm afraid you leave me no choice but to present this behavior to the ethics committee. You know what that means?"

Frank laughed in disbelief, partially out of defiance. "You trying to fire me? I'm your superior you little pee on."

Ed Flannigan stood tall and spoke firmly. "You *were* my superior. For starters, I'm on the ethics committee, and for two, I helped write the handbook. I've been here longer than you and I know the procedure." Frank was for once silenced, though still half-smirking while glaring at Lee. "You can wipe that smirk off your face Frank. Your reign of terror here is through. I can't tell you how glad I am to say that."

"Through?" Frank was indignant.

"Yes, through. You harassed Ms. Clark, our former COO a month ago, and now I caught you intimidating an employee, threatening his job, and provoking a fight. And you didn't know yet, but the Executive Assistant, the blonde, she just placed a complaint last Friday regarding your unwanted sexual advances...that's now under review. So add it all up!" Frank's jaw hit the pavement with a resounding thud as he stood there in disbelief. Flannigan continued. "Lee get inside, we'll talk this afternoon. As for you Francis..."

"It's Frank!" he interjected.

"Your mother named you Francis, I'll call you Francis."

"Watch your mouth...," Frank warned.

"As I was saying, don't get irate it'll just make things worse for you. We can do this the easy way or the hard way...your call. If you leave now, we'll be in touch and upper management will contact you for an exit interview. Ironically, Mr. Johnson and his staff will mail your personal items. Understood? We have witnesses, complaints, and now reason to terminate. I know that for a fact." Mr. Flannigan's last statement ended the discussion. Lee began walking inside and as he passed Francis Frank Harrison, he simply smiled, knowing he wouldn't be there to cause trouble.

Frank stormed off in the direction of his car. He yelled back at them. "You'll be hearing from my lawyers!"

Mr. Flannigan was a skinny, nerdy looking older man, but right then and there he commanded the respect reminiscent of a four star army general. "You don't have a case!" he yelled back towards the fleeting Francis Harrison. He watched Frank's every move until he drove out of the parking lot. He then re-tucked his shirt and adjusted his belt like a sheriff in the old west, then headed inside to consult with Lee about what just transpired.

Later that day in Mr. Flannigan's cluttered office he conveyed to Lee that he'd been doing a stellar job as manager, and his position was rock solid with the company. "I'm proud of you son. You held it together out there," Mr. Flannigan said referencing the scene earlier that afternoon.

"Thank you," Lee responded quietly.

"I don't claim to know all the details between you, Ms. Clark, and Frank. I don't need to know either, but I overheard your conversation."

"We had a big misunderstanding, that's all," Lee said.

"Well...whatever the case may be, if you're with Ms. Clark, you're a fortunate man. There were a few whispers in the building that you all were dating but ...I didn't want to pry. Anyway, how's it going for her over in London? The distance has to be rough."

"I don't really know, we don't really speak much lately."

"Oh, the time difference, I see."

"It's not that," Lee said and lowered his eyes.

"I'm sorry you're telling me you all broke up. I'm sorry. Excuse me for being so brash."

"It's okay Mr. Flannigan, but yea, it's over between us."

"I see, well hang in there, she's not the only fish in the sea." Mr. Flannigan slapped the desk in optimism.

"Thanks again for everything Mr. Flannigan."

"No problem Lee. I was just glad I was there at the right time."

"Me too," Lee said while standing.

"Have a good night Lee, see you tomorrow."

Lee left out the building with tons on his mind, especially how he planned to propose to Simone on the ever nearing weekend.

Chapter 38

After completing the task of patiently wading through bumper to bumper traffic, Lee arrived home. He routinely entered his home and was greeted by a unfamiliar smell that smacked him across his face. The delightful aroma of a home cooked meal teased his sense of taste as he cautiously peeked around the corner of the still naked living room and into the kitchen.

"Hello?" he called out. No response. No signs of life. There was a roasted chicken with cornbread stuffing on the counter. Alongside the main dish sat a bowl of rice pilaf, and a fresh vegetable medley, along with the scent of baked bread, or rolls of some sort. He was used to meals consisting of pizza and beer, or burgers and beer, or anything and beer. He would add that nutritious combination to a night of watching ESPN and that was constituted as dinner.

"Surprise!" He turned to see Simone and Shawn both, all smiles hurrying over to him. They were hiding upstairs awaiting his arrival home.

"What's this all about?" he asked them, totally caught off guard. His arms were extended as embraces were exchanged.

"We wanted to surprise you. Liz called and said you had a really horrible day at work. I thought this might cheer you up," Simone said with her head on his wide shoulder.

"We got you didn't we?" Shawn added.

"Yea you did." Lee laughed, feeling good to be home and have those smiling faces there to welcome him. This was a blessed change from the solitude he had adapted to for so many years living alone. Hand in hand, they filed into the kitchen, when Lee realized Simone had no house key.

"How did you all get in here anyway?" he asked her.

Simone began the explanation, "I used the spare key you hid outside. Why? Are you mad I just came in?" He hadn't yet given her a key of her own, to come and go freely. Besides, Mr. Hart would rather see a marital arrangement in place, since he was tired of Lee's past game playing. The houses were backed up to one another, so spending time together was no obstacle.

"No I don't care, come on...," he said laughing almost uncomfortably.

Shawn scurried to the family room and shouted back, "Tell me when we're gonna eat." He than began promptly playing the video game system hooked up to the large screen television.

"Be honest, if you don't want us in here when you're not home...say something," Simone said. She seemed somewhat disheartened as her eyes slid into a changed mood.

"You know it's not like that. I've got nothing to hide. How can I keep you out of here? You decorated the place. Speaking of that. When are we getting some living room furniture?" he playfully joked.

She turned and walked back into the empty room, teasing as she looked over her left shoulder wiggling her hand, "I don't see a ring on my finger..."

Lee followed behind her saying, "Not yet."

"Oh, so you have plans LJ?"

"As a matter of fact I do. I have *big* plans."

She tried her best to hide her excitement. "When?"

"You'll see."

"Soon?"

"Soon."

"How soon?"

"*Soon.*"

"Oh, it's like that?" she laughed.

"Yea, come on. Let's eat, you got it smelling good up in here. Thank you for dinner," he said while gently grabbing her by the wrist and pretending to drag her into the kitchen, where the wonderful smells still lingered. Lee's next question would open the door to a world full of wonder and possibility.

"Where is everybody? Your parents aren't eating with us?" he asked glancing over to the Hart's home.

"I thought maybe tonight we would eat together, as a family," she said. Her last words echoed in his head like a canyon. *Family, family, family.* As he looked over into the family room at Shawn, then back towards Simone he felt something he hadn't in such a long time. Contentment, and satisfaction with his life. Work was going well, especially now since Frank Harrison was now removed from the equation.

Most importantly, the woman who loved him was in his home, along with a young boy who called him father. He continued thinking to himself quietly, this is what it's like to be a family.

Lee broke the silence. "I want this everyday. You, me, Shawn, all of it. Us."

"Are you serious?" she asked him, feeling pleased he felt that way. She was still in her work clothes, nice grey dress slacks that hugged her shape, and a cute V-neck top.

"Yes, I'm serious. I've been a fool all these years. I just wish I could make up for lost time."

"It's okay, look at the future," she ushered out her usual positivism.

"I'm going to give you the world or die trying," he told her, leaning in close.

"I don't need the world LJ, all I need is you."

"Well you have me."

"Forever?"

"Forever and more, I can't wait to make it official."

The love filled exchange was interrupted by Shawn's voice as his head came popping up, prairie dogging over the couch. "Can we eat now?"

"Yea, come on, let's all sit down," Lee said as they started pulling plates and cups from the well organized cabinets Simone had arranged so neatly. As the evening progressed Lee felt a level of comfort unparalleled to any he'd ever experienced. The frustrations of the day were washed away as if they were carried by waves floating easily in the sea of tranquility.

Chapter 39

Through the remainder of the week Lee spent more than the usual time with Simone and Shawn. He knew without any doubt that this was the way he wanted to live his life. The only quandary was Rita continued to call him at work, pestering him for attention. Each day she would leave a message on his phone, bound and determined to win the war for his heart. His mind was already made up.

That made this challenge more appealing for Rita. She wanted to win. He had a certain amount of skepticism about her claims of love and devotion. Rita was a hard nosed business woman who always had her way. It didn't matter if it was in the boardroom, classroom, or in this case, love.

A lengthy three weeks passed since her departure for London. The city itself wasn't all that she dreamed it would be and the demands of a Vice President were more than she anticipated. The salary proved outstanding but it never seemed to outweigh the new found pressure the position proposed. She decided that a chance at happiness with Lee was more important than her stress filled career, no matter how bizarre that appeared to her Jackson & Fitz colleagues.

She was determined to walk away from the job, the salary, and any parental expectations. Honestly, she would be leaving everything behind. She fondly recalled how simplistic life was when the two of them started down the path of love, and how much easier she could relax once in his arms. She figured, she would move back home, sell the condo, and move into Lee's new house with him.

Humility had won out over success, and love indeed was stronger than pride at that moment in time. Rita was positive she'd be able to find another job somewhere, with all her qualifications, even if it meant not earning six figures per year. She could be perfectly content just being in love with Lee, having that warmth and support that her life now lacked.

Despite his faults Lee was a charming man, who was loving, kind, and always treated her like a lady. She remembered how he'd open doors and pull out chairs, simple things most men in the twenty-first century scoffed at. He would always provide a listening ear, so intently paying attention when she went through drama or work related chaos. She wanted to return the favor to him, and planned to do so in a large scale way by being sensitive to his needs.

All he wanted was for her to stay in town. Every past decision she made was self-scrutinized, as she blamed herself for blowing the chance for her hearts contentment. Knowing she possessed one last shot to garnish his approval, she planned to do the unthinkable. Relinquish her job title to pursue a life by his side. Not in front of him. Not in back of him. But at his side. Never in her wildest dreams did she think in three weeks she could be reduced to a memory in his past, from being the love of his life.

It was Friday and Lee had successfully dodged all Rita's phone calls at work, also deleting her barrage of emails. His non response worried her and her last attempt to get his full attention. Armed with her final decision to return home and sacrifice her prosperous career to be with him, she began a conquest of obtaining a phone number so he could be alerted to her plans. She dialed the number for information service on her phone trying to locate a listed number for Lee Johnson Jr. Her disappointment was great in the fact he refused to return her calls all week long. She was sure this new information would change his mind, especially since their last conversation was mildly promising.

After the telephone operator proceeded with the formalities of inquiring what city and state Rita spoke clearly into her phone, "Mr. Lee Johnson Jr."

"We have a L. Johnson listed ma'am. Would you like that?" the operator asked her.

"Yes please. I'll try that number."

"I'll connect you," the nasal voiced operator stated with the enthusiasm of a postage stamp.

"Thank you," Rita nervously replied, startled to consider the real prospect of Lee having a home phone number. All the time she had known him all she knew of was his cell phone, and he kept that on his person at all times. He never had a home phone line to speak of. The anticipation of reaching Lee to enlighten him in regards to her final decision forced her heart to beat with the force of a marching band, while still speculating why he never told her about a home number. First she had to make sure this was indeed his number before drawing any conclusions.

Someone answered. "Hello." The voice was unrecognizable. It almost seemed feminine, but not quite. "Hello?" they said a second time.

Fully cotton mouthed and nervous she spoke words, "Yes, I'm looking for Lee Johnson." Her tone was puzzled and unsure as to if she had the right number after all. The operator did say L. Johnson, and there was no guarantee that the L stood for Lee.

"Can I tell him who's calling?" the high toned voice asked.

"Um, who is this?" Rita uncomfortably asked back, "I'm not sure if I have the right number."

"I'm not allowed to give out my name over the phone."

Rita was now completely perplexed by this peculiar verbal interchange. It indeed was the right L. Johnson, and inside his home on the phone was ten year old Shawn. As Shawn explained his inability to reveal his name to a complete stranger, Simone's ears instantly perked up. She was now a mother hen, seeking to protect her only child her attention was turned to the phone.

Rita continued her probe. "Okay, well is Lee there?"

"I'll go get him," Shawn agreed. He put the phone down on the leather couch in the family room and yelled out the back sliding door where Lee was outside cutting the grass, while listening to his MP3 player headphones.

"Dad! Dad!! Telephone!" Shawn screamed with all the force his little lungs could muster, trying to corral Lee's attention.

"Who is it?" Simone intervened, referencing the unknown caller on the line.

"I don't know, some lady who wants Dad," Shawn said, still rather loud, as he hovered over the couch.

"I'll take the call for him, and lower your voice Shawn. There's no need to talk that loud in the house."

His loud talking and yelling was the reason for Rita's look of shock and agony as she nearly dropped the phone.

Lee had a son? What?

Shawn walked outside into the backyard and under the golden sun. Rita's mind at that moment went completely blank, causing her nervous system to begin malfunctioning. Bitter tears streamed down her face as mascara began to smudge and run forming black marks on her high cheek bones. The phone quivered in her hand as her stomach now ached along with her head.

He had a son? He lied to her all this time?

Everything was blurring in her vision, but her ears opened wide as the Grand Canyon as she heard clearly the conversation between Shawn and Simone. Most of all she would never forget how a little boy she never knew existed, just called the man she loved so deeply,...Dad.

This was the atrocious type of shock she'd now endure, a total blindside in her faith. Her hopes, dreams, and world were crushed with a few simple words.

A voice she had heard only once before in a hospital hallway answered the phone pleasantly. "May I help you?"

Rita built up the strength, using all her energy to speak. She was beyond broken, she was shattered whole. "Yes," she spoke so soft and timid. Desperate.

"Can I help you?" Simone asked again.

"I called to speak with Lee!" Rita yelled, now enraged. She had let go of all inhibitions, her usual steady composure, nonexistent. Simone instantly knew who this was, and she wasn't backing down.

"You've got a lot of nerve calling *our* house."

"Our?"

"Did I stutter?"

"I can't believe this," Rita said as her high dropped down to the lowest of lows. Her crying was now openly heard. All of these months Lee hid a pitch-black secret from her. This man she once loved had secrets slowly revealed about his past. But this was more than a secret. This was deception of the highest degree. Treason to the fullest extent of the word.

She'd been conned, lied to, cheated on, and hoodwinked. Any hospital could admit her easily with a swift diagnosis. Her illness? A patient suffering, from a broken heart.

Simone stood in the family room looking out the window watching Lee cut the grass as Rita sobbed into the phone. Her devastation was openly exposed like nakedness.

"What do you want?" Simone continued berating her, pummeling her already fragile psyche with a bombardment of questions. Simone's tone resembled a drill sergeant, and her questioning was on par with military interrogation. "Don't you know it's over between you two? Why do you think he doesn't want to talk to you? Will you ever leave us alone?"

Rita fell to her knees, tearing her nylon stockings, her dress strap slid off her left shoulder, with her upper lip wet from the crying mix of tears and mucus. Her size eight heels were removed from her feet, being tossed east and west. "He has a son? With you?" She barely got her questions out as she curled into an upright ball, and activated a constant rocking against the bed.

"You heard our son call him Dad didn't you?"

Indeed she did, still in disbelief. "Why didn't he tell me?" Rita begged.

"Can't you see he played you...he played you."

"No!" Rita yelled, partly in defiance, but mostly to get Simone to stop talking. The damage had been done.

"You thought you were so smart. Ms. COO. Miss move to London. Well how does it feel? He's back with me now. We're a family again."

"Again?" Rita whispered. Then she went silent as she pulled at her hair, still reeling from the word Dad that replayed in her mind. She retraced the past ten months of her life, figuring out why she never picked up on his pack of lies. She never missed a detail. How did she miss this?

"Are you married? Please... at least tell me that," Rita asked between sobs.

"What do you think? Are you stupid? We have a son. I moved back home. You call our house, to a number that you obviously found somehow. And now you're on the phone talking to me. You're a smart girl. Figure it out." Simone decided to answer the question, by not answering the question, allowing Rita to draw her own conclusion. It felt evil to deceive, yet necessary so her love could survive.

Unable to communicate any further Rita simply wept into the phone, defeated, beaten, and mentally manhandled. Her once picturesque exterior now matched her inside feelings of horrific pain.

"Don't you ever call back! You almost broke up our family once. Don't ever try again!" Simone wasn't asking, she was ordering. Her own years of frustration partially the cause of her emotional outburst.

Rita turned off the phone as it slipped from her palm, falling clumsily on the floor near her shaking legs. It was unmistakable to Simone that Rita was gone for good. No woman had a throat big enough to swallow that much pride and call back.

The weight of truth and half-truth thrown on Rita's mind left her avalanched with pain. She had learned the hard way that if someone enters your heart for a moment, if you let them they will stay for an eternity. She lay on the dry itchy hotel suite carpet wreathing in pain, her chest heaving rapidly in and out from the crying.

He had a son? He was married?

Nausea set in along with the harsh realization that she'd been lied to by Lee Johnson, the man with no conscience. It appeared that the man she was prepared to trade in everything for, even her lucrative career had purposely deceived her for the past ten months while separated from his wife and young son. She was now unable to trust a man again. Never again.

She always had her suspicions surrounding Lee. He seemed to hide things from her, and withhold feelings. In her mind, now she knew why he was so terrifically mysterious.

When she picked up the phone to call him, she never imagined that this would be the response received. Instead of reconciliation and a second chance at true love, she now wallowed in devastation and immeasurable pain. The hurt caused her to cry all night until tears could no longer form in her burgundy wine colored eyes. Her soul itself was battered, with a heart crying out and screaming. *Why?*

Chapter 40

A half hour passed after Simone's talk with Rita when Lee stepped inside dripping of sweat after finishing up cutting the grass. Simone met him at the door with a tall glass of ice water to quench his thirst.

"Are we still going out tonight to the furniture store?" Lee asked.

"That sounds good," Simone replied while wiping off the counter top and straightening up the kitchen dishes. She was ridding her body of nervous energy, hoping he wouldn't find out somehow Rita called. She planned on keeping that incident hidden, acting as if nothing of importance transpired.

Lee planned to propose to Simone on Saturday which would usher in a new way of living. "Let me wash up, I'll be ready in like twenty minutes," Lee said while finishing his glass of water, wiping his mouth with the back of his hand.

"Alright, we'll be at Mom's so I can get changed too. Just meet us over there."

"Okay, love you," he agreed.

Lee rushed up the steps eager to shower and change, then go out with Simone for shopping and dinner. He had no clue Rita had ever called the house. Ironically it was Simone's idea to set up a phone line for the house. She made the arrangements earlier that week for the phone and internet service. They had discussed the matter of marriage again, and since they both agreed it was imminent, she suggested the home phone line to conduct business matters. Lee agreed, but requested his name listed as L. Johnson thinking he could somehow avoid contact with Rita. That plan, however clever, still failed plummeting Rita into a pit of despair.

Lee quickly showered and changed still left with a few empty minutes before going to pick up Simone to go shopping. Shawn wanted to stay behind with Mr. Hart to see another one of the summer blockbuster movies on the silver screen.

Lee dialed his cell phone while alone in the quiet home, finalizing plans for tomorrows long awaited proposal to Simone.

"Charlie's Lounge. Talk to me."

"Keith, what's up boy? How's the club?"

"Just wrapping up happy hour, we got a nice crowd in here."

"You been holding it down."

"No doubt."

"How's school going?"

"Good so far, real good."

"That's what I wanna hear."

"I'm not gonna let you or Uncle C down."

"I know." Lee gave his vote of confidence, though he still sometimes worried.

Keith knew why he was calling, and wasted no more time. "You're calling about tomorrow right?"

"Yea," Lee said as he paused and waited.

"I talked to their manager yesterday. He said they'll be here."

"You sure?" Lee asked excitedly.

"Yea man. Pieces of a Dream will be here by eight."

Lee was worried because the last time they tried to book a major jazz act, the show was cancelled at the last second. Even though it was a scheduling conflict, it was still disappointing.

"Hey Lee," Keith said.

"Yea?"

"You sure you wanna go through this?"

"One hundred percent."

"I know I clown around a lot but if you're sure. I'm proud of you. Simone's cool."

"Thanks Keith."

"Whatever happened to old girl Rita anyway?"

"I've been dodging her all week. She keeps trying to call me. I'll probably call her one last time after everything's official with Simone, just to let her know. Out of respect."

"Man...don't call," Keith said.

"I owe her that much," Lee said.

"I wouldn't call. That's all I'm saying," Keith warned again.

"I feel you. But, we'll see. Look, I gotta run but I'll see you tomorrow. Thanks again."

"I'll be here," Keith said as he watched the crowd continue to grow.

Keith had taken his responsibilities at the lounge with utmost seriousness, which surprised all onlookers. Lee was feeling good about his friend's new found seriousness, as it seemed he was amidst a life transition of his own.

Simone began calling Lee's phone just as he reached the door to leave. "I'm running late. Give me another half hour, tops. Okay?" she said.

"Yea, no problem. Take your time," Lee responded, while sticking his head in the refrigerator seeking out a snack to munch on.

He took the allotted time to reflect on his relationship with Rita, coming to the harsh realization that it never could've worked. His heart was never really in it, only the idea of snagging a woman from society's high class was the reason for his excitement. Rita was so unusual than most women he dated previously. Not that she was any better, just different.

That difference intrigued him, along with her manner of speech, her business classic style, and her foreign looks. There were times he felt pride in being with her, other times shame. All those emotion transcended into eventual frustration of not being able to be himself. He was caged in, far from free. Dissatisfied. His fear was she would be judgmental of him, and his past transgressions, though once revealed she truly understood.

Their backgrounds were as different as democracy and communism. His self doubt ate away at him. He never fully believed in the empty words I love you. He only focused on his next move, or rather his next line. He fed her so many compliments it was a wonder her head didn't explode. After six months of that what could he do? Cut the whole thing off? How could he give up when everyone said it would fail? Defiantly, he pressed on determined to prove the doubters wrong.

He never erased the memory of Simone from his mind either. He believed that by dating Rita he could prove to his heart that there was something better out there than Simone Hart. His heart never bought in to that thought. The secret love at work never helped matters. Neither did the fact that Rita lived in the same building his father died in.

The thought of spending time at a building associated with so much pain impaired his ability to relax at her home. It served as no oasis, but rather an evil torture chamber. Doubt from so many places corrupted his heart, leaving it hard and coarse. Rita was right. His male pride was part of the reason for holding on to the notion of a life spent with her.

Without even become conscious to what was happening, he had fallen out of love with Rita well before things officially ended. Before Simone's return. Even his planned proposal to Rita was rushed and sloppy, trying in a last ditch attempt to prove to Uncle Charlie and Keith that no woman, no matter how sophisticated was out of his reach. That fact seemed to prove true. But with consequences. Her love was sincere, but his tainted, never ridding Simone from his mind.

When he began working with Liz, those memories intensified daily, causing a longing to be with her once more. He stood, one day from that reality. One day removed from Simone accepting his proposal and taking the name Mrs. Simone Johnson. How often does a person's dream become reality?

He did his best at juggling the two phenomenal women, and he put forth effort to do so delicately, trying to cause no harm to either one. Little did he know he inflicted a pain into one of them that cut so deep, it would never be mended. For the other, his true love, the future was heavenly, a life with Lee. A man who for once appeared to own something of high value, inner peace.

Chapter 41

Saturday night arrived, and Lee waited nervously in his Durango for
Simone to exit the front door of the Hart's home. They planned to spend
the evening at Charlie's Lounge, and take in some smooth jazz. He had set
everything in motion for the special night, giving everyone a heads up. The
Hart's would stay home and watch Shawn, but they knew his plans. Liz
and Ray were to meet them at the lounge at seven, they too were informed
of his plan.

Keith promised to have Pieces of a Dream perform at the club. Lee
felt his uncle could still be part of the occasion somehow by his proposing
at the lounge in the midst of family and friends. Usually he was private,
but after all these years of off again on again love with Simone he wanted a
full-fledged celebration to breakout. He and Keith were regulars at
Charlie's Lounge for years, and everyone in town knew who they were. This
would be a night to remember.

Simone exited the house and nearly suffocated Lee with her
beauty. She took his breath away from him and threatened to not give it
back. Everything about her was perfect, from her hair to her smile. Most
importantly, her heart was beautiful. She had endured years of his
immaturity, and still gave him this final chance. She had filled his heart
and new home with the sound of laughter.

Lee put the ride in reverse and pulled off towards the main road.
Idle chit chat passed the time as they made the twenty minute commute
across town, arriving right on time at seven. This would be Lee's first time
attending the club on a weekend as owner, no longer just a patron. He still
found it hard to grasp the fact that he owned the lounge. His uncle left him
financially secure beyond his wildest imagination would've ever thought.

He was holding the two karat princess cut engagement ring he'd
purchased over ten years ago in his jackets inner pocket. It was still there

as he checked one last time before entering the lounge.

Keith ran over to meet them once establishing eye contact. He had his head down and pursed his lips. "Sorry man, they cancelled. They said something about a flat tire..."

"What?" Lee asked, feeling beyond disappointed.

"Got ya," Keith laughed, punching Lee in the arm playfully, and then in the chest. His fist connected with the box the ring was housed in. Lee was in no mood for jokes. He was nervous enough about the night as it was.

"What's in your pocket?" Keith asked, rubbing his knuckles. Lee ignored the question and slyly shot him a look back that screamed, shut up. The couple weaved through the crowd down towards the stage where Liz and Ray were stationed in a reserved booth. They had already started sipping on the complimentary bottle of champagne.

"This is nice Lee," Liz commented, "You all look so cute together."

"Thanks," Simone answered back smiling.

"Ray, you going to get up there one day?" Lee asked nodding towards stage.

"I have a bass man already, and I'm holding down the drums. It's coming together. We need a guitarist and somebody to tackle them keys," Ray said using his hands to play the invisible piano in front of him.

"Let me know when you're ready," Lee said, reminding him of the offer to play at Charlie's Lounge.

Simone had already snuggled underneath his arms, as everyone looked around at the robust crowd that was forming. It appeared that everyone was out tonight.

"You all have a name yet?" Lee asked about the slow forming band.

"Yea...Trace," Ray said.

"That sounds classy. I like that," Lee nodded.

Liz was all smiles as she and Simone commenced to whispering back and forth. Keith reappeared at the booth carrying a second bottle of champagne swimming in a bucket of ice.

"It's a special night. Drinks are on the house." Keith's smile and wink at Lee was giving away the planned surprise. Lee wanted the proposal to be a total shock for Simone. But between Liz's wide eyed grins and Keith's carelessness, that wasn't going to happen. Sensing that his cover was going to be blown he excused himself from the table.

"Simone, will you come with me for a minute?"

"Yea what is it baby?"

"Nothing, I just wanted to talk to you before the band comes on." Ray and Liz nodded in marital unison, turning their focus to one another.

"Lee what's wrong?" Simone questioned as she clung on to his arm as they entered the sidewalk.

"Nothing's wrong. For once, everything in my life is going right," he explained as they walked towards his SUV.

"Where are we going? We're going to miss the show," she asked and reminded.

"We'll be back, trust me. They won't start until around eighy- thirty anyway," he assured her. He tried to remain calm while driving a few short blocks and parked. They arrived at a river walk in one of the town's parks.

The two got out and began a stroll along the paved path as the summers night air brought a needed breeze. Lee stopped and sat down gradually on a park bench that overlooked the river and across to a small open field in the distance. The last drop of summer sunshine faded into a caramel colored sunset. Lee's soul was once cold and scarred with emotional pain, but he now appreciated that it was Simone who provided relief.

Lee started to speak, interrupting the silence, "I'm just going to come from my heart with this."

"Lee what's going on?" she asked again. She wondered if he somehow found out about Rita calling. At this instance, she was the farthest thing from his mind.

"You have a real big heart, you know that?" Lee said.

Simone blushed some while he stared into her eyes intently.

"I just want to be here for you, endlessly. I want to be the one to ease all your pain. I must have been crazy to ever tell you we couldn't work out. I'm so sorry."

By the trembling in his lips she knew he offered sincerity and she continued to gaze back at him, rubbing his hand to help him along.

"Take a look at me baby. I'm alone without you in my life. Right now I'm more sure than ever about what I want. You've been there through thick and thin. What we have is love...*true love*." His eyes gave way to the tears unable to be held back as he slid off the park bench and down on one knee, still holding her soft petite hands. He looked at her in all her glowing radiance.

"Lee, what are you saying?" Simone was shocked and in awe, her eyes now misty as well.

"I won't let you down. I need you. I can truly say that there has been no better woman in the world."

Simone blinked her eyes rapidly.

He continued. "What more can I ask for? My love will grow for you more and more each day. For you, and Shawn. I love you." Lee reached into his pocket and gradually revealed the ring he should've placed on her finger a thousand times before.

"I love you," she mouthed.

"Simone, will you marry me? Baby, please say yes. I wouldn't lie to you. I will always be here. I'll never leave."

"Somehow I knew things would work out. My heart told me to keep the faith," she said.

"Is that a yes? I know there were times you felt like giving up. I know I can't but I want to make it up to you. I love you, just say yes..."

"Yes, yes, yes," she said with each word more emphatic than the last. The two embraced tightly and silently, savoring the moment. They could've made a fortune if able to bottle up that moment and sold it. It was beautiful, heartfelt, and satisfying. The feeling exchanged between them felt like the first time they'd ever touched all over again.

"Never let me go," she whispered into his ear.

"I'll never let you go baby, never. I'll love you till the end of time." With that said he slid the flawless gem on her left hand, as she looked at it for the first time. After having that moment together and letting it set in, the two returned to his vehicle and drove back to Charlie's Lounge, experiencing a natural high no drug could ever rival.

They entered the lounge as an engaged couple. Liz could already detect by the fulfilled look on Simone's face that Lee had proposed in private, and she had accepted. As they sat down, they were greeted by a round of hugs and congratulations.

Simone proudly displayed the eye-catching ring that now adorned her left hand, and it was challenging to decipher which shined brighter, the polished diamond or her eyes.

Keith approached the group of four and offered congratulations as well, then hustled on stage at the front of the lounge. The band was coming off stage after tuning the instruments, as Keith grabbed firm hold of the microphone. He would formally introduce them momentarily so they could take stage and do their thing.

Keith took the microphone. "Ladies and gentleman may I have your attention. First off I want to welcome you out to Charlie's Lounge, right here on the east side. Big C we love you baby! We'll never forget you," Keith shouted while pointing to a large portrait that hung on one of the brick walls in the lounge.

Always an emphatic man, Keith was a natural on stage, as the packed capacity crowd went crazy, erupting in cheers and whistles showing Charlie love.

"Before we get it started up in here tonight, I wanna let ya'll know something. Tonight is a special night at Charlie's. You all know Lee, the new owner of this lounge, and Charlie's nephew right?"

The crowd filled with mostly regulars answered back with applause.

"Well let me be the first to say congratulations. Tonight, he and his lady just got engaged and I wanna give it up for them. I wish ya'll the best!" The crowd again responded with excitement, celebrating their achievement. Liz even stood up clapping, followed by Ray and the rest of the customers. Everyone was ready to party and have a great time.

"Alright, you ready for some jazz?" Keith yelled out the question. The response was an overwhelming yes. "I can't hear you!" he shouted back into the microphone, cupping his hand to his ear. "I said are you ready for a show?" He had single handedly worked the crowd into a frenzy.

It had never been so loud in there.

The sound crashed into the walls and vibrated the dusty stained concrete floor. People were spending money and buying drinks like their life depended on it as Keith bounced across the stage, pumping up the crowded room with his yelling.

"Put your hands together and give a Charlie's Lounge welcome, for the first time, ever. Welcome....Pieces....of a Dream!"

The band rushed the stage like a stampede, feeding off the energy in the crowd. The music blasted forth it's first few smooth notes as the band played on.

Chapter 42

The remainder of the memorable weekend went wonderful. Sunday afternoon Mrs. Hart threw a big dinner for the whole family to get together and celebrate the happy occasion. It was decided upon that the wedding would be held in just two weeks, which would take almost a miracle to pull off. But with a mother like Mrs. Hart and a sister like Liz, anything was possible.

They requested a intimate ceremony, in the backyard with close friends and family in attendance. A highly professional celebrated wedding planner was hired and agreed to control the decorating, catering, flowers, and every other detail a wedding demands. It was to be a beautiful site for the eyes on a perfect August afternoon. Keith was making arrangements for a traditional jazz quartet to perform at the event.

Lee still had one task to perform before his wedding day as well. He planned to call Rita, out of respect, to let her know it was his own doubts that crippled their life together. He didn't want his errors to ruin the chance for some other guy. He knew that he had done wrong by her and still felt guilty for blowing off her calls and emails. Rita was a extraordinary person and she deserved to hear the truth from his mouth, not second hand. He manufactured enough courage to give Rita a call after work, he knew it would be evening in London, so she'd have time to talk.

He was parking the SUV when the phone began ringing and he realized that there was only one ways a conversation like this could go. Horrible. He hoped that she would be here usual professional self, unable to be rattled or disturbed by anything. Her corporate background molded her into a personality of methodical thinking. She could process data and input without emotion. Unfortunately, this was different.

Her heart did not consist of spread sheets and account reports, her love was not some audit or stock exchange. She had feelings. Feelings he assassinated by hiding so many lies from her, the biggest being her perception that he was married and had a son all the while dating her while separated from his wife. That wasn't the case, but as far as Rita knew it was gospel.

That was the conclusion drawn from her final conversation with Simone and from his secretive actions. He had always seemed so unpredictable and she prominently viewed it as exciting spontaneity, until now. He on the other hand though he was being forthright with her, not wanting to seem devilish in anyway.

As he exited the car at the river walk and began walking he waited for her answer. At the park he'd take in fresh air while explaining to her what he considered valid reasons for his decision.

She begrudgingly answered the telephone. The time was ten-thirty as she sat alone in her hotel suite. She'd be moving into a new apartment soon, and she couldn't wait for change of scenery. The room was now a jail cell, where she was tormented by her sentence of loneliness. She was watching a BBC news broadcast while sipping a glass of merlot.

"Hello Rita," Lee spoke slow and gentle, like he was entering a room where someone was sleeping.

"Who is this?" she demanded angrily, knowing full well who was calling.

"It's Lee," he said sounding put off.

Without so much as a warning Rita laid into him like a runaway freight train, ending any speculation he had of exchanging pleasantries and saying a civil farewell. "You're a liar, and a coward. I hate you! I hate you!" Lee attempted to intervene. Total confusion entered his mind leaving him flabbergasted. All last week she had been calling, leaving messages, and emailing about getting back together.

What happened?

She continued peppering her words with hatred. "You no longer have a hold on my heart. How could you do this?"

"Do what?" he asked.

"Just shut up! You make me sick…"

"What?" he asked sounding confused.

"I never thought we'd end up this way. No wonder you couldn't marry me...No wonder you couldn't move to London. You thought you could use me? Well you did it. Are you happy now?"

He tried to dodge her verbal jabs. "No, I didn't want to hurt you."

"What did you think would happen?" she asked.

"I don't know."

"That's your line isn't it Lee? You don't know? It's never your fault is it? Well...who do you blame this time? Who?" She yelled into the phone standing hunched over, throwing her wine glass into the wall, letting it explode into tiny pieces. "I never thought I'd hurt like this. Not because of you. My mom and friends tried to warn me. I never thought this would be the price I'd have to pay. My life was in your hands and you crushed me, you..."

"Rita I just wanted to be honest with you."

"Honest? I can't believe that word is even in your vocabulary. You've got a lot of nerve calling me."

"Yea, but you've been calling me all week and I've been dodging you so I figured I'd clear the air."

"No Lee,...if that's even your real name. Let me clear the air! I loved you more than you'll ever know. Despite all your faults, you broke...No. I'm not going there. Just be glad I got you that job at Jackson & Fitz. Consider it, something to remember me by."

"Oh, so you got me the job?"

"Do you think they ordinarily hire riff raff?"

"It's like that now?" he asked.

"Whatever. What if I did get you the job?"

"Then you lied!"

"Just shut up Lee. What does it matter? What do you want? You want to kick me while I'm down?"

"No, like I said..."

He was cut off again, "No! *Like I said.* You took my heart, my soul, my breath. You took it all. Maybe I'll get it back someday, but until then it's goodbye."

"Rita wait..."

"No. This whole thing was a game to you. It was a lie, it wasn't real at all. You used me and I don't know why. For my money? For a job? For my...Why?"

"Rita... I just wanted to tell you..."

"Save it. I already know."

"You do?" Lee was puzzled.

"Yea I do, so save your little pitiful breath. Go home to your family and leave me alone!"

"Rita I'm sorry, I am." Lee was truly remorseful for all he'd done.

"I bet you're sorry. Sorry you got caught. You're a pitiful conniving man. You couldn't handle a woman making more money than you. I promise you this. If you ever try to call me,...you ever so much as email me and I'll have you fired so fast your head will spin. Do you hear me?" Rita was deathly serious as he was all to certain by her tone.

"Yea," he said, feeling now like he was being pimped.

"There's nothing you can say to ever change what you've done. I don't want you to ever even *think* about me, or I'll have you bounced out of Jackson & Fitz and back to that sweat shop you used to call a job. I never should've gave your sorry behind a chance. I never should've stepped my designer shoes into that two-bit dive you call a lounge. *Please.*"

She was insulting and disgusted as Lee didn't bother to fight back with words, he just absorbed the blows she sent flying through the phone. He was still confused by her great anger. She wouldn't stop talking. "That's right Mr. Johnson...I got your game now, and every man out there like you. You don't deserve a real woman like me. Go home to your wife...and to your son, you deadbeat."

"My son?" He never told her anything regarding Shawn, not even an inkling of his existence. He was shocked, paralyzed, and boggled.

"Yea, your son. The one you tried to hide from me. You never even mentioned you had a kid. How could you deny your own flesh and blood you deadbeat? I hate you!"

"Rita!" He tried to interject, to respond. She was speaking so fast it was impossible.

"Leave me alone. Don't ever forget what I said. You call me again and I'll make sure you're fired...that day! I'm talking about gone. Do you hear me? Answer me!" Rita screamed at the top of her lungs.

"Yea," he said, slightly above a whisper. His hands were tied.

"It's *yes* Lee. The word is *yes*. You don't know how sick I was of your broken English. You're a bum. Good - Bye!"

This time Lee knew their ties were terminated. He didn't know how or why she knew everything going on. All he knew was one thing for certain. That conversation he just had with Rita, would be their last misunderstanding.

Chapter 43

Rita had never lost her composure in that way before. She paced haphazardly around her temporary home in the illustrious hotel, her eyes darted back and forth across the suite, focusing on nothing. Her silk robe was wrinkled, with her hair a complete mess sitting atop her head.

She was in desperate need of a listening ear. Lately she'd purposely missed her mothers calls, but right then she was all she had left in the world. Rita stood in her window, facing out into the black foggy cloud filled sky. She speculated on why out of all the men in the world she had to meet Lee Johnson. She elected to call her mother now, and clue her in on the truth.

"Hello dear," her mother said.

"Mom," Rita whined out like a adolescent child after a bad day at school.

"What's wrong Rita? What's wrong?"

"He hurt me...," she let out and began her usual nightly routine of crying.

"What do you mean? Did he hit you?" her mother gasped fearing the worst. She knew first hand what abuse felt like.

"No, no. You won't believe this mother."

"Oh, I bet I would Rita. I warned you, didn't I?" She scolded with no restraint.

"You were right. He was nothing but a bum. Just like you said, a lying bum."

"Rita calm down. Tell me what happened."

"He's married mother."

"Oh my!" she said, clasping at her neckline.

"He even has a child. I never knew any of it."

"Good heavens Rita. I'm sorry...but I warned you. You see, men like him are dogs. To be honest all men are, but these lower class fellows never cease to amaze me. All their lies and baby momma's...whatever they call them. Ugh! How putrid."

Her mother was no real support, only a reinforcement of the idea; men were not to be trusted. Rita had no one else she felt comfortable enough to discuss matters with. If she was forced to hold in emotions this deep, she might soon detonate like a bomb.

"Mom, I don't think I can ever love, or trust again," Rita said.

"I know dear. I haven't trusted a man since the day I left your father. Believe me, I have no regrets. My focus became my career and today I'm first chair in the orchestra, touring the world. Do you know what it would be like to find a man on my level?"

"I just can't believe..." Rita started back in with the crying.

"Enough of your tears. What did you expect? Too marry this numbskull and raise his little snot nosed kids? Join the PTA? Rita please...wake up! You were a COO, he was blue-collar trash. Now look at you. Vice President Ms. Rita Clark. The world is yours my dear. Achieve greatness, that is your true calling. Not rolling around with some washed up basketball star living on food stamps."

"It was baseball."

"Whatever, it's all so barbaric."

"He wasn't on food stamps."

"He might as well have been by the way you described him. Regardless, he was fun for a while. Move on. Focus on your career, and find a man who can challenge you...and your bank account. Agreed?"

"Mother...," she dragged out the word trying to show she needed good advice, not another lecture laced with negativity.

"Don't mother me. I was right, and now my baby is in London crying her eyes out over some ex jock. He should be thanking you on his hands and knees you would ever speak to him, let alone get involved."

"You think so?" Rita asked.

"I know so. You need to wake up and smell the cappuccino. Realize who and what you are. A beautiful, successful, and rich young woman. With all that going for you, who needs a man? Well, you do to a point, but not like this last one. In time the right investment banker or real estate mogul will come along. You'll see. All of your charity work with men is over I hope. Do you understand what I'm saying? I just don't need you calling me up crying over another boy toy of yours. So, he had muscles. Sooner or later you'll see how right I am. I promise."

"I think you might be right. I plan to focus on my career one hundred twenty percent and be the best VP Jackson & Fitz has ever seen," Rita sniffled.

"That's my girl."

"Thank you Mom."

"For what?" she asked.

"For not being harder on me. You were right all along."

"That's right dear, you're class...he's trash," her mother said and laughed haughtily. Rita laughed herself, a small chuckle for the first time in weeks. Ordinarily she never gave in to thinking of class distinction, but she was hurt and it seemed hardly cruel to pity Lee.

"Hey Mom," Rita said.

"Yes dear, make it quick. I'm exhausted and we have a concert in New York tomorrow."

"I promise you I'll never give a man like him a chance again. *Never.* I don't care how nice and sincere he seems. The next man better make six figures or he can forget it. I tried that whole understanding bit. I gave him a chance and it blew up in my face, and now I can't stand him. That'll never happen again. *Never.*"

"I know, I know. Just look at me. I'm perfectly happy. Who knows, maybe you'll end up being President of Jackson & Fitz one day. Then you settle down with Prince Charming, if he even exists."

"Thanks Mom."

"That's what I'm here for, smooches."

"Love you." Rita hung up the phone then fell backwards, landing on the bed, her eyes scoping the ceiling.

The sad truth was she really did award Lee her heart, and he took it and trampled it six feet into the ground. Putting a born and bred princess with a blue collar ex jock was like mixing vodka and milk.

The first few months were fine, before getting to know everything on a deeper level. After less than desirable personality traits appeared and the glow of love died down things became undone. Rita now knew she would never date a man like Lee again. No matter how nice, friendly, or handsome.

Rita felt just as her mother forewarned. Those kind of men were not to be trusted, at all. All men she would meet from that point forward would suffer for Lee's indiscretions. She had joined the ranks of other successful women with powerful jobs who would preach their gospel of repelling any man that didn't have an executive title attached to his name.

Maybe she'd never discover love again, or even seek it out at all. Who even knew if true love actually existed? Maybe it was a figment of imagination? As Mr. Sander, the former Vice President at Jackson & Fitz reminded her, the company is first priority, the *only* priority. There was still opportunity to climb even higher on the corporate landscape which had now brought her into Europe. Also there was the lure of additional compensation, incentives, prestige, and praise from her constituents that were comprised of men.

Rita Clark could hold her own with those masculine counterparts and if necessary she'd make them ignore her obvious femininity. No longer would the draw of love lure her in as if a stranger lurking in the dark where she'd be vulnerable and fall victim to harm. She tried that once, whole-heartedly. The outcome was pain…heart wrenching pain. That night she sent strict orders to her heart, letting it know that she'd experimented with love for the last time.

Chapter 44

That week and a half before the wedding was filled to the maximum with preparation for the fast approaching wedding. With the life changing event only a solitary day away Lee was unruffled and not touched by the least bit of nervousness. Rita's last stinging words were now pushed back into the far recesses of his mind, while he only focused on future events. Joyous ones.

On the Friday before the wedding he returned home from work to find the flamboyant wedding planner in the backyard obsessing over the construction and expensive decorating in the yard. Lee's mother was in town for the wedding and had arrived days earlier. He noticed from afar that his mom and Mrs. Hart were pointing to different things in the yard that deserved attention. Mr. Hart was inside partaking of a well deserved nap. Liz and Ray were coming by later that evening to also lend a hand.

Outside, a large white canopy would be erected, with all white chairs attached with large bows on the back, placed over whitewashed flooring. That is where the ceremony would take place. Fountains were being installed along with added landscaping, and plant life. At least fifteen to twenty workers zipped around the yard, frantically handling various tasks to pull it all together. Lee stepped outside on the deck and waved to Simone who arrived home before him. She was in the yard as well, discussing final flower bouquet selections, explaining the appetizer choices and so on.

Upon catching sight of Lee she excused herself and came over to join him on the deck. "Can you believe this? I want to pinch myself."

"I know this is crazy," he said, "My only regret is not doing this years ago. I love you so much. I can't believe you're still here after all I put you through."

"Of course I'm here. I love you too. This is all I ever wanted since we were kids. Tomorrow it will be a reality. We'll be one at last. A family."

"I can't wait," he said back.

"Shawn is so excited too, he hasn't stopped talking about his little tuxedo and how he got to help pick out the cake." Lee laughed about Shawn's enthusiasm as he suggested they move inside for a smidgen more of privacy.

"Did you get all the paperwork for the adoption to be finalized yet?"

"Yes, actually I did. I meant to bring it over earlier. Daddy's been moving our stuff over here all day."

"Yea, I saw that. Is everything here now?"

"Yea, just about. Oh, don't forget the furniture truck should be here soon with the living room set."

"I was wondering when that was coming," he said.

"Hey Lee?" Simone asked sounding apprehensive while she was fishing out a bottled water from the fridge and offering one to Lee.

"Yea, what's up babe?"

"I ordered some new bedroom furniture too. I used the debit card from our new account to pay for it. I hope that was okay." Simone was still uneasy and getting used to the idea of a joint account with Lee, especially since Uncle Charlie left him such a hefty inheritance. That money was still being managed by a financial advisor.

To her, it still felt like Lee's money and not their money, but he insisted it was. The advisor gave him a budget to work with to help with the wedding cost, the additions to his household, and a new car for Simone. Up until that point she had been borrowing her mother's Ford Taurus to get to work since she sold her car when she left Atlanta. Lee surprised her with the purchase of a new white Honda Accord. She was awed by his persistent generosity.

He continued to assure her the bedroom purchase was fine, as well as logical. He was convinced she would make a tasteful choice. He sought to do anything possible to make her feel at home and realize this was now their house together, not just his. She was still anxious.

"Are you sure?" she asked.

He touched her cheek. "Baby... It's fine. We can leave my old bedroom set in the spare room and Shawn can set up his room. It's fine okay." Lee was once again corralling her into his well-developed arms.

"Thank you baby, you're making all my dreams come true," she said while he held her close.

"That's all I ever wanted to do," he said, using a sweet tone. He next changed the subject, "I want to fill out the adoption paperwork as soon as possible. I love Shawn, I really do. I want to make it up to him for the times I disappeared."

"Lee, there's no pressure. You don't have to rush this."

Lee stepped back and placed his hands on her upper arms, and looked upon her with remorseful eyes, "Yes I do. I'm doing this because I love you both. He's my son, and tomorrow you'll be my wife. I can't wait." He hugged her once more silently screaming out sincerity.

The doorbell rang, interrupting the precious moment as Lee unlocked the front door. The sun stretched its long arms of light into the house. At the door stood the furniture delivery guys, eager to transport the living room and bedroom furniture that Simone selected for the home, and call it a day. As the two men wrestled in the cumbersome furniture Lee retreated to his bedroom to fill out the adoption paperwork that would legally make Shawn his son.

The last piece of furniture was positioned and the yard became still. Night fell slowly across the sky filling with diamond like stars. Lee and Simone strolled beneath the vast blanket of twinkling brilliance hand in hand, noticing the intricate details that transformed the ordinary backyard into a modern day garden of Eden. Truly a paradisiacal setting lay before their eyes, used to commemorate the wedding day that was now well under twenty four hours away. The wedding planner had outdone himself, holding true to his well referenced commendation. It was a truly breathtaking sight to behold.

The next day's weather forecast was clear, sunny skies on the horizon. Lately, everyday had been bright as he spent time with the woman he loved. Each day surpassed the next in rich splendor and satisfaction. Their love would reach unprecedented new heights while they exchanged vows, rings, and undying expressions of love. It would be a day neither would forget, sprinkled with memories to last three lifetimes.

As Simone tip toed across the lightly dewed lawn to her parents home for the last time, Lee's mother emerged from the home, and after hugging Simone she walked out to meet her only child.

"You ready for tomorrow baby boy?" she asked in a motherly manner as she placed her arms around his waist. "We had a lot of memories in that house didn't we?" she asked.

"We sure did. Thanks Mom for everything. You raised me right."

"You were a good kid growing up. Your father would be so proud of you. He loved you so much. He always wanted a boy and to watch him grow up." Mrs. Johnson wrestled back tears as she spoke of her late husband. Most times Lee never discussed his father, not even with his mother. But he finally felt peace inside and let down the guarded wall he put around that sector of his heart.

"I wish he was here Mom. I barely remember him, besides the pictures you have and stories you told me."

"He was a great man Lee...a great man," she said and sighed, staring into nothing. "He would've done anything for anybody, especially his family." Lee nodded in respect for his fallen father's memory. "Now that Charlie's gone, you're the only man in the family now. You've got a lot of responsibility on those shoulders of yours."

"I know Mom," he assured her.

"Charlie left you in a position to take care of yourself, just like your father did for us when you were growing up."

"I'm not going to blow through the money, come on..."

"I'm not saying you are. But you have a family now. Simone loves you and needs you, she always has. But Shawn needs you now too. You're a father and that's a big job. Remember everything I taught you and remember your father's example. He never neglected us, and always put our needs first. That's what a real man does."

"Don't worry Mom. I'm not some silly kid anymore. I'm not out there in the street like I used to be, drinking and hanging out. All I want is for Simone to be happy and to raise Shawn in this house."

"I know baby. I really just wanted to tell you how proud I am of you. You've come a long way. I was worried about you for a minute…"

She laughed out loud.

"I was worried too. My life had no direction after baseball. That was all I cared about…going pro. But now I'm back on track. My life has purpose again."

"That's my boy," she said as she squeezed his hand for the last time before his wedding.

"I love you Mom," he told her as they stood in the backyard. The air was beginning to cool, as the night pushed on.

"I'm proud of you baby." Mrs. Johnson smiled and walked back over to the Hart's where she was staying while in town, leaving Lee isolated with his thoughts. This was the first time outside of his baseball accolades that he could honestly say he was proud of himself too.

Chapter 45

The joyous occasion went flawlessly as intended. The wedding was behind them followed by a honeymoon in New York City where they roomed at the Waldorf Astoria Hotel located in midtown Manhattan. Simone had never been to the famed big apple, and they took in each and every one of the sites. Dining at fine restaurants, shopping along Fifth avenue, Broadway shows, even a visit to the Apollo Theatre.

Due to Lee having already missed two weeks of work the previous month and Simone was still new at Rockstone Industries they opted for a three day trip, and planned an extended vacation for a later date. Once back home and settled in, the life as a family took shape.

A year passed quickly and everyday was still a source of pleasure. Everything on the home front went exactly as planned, including the adoption. Inevitably, change had to occur.

Clear out of the blue Lee came home from work one day to find pamphlets and books spread out over the kitchen counter that all pertained to a certain subject matter. The subject was infant care. This was what Simone viewed as a subtle hint to alert him to the fact she was pregnant with his child. His life would change once more with the new addition to the family.

The pregnancy was normal. Cravings, mood swings, swollen ankles, the usual. Two weeks from delivery and time rolled on. The baby could arrive at anytime and everyone was ecstatic about bringing a new child into the family. The couple decided not to find out the sex of the baby until delivery, which added to the anticipation and suspense factor. It had been a year and six months of marriage as this bundle of joy was prepared to arrive on the scene and turn their lives as well as the perfectly kept home upside down.

Simone was off from work, and staying home while Liz cared for her everyday. She was granted temporary leave of absence from work by her supervisor, who conveniently happened to be her brother-in-law. Lee would work harder than normal at work to cover Liz's work while she had time off. His mother planned to return to town the minute Simone went into labor. She was jubilated with the prospect of laying her eyes on the precious little baby.

Keith was caught up in the excitement too, pressuring them to name the newborn after him if it was a boy. The funny thing was, he was serious. Now, fulltime manager at Charlie's Lounge he also had completed his degree in hospitality management. He'd done more than find a job he absolutely loved, he excelled at it. Charlie's Lounge was reaching another level, with visitors now streaming in nightly from the city. Weekends were especially busy as many nationally known smooth jazz acts were being booked to perform sets at the lounge that grew in popularity.

Ray's band Trace was formed a year earlier and performed regularly at the lounge just as Keith promised. Things were looking up for everyone secularly, including Lee. He had been promoted to District Mail Manager, which meant overseeing operation in neighboring states facilities as well. He was grateful to Mr. Flannigan's steadily increasing faith in him as a supervisor. Mr. Flannigan had easily transitioned into the position once held by Frank Harrison. Any minute at work Lee anticipated receiving the call from home to head to the hospital for the delivery of his son or daughter.

As always, his cell phone was on him. Each time it rang, he jumped, thinking that was *the call*. On a Friday, making the routine commute his phone rang. The buzzing vibration from the phone nearly caused him to swerve into oncoming traffic.

"Lee...this is it!" Liz yelled in the phone.

"I'll be home in five minutes," he said, his heart pounding.

"No, there's no time. Meet us up at County General. We're on our way."

"We who?"

"Me, Simone, and Mom."

"Where's Shawn?"

"He's riding with Dad. We called your mom, she's taking the next flight out. Meet us there."

"Emergency room?"

"No. Maternity. Remember orientation?"

"Oh yea, see you there. Tell Simone I love her"

"Okay Bye."

The last time Liz called him frantically and said to meet at County General, there was horrible news to follow. Hopefully, this time things would be fine. As he arrived at the hospital he burst through the double doors like he was entering an old west saloon, his head spun in every direction, trying to figure out which way to turn. The hospital was set up like a completely ridiculous maze.

An older nurse with Mickey Mouse scrubs approached him, noticing he needed assistance. "Can I help you sir? You look lost."

He was lost. Shut up and help. "Yea, my wife is in here somewhere. She's in labor. I'm supposed to meet her here."

The nurse seemed unfazed by his hurried explanation.

"Name?" she asked calmly.

"Lee. I mean Johnson. Simone Johnson."

"Let me check with admitting," the wrinkled nurse said. Her face resembled a melted candle. She slowly shuffled down the hallway.

Out of the corner of his eye Lee caught sight of Shawn and Mr. Hart down a long corridor. He took off running in pursuit, leaving candle face in the dust, his shoe laces flapping against the blue and gray tiles beneath his feet.

"Dad!" he called out, grabbing hold of Mr. Hart's ear.

"Lee this way, she's going to deliver this baby any minute they're saying. Get in there." Mr. Hart shoved him towards a delivery room crammed with doctors and nurses. How many people did it take to deliver a baby? Liz was on one side of the bed and Mrs. Hart on the other as his eyes fixed in on Simone who laid in obvious discomfort, she was being prepped for delivery.

"Lee," Simone cried out, attempting to look over the shoulders of the crowd surrounding the bed.

"Are you the father?" a nurse asked rushing out her words.

"Yes," Lee said, with his eyes still on Simone.

"Let me get you some scrubs. Come with me, your wife will be fine."
Lee followed the instructions, promptly entering a nearby bathroom to
change in true Superman fashion. Once in hospital gear he said a quick
prayer before departing from the small bathroom. The nurse let Liz and
Mrs. Hart know that it was time to begin the birthing process. They
regretfully left the room after kissing Simone's forehead goodbye.

It was then Lee and Simone in the room together with the doctor,
an intern, and nurse to begin the process of delivery. He squeezed her
hand and kissed it, letting her know everything would be fine. He'd be
there every step of the way. They had been there before with Shawn's
delivery, eleven years earlier. That birth was a bittersweet occasion
because of how the pregnancy came about, whereas this was their first
child together as a married couple.

"I love you. You can do this," he said bending down to her ear. The
doctor instructed her to begin pushing. Push she did, and with each effort
squeezing Lee's hand until it went thoroughly numb. Two hours of labor
and Lee's crushed hand later, a baby boy was brought into the world to
proud new parents.

Chapter 46

After being cleaned up and established in a recovery room Lee and Simone spent the first few moments together, alone with the new baby.

"What do you want to name him? You choose."

"I'm not sure yet," Lee said.

"How about Lee Johnson the third?"

"I don't know...let me see," he said looking at his beautiful wife and new baby boy as he held his chin which bore a healthy five o'clock shadow.

He recounted all the changes over the past two years. He couldn't help but think of Uncle Charlie, and how his advice about settling down and generosity changed his life. Everyday he missed his uncle and how they laughed and joked so many nights, often until dawn.

Lee broke his silence, "Charlie. I want to name him Charlie."

Simone looked down and smiled lovingly at the tiny person pressed against her chest. "Charlie...I like that."

Lee smiled back, both of them knowing why he selected that name. A knock at the door soon followed. A nurse unobtrusively peeked her head in the room. She asked quietly, "Are you up for visitors?"

"Of course," Simone answered, her face coated with pride as the family entered the room, anxious to meet the newest family member, Charles Lee Johnson.

A few days later, Lee found himself leaving the safety of the hospital and driving the new family home. A small crowd of friends and family welcomed them as they stepped across the front door for the first time.

Before turning in for the night Lee walked down the dim lit hallway to check on Shawn. He watched him sleeping peacefully in his room that was decorated floor to ceiling with baseball paraphernalia. Lee's own dreams of the past nibbled at his mind. There was a time when he believed that success was defined by getting to the Major Leagues and scoring a multimillion dollar contract. But as reality set in on his life those dreams faded away like clouds in a blue sky. They were replaced by real dreams.

His life came full circle over the past two years. He'd gone from hanging out every weekend with Keith, to dating a highly successful business woman, to marrying his childhood love and having a new baby with her. Things were different too because of the loss of his uncle, now owning the lounge, and watching Keith do an incredible job running the place instead of mooching from it. It was hard to believe.

He even lived in his old house, and coached Shawn's little league team, reigniting his love for the game of baseball. Life has a funny way of showing you what's important, he thought as he entered the master bedroom. Simone was in bed resting. The baby was finally asleep in the bassinette next to the king size bed.

He tapped her shoulder. "Simone, are you up baby?"

"Yea I was just resting my eyes," she answered nearly in a whisper.

"I don't want to keep you up. I just wanted to say how happy I am."

"I'm happy too," she said with her tired eyes still closed.

"Ever since you came back in my life I haven't stopped thinking about how grateful I am you gave me another chance," he said while running his hands through her hair.

"Lee it's okay. Stop beating yourself up over the past. You're a great father. I'm proud of you for all you do for us."

"You mean that?"

"Yes...I do," she answered, her eyes still shut tight.

Lee rose out of the bed and tucked the blankets in around her, then laid back down just staring at the woman he adored with every fiber in his body.

Simone had always given him so many chances and he knew he'd never be able to repay her for that, but he would try. She was truly a beautiful person inside and out, and she gave him the greatest gift a woman can bestow upon a man. *She taught him how to love.*

Chapter 47

Over the next few weeks the adjustment to life with baby took its toll. Lee began to feel like he suffered from sleep deprivation and wondered how Simone could get up every two hours and care for the screaming child. He was slowly but surely realizing just how much stronger a woman could be than a man. Work remained routine, and busy as ever.

The company grew with the speed of a European bullet train. Mr. Flannigan called a mandatory meeting inside the boardroom to discuss what he termed as exciting news. The management staff assembled inside the room as the presentation began.

"Thank you all for coming. We have some exciting news to announce. The company has decided to expand its horizons," he said while sweeping his hands left to right. The group of department managers seemed disinterested, some pretending to be taking notes, others fighting back impending drowsiness. A small handful, including Lee attempted to focus and stay interested in the dissertation.

"Jackson & Fitz has decided to expand into the far east, that has come down from headquarters. Any questions?"

"Where are we expanding?" someone asked.

"Glad you asked that. China. Beijing, to be specific. We're globalizing and are going to diversify our assets. The Chinese yen is up, and we're going to strike while the iron is hot. Now, you're probably wondering what this has to do with you. Right?"

Heads could be seen shaking up and down as some looked nervously on, now listening to every word. One employee stood asking, "What are you trying to tell us, job cuts?"

"No, no, no, opportunity. Follow me, it's positive, trust me." The skinny man Lee had come to know wiggled around in his tweed suit jacket.

"Lee, open this box will you?" Ed Flannigan asked while sliding a large cardboard box in his direction. Lee opened it with his pocket knife, and then pushed the box back down the table.

"Thank you," Ed said while removing a copy of World Business Executive Magazine. "Inside here is a feature article about our company. We've caught the eye of the global market, pat yourselves on the back people," he said while clapping.

"We're all getting bonuses this year," some optimists muttered, while others clapped in enthusiasm. Smiles filled the room as dreams of a bonus check penetrated greedy minds.

"I want you all to read the article, and see where we're headed. China is booming and we're trying to get in on the ground floor. Please take a copy on your way out. Take a few minutes to look it over in case you bump into one of the executives. They are extremely excited and proud as you can imagine. Thank you."

With that said, the brief staff meeting concluded. Lee brought a copy back to his office where it sat on his desk next to his growing collection of family pictures. Somewhere around 4:30 he finished up the last bit of paperwork and took the advice to at least skim the article. Most of the terminology used needed translation from a financial expert. Information like this was not of great interest to the average Jackson & Fitz employee, but being a team player meant drudging through the company's new-fangled plans.

As he turned the page he was taken back to a different time. Before him was a face he hadn't thought much about in a year and a half. There was a half page color photo of the new face of Jackson & Fitz Asian Operations. Ms. Rita Clark, CEO.

The column went on to praise Ms. Clark's devotion and attention to detail. She had been chosen to spearhead the company's premeditated drive into the Chinese business market. There was a quote highlighted by Mr. Donald Sander, Executive Board Member and former Jackson & Fitz Vice President which read, *"Ms. Clark is the sort of executive a company can only dream of hiring. Leaders like her arrive only once in a lifetime."*

Since her final conversation with Lee she had nose-dived head first into the position as Vice President of International Banking. She exceeded all expectations, doubling the company return on investment in eighteen months. She also facilitated a banking acquisition in Glasgow which brought the company supplementary assets into the millions of dollars.

Ever since the breakup she took to heart the recommendation of Mr. Sander and of her mother. She focused on her career like a sniper, handling each task with devoted single mindedness. That relentless exertion now landed her the highly touted CEO position in China.

The article continued to indicate her honors and awards earned, most prominently the World Business Executive Diamond Award for outstanding International Executive. In the picture featured in the magazine her disposition shouted more of a military leader than executive. Her ghastly decomposed heart was noticeable by the look in her eyes. Lee in spite of everything smiled, as he looked at the woman whose outer shell was still alluring.

Rita was tremendously powerful in the business world, but now a stranger to him. Almost a figment of his imagination as he looked on at the picture, reminiscing. No one would ever believe that there was a time when he knew her so well, or that she possessed a playful personality, or that she'd ever frequent a small nightclub like Charlie's Lounge.

She was pictured standing behind her desk in a navy blue professional women's business suit, staring into the camera with a half-smile. Her beauty was still undeniable, but masked by her stark look of seriousness. He held the magazine close to his face, within inches, and then let it fall, plopping down on the desktop below.

She had indeed done what she set out to do. She had achieved the highest form of success in the male dominated cutthroat world of big business. Part of Lee still felt apologetic, because she let pass a possibility to be happy for simpler reasons. Another part of him swelled with pride for her because she was living out her dreams, even though they were vastly different from his own. Exciting opportunities lay ahead for them both in the future, he with his new family, and her in a land far east.

Lee closed the magazine, and logged out of his computer for the night. Everyone had already left as he sat alone in silence, still recalling their twisted rollercoaster ride. The phone rang. He cautiously answered. "This is Lee Johnson. May I help you?"

"Lee what's wrong," Simone was asking. She could tell by his voice that he had been thinking heavily.

"Oh nothing babe, I'm just finishing up. I just got caught up here."

"Don't forget to stop and pick up some paper towels."

"No problem. I'll be home soon. How are the boy's doing?"

"Good, Shawn's outside playing and Charlie is asleep."

"Tell Shawn we'll play catch when I get home."

"Okay, he'll like that. I love you."

"I love you too. Sorry I'm running late. I just heard something about somebody that used to work here that's all," Lee said.

"What's wrong? Are they okay?" she asked sounding concerned.

"No...yea, they're fine. They just got a big promotion, that's all."

"Well that's good," Simone said.

"Yea...yea it is," Lee continued, "Hey Simone? Thank you."

"Thank you for what?"

"I just want you to know how much I love you, that's all."

"Okay...love you too, see you when you get here," she said.

"I'll call when I'm close. Sorry again for running late."

"It's no big deal Lee, just be safe," she said.

"I'll be home soon...and Simone."

"Yes?" she said back.

"Thanks for always being so understanding."

He hung up the phone and smiled, grabbing his keys off the desk. Lee hit the lights and headed towards the door. As he closed the door to the office he pulled out his keys to lock the door. As he walked into the hall and pushed the down button for the elevator the phone rang again in his office.

With the building now nearly deserted he heard the faint ringing. He thought about going back in the mailroom as the doors opened wide. He let the call go to voicemail as he stepped inside the elevator. His family was waiting for him at home.

About the Author

RL began his journey to become an author in unconventional fashion. Always a gifted story teller, a friend's suggestion to try his hand at writing ignited a spark inside of him that unleashed a fire. The story began to spill into a notebook and eventually into the instant classic debut novel, *The Last Ms. Understanding.*

RL Taylor writes from the heart as he interweaves personal experiences into his work that give each story told raw emotion and a dangerous sense of reality. Readers are sure to enjoy the real life situations and social issues within the pages of each book.

RL Taylor has earned a Bachelor of Business Administration and has a secular background in Manufacturing. He resides in the Midwest with his wife and family.

His next book, *Champagne, Jellybeans, and Chocolate* will be released in 2009.

Sign up for updates and more book information at:
www.rltayloronline.com

THE LAST MISS UNDERSTANDING, a poem by *CeeGii*

I understand...at what cost
What made me a man I loss
Now lost,
I count the cost of what...I understand

Bottled up emotions in the form of rage I drink daily
Magnifying my comprehension of commitment
Whom do you hold when all arms are warm and inviting?
Whom do you run to when love has already won?

Like oxygen or pure H2O, that's vital for life
Your feelings and understanding, sustains my heart
Like the suns light that's miles away, once it reaches us, it's already in the past
Your love ignites my wayward course

Love is no longer halting to the sentiments of sentimentality
But as alive and active, with wisdom and thinking ability
No more mistakes, misfortunes, miss breaks, miss opportunities
I've chosen you for truly being...MISS UNDERSTANDING

Bonus- Excerpt from: *Champagne, Jellybeans, and Chocolate*

Chapter 1

The rapping on the window began again, startling him.

"I said wake up!" The persistent tapping against the driver's side window of the Chevy Malibu woke Royce Tyler from his deep sleep. It was the first night of decent rest he'd had in weeks.

"Get out of here! What does this look like to you? This is a park, not a campground." The city maintenance worker frowned heavily. His lip curled into a snarl as he banged his tight fist against the foggy car window.

"I'm moving, I'm moving," Royce mumbled while he adjusted the car seat to the proper upright position. He yawned wide and with a swift wipe of the eyes, he fired the modest V-6 engine. Rough idle. The well worn car needed a tune-up in the worst way.

"I'm sick of you bums camping out here. I've got your license plate number. I'll report you," the man said. A flurry of foreign words followed as he pumped his fists in frustration and disgust.

Royce kept his head away from making eye contact and accelerated slowly out of the parking area. He passed the sign to his left that read, Prospect Park. Once the maintenance worker vanished from view the shame set in. It rarely left. Shame had become his shadow that followed him ubiquitously, similar to a younger brother. He'd been sleeping in his car for over a month.

At first he'd park in a 24-hour grocery store or a deserted parking lot. But those places had sometimes grown too hectic, too risky. Someone might see him sleeping there. They'd see all the crumpled cardboard boxes and plastic bags he had overcrowding the dinged-up tan mid-sized vehicle. They'd ask questions. He'd be forced to answer them and tell them the truth. He was homeless.

* * *

Paula Daniels rolled over in her king-size bed and peeked at the alarm clock next to her. 7:30 already? She had an appointment scheduled for 9:00 a.m. sharp downtown with a group of physicians from Mercy Health Systems. The hospital had just been approved to carry out a brand new research study in their oncology department. Being late for their appointment would be no way to make a good impression with the busy staff.

She'd exerted great effort to become the top pharmaceutical sales representative for Form Tech Incorporated. The group of potential clients meant a large commission and bonus. She hoped a lucrative partnership between Form Tech and Mercy Health Systems would be facilitated.

She hurried off to shower as her ivory colored 500 thread count sateen sheets were tossed into a heap at the foot of her cherry wood sleigh bed. She took a few steps and glanced out her twenty-first story window. The sunlight poured inside the room and woke her up like a pep talk. She loved the expansive view. One of the many reasons she rented the one bedroom luxury apartment. Paula yawned as she entered her Italian inspired bathroom.

After a quick shower an outfit was selected from one of the endless business suits that hung inside her walk-in cedar lined closet. Once the plastic was detached from the all black ensemble she tossed it hurriedly towards the floor. Paula dressed in record time and exited the apartment. She turned and marched down the hallway. Time evaporated at an alarming rate. The elevator ride downstairs seemed to last forever.

A quick peek at her watch showed 8:25 a.m. as she skipped out the high rise apartment buildings front door. She smiled at Harvey, the buildings awkward doorman who salivated over her on a daily basis. Her favorite coffee shop, Baby Bean, was one block east. If she hurried, she'd have time to grab a tall caramel latte to enjoy on her six block cab ride north to Mercy Health Systems Hospital.

* * *

The thirty year old brown linoleum tile felt ice cold as Royce changed into his dress socks inside the cramp bathroom booth. He lowered the yellow tinted toilet seat and sat down to slip on his worn in coffee brown Stacy Adams loafers. He zipped up the worn-in duffel bag after stuffing the remainder of his garments inside. Royce stood and a sigh escaped from within. The shame followed thereafter.

As he exited the foul-smelling booth an elderly afro wearing janitor with wrinkled copper skin entered the two-star downtown hotel restroom to clean up before the morning rush. The Skyline Inn wasn't known for upscale clientele. Most times, cheap skate visitors from out of town, or young kids seeking a party would rent out a room at the family owned establishment.

The janitor's old face glared at him with inquisitiveness as his eyes followed Royce's hand clutching the duffel bag. Royce moved past him and gave a polite nod while beginning to wash his hands. Where else could he go to wash up and change?

The Skyline Inn was ideal. It was seldom crowded, with an easily accessible bathroom, out of the front desks view. Perfect. He'd tried washing and changing in other locations. This worked best and he'd taken full advantage of its convenience for the past week. Friday had arrived and sadly, two other days the same janitor spotted him in the restroom before nine a.m. with the same tattered red duffel bag tucked under his arm.

Royce dried his hands with a few paper towels and took a final look in the smudgy mirror. The janitor kneeled down and promptly began to attack the urinals, only pausing briefly to look over at Royce and grunt. He followed the grunt with a laugh. Royce immediately ceased fussing with his tie and walked out the door, head down. His clothes weren't too wrinkled considering their escape from a garment bag. He smoothed the front of his jacket.

Friday was the one day he'd been in anticipation of all week. He'd applied for a sales position at Xpert Paper, a well known paper and graphic arts supplier. The pay would be based on an average salary plus commission.

Royce walked outside the hotel side door and approached his car. He opened the door and shoved the duffel bag into the front passenger seat. Driving a few blocks north he wheeled into a parking lot and brought the car to a halt. He hopped out and scoped out the area, quickly leaving the scene. Part of him felt horrible for parking at the hospital in a spot designated for clergy. But the parking was free and at the moment that was all that mattered.

The Xpert Paper office location sat a mere two blocks away. He smoothed out his suit one last time and began the short commute. Halfway down the block a taxicab pulled up to the sidewalk next to him. The mud thrown from the cabs tires in the road nearly splashed against his light tan suit. He jumped back to avoid the potential mess.

An attractive leg stuck out from the back seat. The leg was followed by a hand carrying a briefcase. Royce paused, and then followed the leg up to the torso, all the way until he reached the angelic face of Paula Daniels, his girlfriend from college.

He gasped. She once owned his heart, along with a trail of other men who reminisced over their brief time with her. He hadn't seen her in years.

He never dreamed he'd see her like this; living in a car, jobless, and stripped of all his confidence. But there she stood, staring back at him with her same electrifying smile. She hadn't changed a bit. She'd only gotten better with time, aged like a fine wine. She closed the cab door and approached him. He had nowhere to hide, and no way to explain.

He was homeless.

Sign up for updates and more book information at: www.rltayloronline.com

www.ingramcontent.com/pod-product-compliance
Lightning Source LLC
Chambersburg PA
CBHW031955240626
47153CB00003B/997